I0741193

Books by Edison T. Crux

Tale of the Wisconsin Werewolf
Tale of the Gévaudan Beast
Tale of the Twin-City Vampires

Websites

edisontcrux.com • enoctales.com

wisconsinwerewolf.com • twincityvampires.com

Edison T. Crux

Tale of the Wisconsin Werewolf

The Enoc Tales Book 1

Enygma Enterprises
Rockford, IL

Enygma Enterprises
P.O. Box 1284 Beloit, WI 53512
www.enygma-enterprises.com

The Enygma Enterprises name and logo are trademarks of Enygma Enterprises.

The characters, locations, and events portrayed in this book are fictitious. Any similarity to real persons, living or dead, is coincidence and not intended by the author. To the extent any real names of individuals, locations, or organizations are included in this book, they are used fictitiously and not intended to be taken otherwise.

Cover design by Edison T. Crux, made from the wonderful stock images by Wyldraven (wyldraven.deviantart.com) and wookiestock (wookiestock.deviantart.com). Used with permission.

Publisher's Cataloging-in-Publication Data
Crux, Edison T.
Tale of the Wisconsin Werewolf / by Edison T. Crux.—2nd ed. p. cm.
Summary: Something is strange in Elkhorn. Fifteen tear-old Will Lewis winds up in the middle of the town's biggest mystery, as sightings of the Wisconsin Werewolf keep pouring in.
ISBN 978-0-9858873-4-6
[1. Supernatural — Fiction.] I. Crux, Edison T.   II. Title.
2012948944

For Katie,
who has always been my number one fan.

Contents

Introduction:
Dreams

Have you ever dreamed of doing something great with your life? A huge goal, like becoming a doctor. Climbing a mountain. Being a TV star.

Or telling stories for a living.

Yeah, so have I.

This all started as the crazy dream of a fifteen year-old kid. That was so many years ago, and a lot has changed since then… But the dream persisted.

To be honest, it still amazes me that I'm standing here, writing the introduction to a book I have been

Dreams

imagining for so much of my life.

It's funny; I wrote a novel, yet here I am at a loss for words.

Any of you with a dream should understand. Picture yourself, at long last, looking at the final product after years of hard work. Accomplishing your dream doesn't happen all at once; you keep working and believing, day after day, until you are surprised to see yourself where you always wanted to be.

Frankly, I'm speechless.

Tale of the Wisconsin Werewolf started as a feeling. My father and I made a habit of visiting Elkhorn ever since I heard the real legend of the Bray Road Beast. We called it "investigating," but more than anything it was a father-son adventure of the mind. We drove up and down the dark country roads, trying to imagine what people were seeing around here. One day, as I leaned against the car on the side of Bray Road, I said to my dad "There's a story here."

And ever since, I've been trying to tell it.

I was a kid when this started, no older than the book's main character. While telling this tale, a funny thing happened; I grew up. I looked in the mirror and realized I

Introduction

wasn't a kid anymore.

But that spark, that passion in my dream, was still there.

If you have a dream, my advice is this; never give up on it. It might take years, and it will certainly take lots of work.

But it's worth every moment to finally say "I did it."

Edison T. Crux
Author & Entrepreneur

Part
1

Prologue: Retribution

Retribution.

That is the reason for my existence. Retribution.

A trail of despicable choices brought it to this. With every decision, a justification; the wrong choice looked right and the right choice looked too hard. He dug this hole. Now the weight of a thousand selfish deeds pile up, one by one, until he is buried in them. His actions forged his tomb.

Retribution.

He must pay for his sins. Intention does not excuse action.

Under the cover of the starless night I find him, pacing sleeplessly in his home. Is he troubled by what he has done, or worried that he could be held accountable?

Retribution.

I look through the window. The room is illuminated by nothing but the gentle glow of the hearth. He does not see me. Not yet.

With a mighty leap I shatter the window. He turns to see his punisher standing in the wreckage of broken glass. The man is afraid, yes... But not surprised. He knew this night was coming.

Prologue

Retribution.

We stare at each other. Orange light from the fire ebbs and flows over his face, pulsing like the beat of a heart.

"I... I never meant for it to come to this," he says. If he only knew the irony of these words. From his mouth they are hollow and meaningless.

I growl, and he steps back. Coward. He knows better than anyone that there is no escaping his fate.

"P—please!" he whimpers. "Don't kill me!"

The fire blazes brighter and faster, keeping pace with the fool's heart. I bare my teeth in a snarl and he runs. Runs! Like he has a life worth sparing. Like he doesn't deserve what's coming.

He retreats no more than a step when I pounce, a predator claiming its prey. Deep cuts turn his back to bloody canyons.

Retribution.

The man falls. He attempts to crawl away, but I won't allow it. My powerful claw sinks into his side and flips him over briskly.

I want him to see me as he dies.

He yelps as his fresh wounds hit the floor. His eyes reveal a pitiable array of emotions; hopelessness, desperation, terror. Not a trace of willingness to pay the price of his deeds.

"D—don't do this to me!" he cries. "It might not be too late. We might still be able to—"

A sharp growl interrupts him. I press my horrific face to his. The livid fury in my eyes send a clear message. Look at me, these eyes say. Look at me and tell me it's not too late!

Tears drenched the fool's cheeks. "Please..." He mutters one last time.

I grab him by the collar, and hurl him into the fireplace.

I watch as the flames consume him. Embers flicker out from the hearth and catch the carpet. Before long, the room is blanketed with a hungry fire.

His last moments alive were a living Hell.

Retribution.

Chapter 1:
Funerals

This was a winter of funerals.

Last time the ground was clear of snow, fifteen year-old Will Lewis was happy to say he had never been to a funeral. That might not be something to brag about, but rather to give thanks in the silence of your own mind. In fact, Will's childhood was free from any tragedy worse than a bad flu season.

That is, until recently.

For the second time this season Will stood with his parents at Hazel Ridge Cemetery. You needed no directions to find the grave-side service; dozens and dozens of mourners in black coats stood out against the white snow and gray headstones. There were almost as many living as there were dead in this quiet Wisconsin graveyard.

As family of the deceased, Will and his parents were flooded with condolences. Despite the cold air Will felt hot and uncomfortable, and not just because of his suit. It was awkward to greet an endless stream of teary-eyed people he

Chapter 1

barely knew, if at all. One man Will hadn't met until that moment gave him a tight, sobbing hug.

I should be used to it by now, he thought. *We went through this a few months ago.*

But last time was different, wasn't it? Grandma Eleanor had *Creutzfeldt–Jakob* Disease, a fatal condition that slowly stole her personality and memories. Sure, she started getting better, but when a heart attack claimed her life the people of Elkhorn already pictured a world without sweet old Eleanor Amon.

A heavyset woman in a black wool coat joined them. Will was grateful to see a familiar face. Her name was Julie Baker. Although Julie and Will's mother were best friends growing up, they rarely saw each other after Cassandra Amon moved to Beloit to become Mrs. Lewis. But old friends become close in a hurry when surrounded by strangers.

Mrs. Baker and Will's mom met eyes. Silence was enough of a greeting for them.

"How are you holding up, Cassy?" Mrs. Baker asked.

"I'm here," she said quietly, and left it at that.

Will expected his mother to be in tears. Certainly more than a few were shed at her mother's funeral in December. But today, Cassandra Lewis (previously Amon) stood with her head held high and her eyes determinedly dry. Will swelled with pride at that fact.

After all, they were about to bury her father.

It was no great shock to Will that his grandfather, Connor Amon, passed away less than two months after Grandma Eleanor. Wives usually live longer. Husbands, it seems, often follow closely behind their dearly beloved. It's almost as if they lose more than a spouse; that some vital part of their being is torn away, a wound that will eventually bleed the life out of them.

Connor felt responsible for his wife's death. One look

Funerals

in the grieving man's eyes was all it took to see that. He hadn't been the same since Eleanor was diagnosed with CJD. You see, Connor Amon wasn't just a neurologist; he literally wrote the *book* on neurology. Textbooks with his name on the cover were required reading at medical colleges nationwide. But even the great Dr. Amon couldn't cure his wife.

No, it didn't surprise Will that Grandpa Connor had died. What surprised him was *how* he died.

Another group of bereaved strangers offered condolences. Will sensed his mother's well-contained tears on the verge of breaking. He wasn't the only one who sensed it; Will's father took the initiative of shepherding the new arrivals towards the memorial display. The mourners fussed, but John Lewis left no room for argument. He was stern. Held to his word. And loved his wife and child deeply, even if he rarely showed it.

The interruption averted, Will's mind returned to Grandpa Connor's unusual death.

This is what Will was told: Late last Wednesday (which always sounds better as "the night of February the 10th"), one of Connor's neighbors reported smoke coming from the doctor's house. By the time the fire department arrived, it was too late for poor Grandpa Connor. They said the fire was an accident.

It wasn't a bad story. The only problem is it wasn't true.

Will spent the following nights with his ear to his door, listening to his parents (some might call it *eavesdropping*, but Will preferred to think of it as mere curiosity). He couldn't hear them clearly, but from the words he could make out (*"arson," "broken in," "intruder"*), Will pieced together a theory.

Connor Amon was murdered.

Everyone was beckoned to the coffin, filling up the

seats under the canopy. The clergy was about to begin the grave-side funeral service. As the clergy made his eulogy and read a few verses from the Bible, Will puzzled over his theory. There was one important element that didn't make sense; who would want Dr. Amon dead?

He was a doctor, not a lawyer or business executive. He was never accused of medical malpractice, in fact he had an outstanding track record. Surely no one could murder him based on his profession.

Connor was charitable. He didn't live luxuriously, and donated more money to the library, schools and hospital than most people made in a year.

Will's mother was the primary beneficiary of Connor's estate. She had the most to gain financially, but was miles from Elkhorn at the time of her father's demise.

Who, then, would murder Connor? As far as Will could figure, no one else had anything to gain. Except, perhaps...

Will looked through the crowd, but couldn't find him. At last, when he craned his neck around he spotted the person he was looking for.

Barbason Amon.

Separated from the mourners, the old man was leaning against a mausoleum watching the funeral service with mild attention. His long, thinning hair was a mess of tangles and split ends. That face could have been carved of wood; sharp features, deep eye sockets, a rough stubble, and a flat, emotionless face. Barbason was Connor's younger brother, although few would have guessed it. Connor's enthusiasm kept him youthful, while Barbason aged faster than his time.

Could Uncle Barbason have killed his own brother?

Doubtful, Will concluded. His great-uncle was antisocial, but he never seemed dangerous. Just an old man who minded his own business, and would thank you to do the same. He did remember the brothers talking in hushed voices at Grandma Eleanor's funeral, however. That was unusual, but hardly reason to worry.

As the eulogy finished, Will began to think his imagination got the better of him. Maybe Grandpa Connor hadn't been murdered. Maybe it really wasjust an accident.

… Or maybe there was more to it than Will knew.

After the service, people lingered. No one seemed ready to leave Connor's side, so they stayed and talked to each other, despite the brisk chill nipping at their skin. Will didn't expect his family to stick around; mourning alongside strangers might be comforting to some, but not to the Lewis'.

Will's father pulled him aside.

"Son," he said. "Your mother and I need to speak to your uncle. Would you be alright for a few minutes on your own?"

Will knew that tone. It was a *don't argue with me* tone. The way he said it wasn't mean, but it *was* adamant. Will nodded, and his parents left a trail in the snow leading to the mausoleum Barbason had claimed. The old man sized them up as they approached.

Not wanting to intrude, Will took a stroll down the cemetery path. His eyes idly read the names on headstones while his mind continued to question the newest resident of Hazel Ridge.

In his lack of attention, Will walked right into somebody. They both staggered to keep their feet on the ground

"Oh, I'm sorry," Will said. His arms flailed as he tried to keep his balance.

Chapter 1

"It's fine," said a girl's voice.

When Will looked up, he almost *did* lose lose his footing. The girl he bumped into had to be around his age, give or take a year. It took a single glance for Will's heart to speed up a notch. The girl's red hair was silky and smooth, flowing from her winter hat to below her shoulders. She had a kind of carefree youthfulness that shined through her face. When she met his gaze, Will blushed; those eyes were such a brilliant shade of green they almost sparkled.

She was the prettiest girl Will ever met.

He forced his eyes away. Will was embarrassed enough for bumping into her, he didn't need to make it worse by staring. But when silence followed the girl started to walk away.

"Are you here for the funeral?" Will blurted out. It sounded stupid, but he had to say *something;* he didn't want her to leave yet.

She turned towards Will. "Yeah. My dad knew him, and wanted to pay his respects." She smiled. "He dragged me along."

Will laughed. It came out at a higher pitch than he hoped.

"How did you know Dr. Amon?" the girl asked.

In the distance, Will noticed his parents talking to Barbason. It didn't look friendly. "He was my grandpa," said Will.

"Oh wow, I'm sorry," she said. The girl examined him more closely. "Do you live around here? I don't recognize you."

Will suddenly wished he was from the area. Suddenly Elkhorn was much more appealing. "I live in Beloit, actually. It's about a half hour drive." It was a struggle to sound casual; Will thought his heart had taken on life of its own, beating at such a frantic pace. He couldn't remember when he last had feeling in his legs.

This girl, on the other hand, seemed perfectly at ease. "Ah, that explains it. I've got connections around here, but you're outside of my reach!" She smiled and held out a gloved hand. "My name's Eliza."

Will felt queasy as they shook hands. Captivated by her smile, he momentarily forgot how to speak. The memory returned with a crash, and finally he understood he had to introduce *himself* too. "I'm Will," he said at last. "Will Lewis."

"Well, nice to meet you, Will," said Eliza. "I should probably find my dad before he thinks I'm avoiding the funeral."

"Yeah, I need to get back to my parents too." Will tried not to sound disappointed. He was in no hurry to see her go.

Eliza winked. "Who knows, maybe we'll see each other next time you're in town."

With Grandpa Connor gone, Will didn't see any occasion to return to Elkhorn. He made a mental note to think of excuses to come back, just for the chance to cross paths again. Eliza waved and headed off towards the canopy, where the number of people finally started to diminish.

For the first time all day, Will's mind wasn't on his grandfather's death. In fact, he was quite proud of himself; he talked to a pretty girl, and didn't make a *complete* fool of himself (well, aside from blindly running into her and nearly knocking them both over). He would probably never see her again, but his mood had certainly improved.

Within minutes, that would change again.

Will strolled down the paths, using his memory like a video; it rewound to meeting Eliza, paused at every smile, then replayed the scene over and over. His knees still felt a

Chapter 1

little shaky, but at least his pulse stopped its crazy tap-dance.

Just as Will pictured that last, playful wink, there was a commotion by the canopy.

Will rushed back. The sight coming into view shocked him; it was his father, fist clenched around Barbason's collar, pinning the old man to the mausoleum. Only a handful of visitors remained, but they rushed to break up the confrontation. Will's mother buried her face in her hands, the tears flowing at last.

"What the devil is going on here?" said the clergy. "This is a *funeral!*"

Mr. Lewis and Barbason were motionless, their eyes locked with laser focus.

"Would you kindly put that man down?" the clergy pleaded.

Slowly, Barbason slid down the stone wall. Even as Mr. Lewis released his grip he didn't break his gaze.

Through her tears, Mrs. Lewis managed to smile at her son. "C'mon hun, I think it's time to go," she said, leading Will back to the car. Mr. Lewis finally turned from Barbason to follow his wife.

"Yer father ain't no saint, Cass!" Barbason yelled after them. His voice was gruff, like an old dog's bark.

The words sent a chill down Will's spine. His mother cried. His father walked briskly, jaw clenched.

Will glanced over his shoulder. Barbason's eyes followed them with unnerving intensity. When he was safely in the car, Will realized he was holding his breath. He let out a sigh of relief, and was glad to leave the gates of Hazel Ridge Cemetery.

The Lewis family stopped for dinner at the Elk Creek Bar & Grill. During her youth, Will's mother came here every

Funerals

Friday night for the fish fry. Although it was Sunday and no fish were frying, "The Elk" was a fitting place to honor her father.

It was a quiet dinner. No one said more than an occasional comment on their food (Will's parents both order "Elk Burgers," a local tradition. Being a self-proclaimed vegetarian, Will was happy with grilled cheese and french fries).

Will needed all of his self-control not to ask what the argument was about. Not knowing drove him crazy with curiosity, but Mr. Lewis was gripping his burger tight enough to break the bun. Not a sign of calming down. So Will held his tongue, at least for a bit longer.

Once they were well fed, the Lewis' got back in their car for the trip back to Beloit. It was already dark, and the snow that came in gentle flakes earlier now fell in flurries. Mr. Lewis let the car warm up before driving, and Will sensed an opportunity.

"That was quite a funeral," he said.

Mr. Lewis didn't respond. Mrs. Lewis nodded and said "I think Grandpa Connor would have been happy to see how many people came."

"Yeah." Will tried to pick his words carefully. "It seems like everyone really liked him."

Mrs. Lewis gave a pained smiled. "He did a lot of good, for a lot of people."

The car pulled out of the parking lot. There weren't many cars on the roads in town, but those that were out were driving slowly tonight. The wind was picking up, bombarding the windshield with snowflakes.

"Did Uncle Barbason like him?" Will asked.

This time, silence was his only response.

"I mean, I don't remember seeing them together a lot," Will continued. "Except at Grandma Eleanor's funeral. I saw them talking a lot then."

As they merged onto highway I-43, the car felt colder than it did without the heater. "They... Had very different interests," Mrs. Lewis finally said.

"What were they talking about? Do you know?"

Mr. Lewis spoke for the first time since dinner. "You would have to ask your great-uncle."

"Was that what you asked him?" Will said. Once the floodgate of questions was open, he couldn't stop himself.

"That's not important," Mr. Lewis said.

"He sounded angry."

"He might have been."

"What were you talking about?"

"Nothing."

"Was it about Grandma Eleanor?"

"No."

"Grandpa Connor?"

"Leave it alone, son."

"Was it about Mom?"

"That's *enough*, William," Mr. Lewis said loudly.

Will shrunk into his seat. He found his boundary, and pushed it one question too far. He had a feeling it was going to be a very quiet car ride.

They drove through the snow without another word. Will watched the open countryside; even though it was night time, the sheet of snow reflected enough light to see the passing landscape.

Something caught his attention. In the distance, a dark spot stood out against the backdrop of white. It was too far to make out any shape, only the indistinct silhouette of an object not covered in snow. Will thought it was odd, and wondered with only half-interest what it could be.

Then the silhouette moved.

In that moment goosebumps covered Will's body. He

didn't expect it to be *alive*. There was no mistaking its movements; the mystery spot was some kind of animal. And, judging from the speed and direction, it was an animal with a purpose.

Will had a grim realization as he traced its path. *It's headed towards the highway!*

"D-Dad," he said, his voice quivering. "What's that?"

Mr. Lewis glanced over for just a moment. In this weather, he needed to keep his eyes on the road. "Probably just a cow, son."

As the shadow got closer, Will saw two tiny yellow lights on the creature. *Eyes,* he thought. *Its eyes are reflecting light from the cars.* Will had the horrible impression the eyes were looking right at him.

"Seriously Dad, what *is* that?" he said. He was quickly rising to panic.

What came next happened so fast, Will could barely keep up.

Within seconds the silhouette was nearly to the road, on a collision course with their car. Will had just enough time to wonder if the creature was aware of the speeding vehicle before the shape (huge from this distance) leapt high off the ground. A moment of silence. Then, with a thunderous boom, the car shook violently off its lane. The metal roof sunk in from the weight of impact.

That thing landed on us!

Mr. Lewis swore. He tried to regain control of the car, but the back wheels fishtailed in the fresh snow.

Before Will could grasp one thing that happened, another interrupted him.

Will started to say "What's going on?" But his voice caught in his throat as he saw it; the dark shape of a gigantic claw swinging in front of the windshield. The sound of shattering glass was nothing compared to the relentless

Chapter 1

howling of the wind, hitting them headfirst at over 65 miles per hour. Will covered his face before being showered in glass shards.

He couldn't see, but he could feel. He felt pain as dozens of cuts lacerated his body. He felt freezing wind choke the breath from his lungs. He felt the car sway dangerously.

Will peered out from the cover of his arms for just a second. His eyes instantly dried up and stung, but he caught a glimpse of what was happening.

That claw reached forward, pinning Mr. Lewis to his seat. He wasn't moving.

Mrs. Lewis was struggling to free her husband. She was drenched in blood, large pieces of glass still caught in her skin.

And, barely visible against the dark background, was the face of the creature.

Will couldn't see its shape or features. But he saw those eyes; two glowing yellow embers taken from the hearth of Hell.

The car shook again.

The wheels turned, out of control.

They left pavement.

Spun wildly.

And then, with a final ear-splitting crash, Will was unconscious.

In the land of dreams, nightmares are king. You might go years without having one, but when they do show up they demand your attention like no other dream can.

Time means nothing in nightmares. For that reason, Will had no idea how long he was sleeping. But whether he was out for an hour or a week, he spent every second of it locked in perpetual memory of the car crash.

Many details evolved with each replaying, becoming something they never truly were. The landscape changed to a much grander setting than I-43. Snow flurries became an all-out blizzard. And despite the wind stinging his eyes Will started to see the entire event unfold, as if watching it on TV while safely curled up at home.

Each time, the creature became more terrifying.

Even in his dreams, Will never got a good look at it. Fear of the unknown is highly distilled. It leaves your imagination to come up with one horrific possibility after another. The only thing Will could clearly see were the eyes. They haunted every moment of his dreams.

Those eyes lingered in Will's mind when, finally, he woke up.

Consciousness was a relief. It meant Will could finally escape the endless loop of nightmares. Gradually, he took in his surroundings. He was in a hospital, which didn't surprise him at all. A nurse was next to him, checking his vitals.

"Good morning," said the nurse. "How are you feeling?"

Will squinted, still adjusting to the light. "Sore," he said. His body was covered in dull aches, and his head was pounding. Will had the feeling it would be much worse, if it weren't for the modern miracle of pain medication.

She consulted her chart. "I bet you are. Looks like you're recovering well though."

Will massaged his forehead, to find a large bandage covering it. Several smaller wrappings were scattered across his arms. Suddenly, a question rushed to him. "Are my parents okay?"

The nurse stiffened, but her voice remained even. "Just try and rest for now. Dr. Thompson will be in later."

Not leaving much time for argument, the nurse left.

Chapter 1

Will fell back asleep with an uneasiness in the pit of his stomach.

By the time the doctor came, Will was awake again. Dr. Thompson was an older man, with comically-bushy eyebrows and mustache. His expression, however, was not so comical.

"Ah, hello Will," he said in a husky voice. "How are you feeling?"

That always seemed like a silly question to ask someone lying in a hospital bed. "Alright, I guess."

The doctor took a seat next to the bed. "I expect you've felt better. You suffered from a mild concussion. Aside from that you have an impressive collection of cuts and bruises, none of which severe."

Will tried to move, but a fresh wave of aches changed his mind. He hoped it was almost time for more medication, because he was beginning to feel like one giant bruise.

"Have you felt any dizziness, nausea, or lack of motor skills?" the doctor asked.

Will shook his head.

"Any sensitivity to light, blurred vision, or ringing in your ears?"

"A little bit of the light sensitivity," Will admitted. "But none of the other stuff."

"Good," Dr. Thompson was taking notes as they spoke. "Now Will... Do you remember what happened last night?"

Will's temperature dropped.

He remembered the creature.

He remembered a crash.

And boy, did he ever remember those eyes.

Or did he? His sleep was filled with nightmares, reshaping the event in more horrific detail. Awake now, he wasn't sure how much of it really happened.

Funerals

"I'm not sure," Will said. "I was having... A lot of dreams. It all sort of blurs together."

Dr. Thompson scribbled another note. "That's fine. Post-traumatic amnesia is common with head injuries of this nature." His expression turned grave as he put down his clipboard. "Will, you were in a very serious accident last night. While on the highway, your car slid across the median into oncoming traffic. You collided head-first with another vehicle, resulting in a four car pile-up."

Perhaps Will spoke too soon about the nausea; his stomach suddenly felt ready to empty its contents.

"Are my parents okay?" Will asked.

The doctor let out a heavy sigh. "Paramedics were there as soon as possible... But it was bad. Your father passed away before they arrived. They did everything they could for your mother, but she died on the way to the hospital." He put his hand on Will's arm. "I'm so sorry, Will."

It was like a switch was turned off in Will's mind, shutting off all thought and feeling. He was frozen in his place, unable to comprehend what he just heard. Dr. Thompson kept talking, but the words flowed meaninglessly through the air, the connection from ears to brain lost. He didn't hear the doctor stand up, but the sound of the closing door faintly registered.

Will was alone now.

Alone in the room.

Alone in his life.

He cried. There were no tears. Just deep, hollow sobs. Eventually, he cried himself back to sleep.

It was early morning when Will got the news from Dr. Thompson. The next time he woke up, it was past four o'clock. Mercifully, this sleep was completely dreamless. Will's

Chapter 1

mind was still too numb to think, and certainly couldn't conjure up something as complex as a dream. The nurse brought him a plate of food, which he ate in auto-pilot.

Subconsciously, Will refused to believe that his parents were gone. Since he had no rational hope to cling to, his solution was to forgo thought entirely.

Shortly after Will's meal, the door opened. He expected to see the nurse, or perhaps Dr. Thompson.

But he certainly *didn't* expect his great-uncle, Barbason.

The old man stood in the doorway, hesitant to enter. He finally stepped inside, leaning heavily on his wooden cane.

"Hey kid."

Will had no idea what to say. He could probably count the times he spoke with his great-uncle on one hand. Not to mention, of course, that the last time Will saw him he had nearly gotten into a brawl with his dad. "Hi..."

Barbason sat down. "Ye feelin' alright?"

"Sure," said Will, who felt anything but alright.

"I heard 'bout the accident." Barbason sounded just as uncomfortable as Will felt. "I'm sorry."

"It's okay." Will didn't want to address the issue of his parents. He brushed the topic aside as lightly as he could.

The old man cleared his throat. There was a long, awkward pause before Barbason spoke again. "Listen, they was askin' 'bout ye, and what all ye had as for family. Wanted to know if yer dad had any relatives, stuff like that."

In his denial, Will hadn't thought about where he would live. The more he considered it, the worse it looked. "Dad was an only child. Both of his parents died when I was young."

"Yeah, that's what I was figurin'. I told 'em I didn't think his folks were 'round no more." Barbason fiddled with

Funerals

his cane, keeping his eyes there instead of on Will. "They, er... Well, seeing as we're related and all, they asked if it'd be alright if ye stay with me."

Will tensed up. He didn't like the sound of this. "What did you tell them?"

"Said I'd ask what ye wanted."

"I want my parents," Will said flatly.

Barbason looked directly at Will, his eyes flooded with remorse. You couldn't tell this was the same man who shouted harsh words at his brother's funeral.

"I wish I could do that for ye, kid. I really do. But the best I've got is a roof and a bed. It's not much, but if ye want it... It's yours."

Will laid back on his pillow. He couldn't ignore reality any longer; he was now an orphan. Fighting back tears, he considered his options. If he turned down his great-uncle's offer, chances are Will would live in an orphanage. Maybe, if he was lucky, he might get into a foster home.

The truth is, Will didn't like any of his options. But something about the sadness in his great-uncle's eyes made him feel connected to the old man. They might not know each other well, but ultimately they were still family.

"Alright," Will said. "If you'll have me, I'll stay with you."

Chapter 2:
Welcome Home

Will spent another night at the hospital. Overall he felt pretty good, especially considering he survived a fatal car crash. He discovered a new ache with every move, but these sores didn't require much medical expertise beyond a steady regime of vicodin.

Part of the reason he stayed had nothing to do with his injuries. It was simple; Barbason needed time to prepare his home for a new resident.

Since he had no family or friends close enough to visit, it was a boring night. Eventually Will asked the nurse if she would find him a book of Sudoku puzzles.

Will loved Sudoku.

It started out as curiosity. Every so often he heard it mentioned at school, and caught glimpses of other kids filling out these strange number puzzles. Finally he looked it up online, read the rules, and tried a few practice puzzles on his computer. It was frustrating at first, but before long Will was hooked.

Welcome Home

The nurse returned with a puzzle book from the gift shop. After flipping through the crosswords and word searches (neither of which interested him in the slightest), Will found the familiar 9-by-9 grid of a Sudoku puzzle. He got more relief completing his first row of numbers than from a whole night's worth of medication.

Finally, Will slept.

Around one o'clock the next day, Barbason returned. Once all the release papers were signed, he led Will to his old, faded blue pickup truck. It protested when Barbason turned the key, but a slap to the dashboard (plus a mumbled obscenity) got the engine started.

They drove down I-43 South, the same highway that recently claimed two lives. Although the sky was clear today, Will still felt queasy as they passed that section of road. He held his breath until he was certain no dark shadow was waiting to finish the job. Will gave his great-uncle directions to his house, but otherwise the ride was silent.

When Will's house came into view, he had to fight back tears.

Knowing his deserted home would be a cruel reality check, Will slipped back into numbness. He refused to think about his parents, or acknowledge their deaths. If he could just do that long enough to pack, Will thought he would be okay.

The truck gave a mechanical sigh as it parked. Barbason climbed down, inhibited by his bad leg.

"I threw two suitcases in the back," he told Will. "There ain't gonna be room for no more than that anyhow. Whatever don't fit, well... We can sell, or get ye one o' those storage unit things."

The suitcases looked older than the truck. They each carried one up to the house, but Barbason waited outside while Will packed.

Chapter 2

It was easier than Will expected to walk through his home. It looked just like they left it. Traces of his mom's cooking lingered in the air. Mail was still spread on the table, to be sorted later. The thought that this house was no longer a home seemed silly when surrounded by the subtle signs of family life.

All the same, Will packed. It felt like getting ready for a vacation, although he knew better. This was no vacation, and he wouldn't be returning any time soon. Chances are, this would be the last time he saw this place. But if it didn't feel like goodbye, fine. Will was going to ride this delusion until his work here was done. There would be time to deal with his feelings later.

He packed a few sets of clothes, but decided not to waste much space on them. He could always buy more. Will selected only his favorite books from his bookshelf; *Twenty Thousand Leagues Under the Sea, The Island of Doctor Moreau, Frankenstein,* and *Stranger in a Strange Land* made the cut. As far as Will was concerned, it was classic science fiction or nothing at all. The only nonfiction he packed was a pocket-sized book filled with Sudoku puzzles. It had hundreds of puzzles, half of them completed. Will gathered his laptop and accessories in their travel bag, then grabbed the family photo album and a few pictures off the mantel.

Once the suitcases were full, Will took a final look through the house. There wasn't room for anything else, but it felt like he was missing something. He was randomly looking through drawers when something bright caught his eye. He picked it up; it was a silver watch, still shining like new. Will's mother gave it to him last Christmas. It looked new because he only wore it once or twice. At the time, the watch meant nothing to him. But now it was a treasure, like a gift left from the grave.

Suitcases in hand, watch on wrist, Will left the home

of his childhood.

Barbason helped hoist the suitcases into the bed of his truck.

"Ye ready?" the old man asked.

Will didn't look back. He knew if he did, he would fall apart. With more of a quiver than he hoped, he said "Yeah, I guess so."

They got into the truck, and the Lewis House faded into the past.

The 40 minute drive from Beloit to Elkhorn was awkward. Really awkward. Neither Will nor his great-uncle had any idea what to say to each other. Whenever either of them tried to start a conversation, it was promptly followed by a short response and a long silence. By the time they passed Delavan *(Elkhorn, 6 miles ahead)*, Will gave up on the idea of chit-chat.

They took the exit off I-43, jumped on County Road NN, then turned down Bray Road. It was a scenic, country road complete with hills, curves, woods, and cornfields along the way. It was easy to be distracted; this road had an almost otherworldly feel to it.

At the end of Bray Road, looming like a gargoyle over the intersection, was B.R. Amon & Sons, Inc.

Although Will had never been there, he knew its general history. Technically, Uncle Barbason should be "Barbason Jr." Will's great-grandfather—the *original* Barbason Re Amon—started the construction business back in the 40s. He hoped to pass it along to his two sons, but Connor's goals led him to the field of medicine instead of construction. As far as Will knew, Barbason Jr. worked there his whole life.

Whatever it was like in the past, now B.R. Amon was a ghost of its former self. The white brick building rested

Chapter 2

atop a hill, with its paint peeling and name fading away. The huge garage doors, which took up most of the front, were shut tight.

Barbason parked the truck (which seemed to give a groan of relief) and led Will around the side of the garage. A small white addition was partially concealed from the road, and the mailbox hinted that this was where Barbason lived. The old man unlocked the door, and they dragged the suitcases inside.

Barbason threw his jacket onto a coat hanger with the blind ease of daily routine. Will got a tour, but it didn't take long; they entered into a living room with splintered wood floors, a legless plaid couch that sat on the floor and sunk in at the middle, and an ancient moth-eaten easy-chair. The seats were facing an antique television. With a quick glance at its condition, Will suspected the television was nearing the end of its days. Beyond the living area was a cramped kitchen, complete with a patio table and chairs shoved in the corner to serve as a dining room. Next they went down a claustrophobic hallway next to the kitchen.

"Bathroom," Barbason mumbled as they passed the first door to the left. "The hot water don't keep, so ye gotta take a shower fast or take it cold. My room's at the end o' the hall, and up to the left just goes to the garage." He stopped at the next door, to their right. "This will be yer room, kid. I cleared it out this morning."

They hauled the suitcases into Will's new room. It was a small, barren space that smelled like old dust recently disturbed. It was empty aside from a little desk, a bedside table, and a rickety bunk bed (not to mention thick cobwebs in each corner).

Once, on a dare, Will took a flashlight and looked into a mausoleum. The overall impression of this room was about the same.

Welcome Home

"Used to be my room, back when me and Connor were kids," said Barbason. There was no distinguishable emotion in his voice; just simple, matter-of-fact recollection. "Top bunk used to be me, but I'd do the bottom if I were ye. That thing's been askin' to fall apart for years."

Will set down his suitcase and sat experimentally on the bed. He thought he might prefer the sleeping quarters at the mausoleum. "Thanks," he said.

The old man hesitated, opened his mouth to speak, then decided against it. He limped through the door without a word.

Suddenly, in the stillness of that deserted room, reality hit.

Will thought it sunk in back at the hospital, but it wasn't until he had to call a new place home that everything came into perspective.

My parents are dead, he repeated in his mind. *My old life is gone now. Gone forever.*

He turned over, grabbed his moldy pillow, and cried. A new life was about to begin. And Will didn't think he was going to like it very much.

That night, Will barely left his room. After a few hours he composed himself enough to look for some food. To his surprise, Barbason had a lunch meat sandwich waiting for him.

"Figured ye'd be hungry," he mumbled while chewing his own dinner.

Will tried his best to smile. "Thanks, but I'm vegetarian."

Barbason stared at Will as if he had suddenly spoken a foreign language. He stopped eating and tried to wrap his mind around the concept of "vegetarian." Will didn't know what to tell him; ever since he found out what meat was he couldn't eat it without imagining the animal screaming in pain. He hunted through the fridge for a meatless meal, but his hopes grew dim as he saw the carnivorous preferences of his great-uncle. He settled for peanut butter and jelly, which was about all he felt up to eating anyway.

After dinner, Will unpacked. It quickly became clear that Barbason was right; there wasn't room for more than two suitcases could fit. Despite the cramped living quarters, Will started to feel better as his possessions filled the room. Once most of his things were put away, Will laid down on the old mattress. It took hours for sleep to finally reach him.

The next day Will woke up to a back as stiff as the mattress it slept on. He grabbed fresh clothes to take a shower, hoping the warm water would sooth his aching bones. For a few minutes, it worked wonders. Then Will very quickly remembered what his great-uncle said about the hot water. He stepped out of the shower, shivering. Barbason appeared to be a late sleeper; Will got dressed, ate toast, and cleaned his dishes without seeing his great-uncle once.

Later that morning, Will's cellphone rang. He had no idea who would be calling. Will's parents only gave him that phone "in case he needed it," which he rarely did. The number was unfamiliar, but the voice wasn't.

"Will," said the man on the phone. "This is Mr. MacDonald. I'm your parents' attorney."

He remembered MacDonald. He helped his parents during the few occasions they needed legal documents drawn up. Although rather detached, Will liked him. Something in his dull voice and sharp eye gave Will the impression this man hunted technical errors like a hawk for a field mouse.

"Hi Mr. MacDonald," Will said. He was pretty sure he knew what this was about.

MacDonald cleared his throat. "I need to discuss the

Welcome Home

Last Will & Testament of your parents with you, when you are available."

"Okay," said Will. He wanted to get this over with, but he didn't know when Barbason would be awake. Thinking it rude to invite someone over without his guardian's consent, he said "Let me ask my great-uncle. Can I call you back?"

"Sure," MacDonald said. "You have my number."

Will hung up, and paced the living room. Now on top of his other worries, he began to wonder what would come of his parents' will.

Morning came and went, the afternoon began, yet still Barbason's door remained shut. Will was beginning to worry when the old man finally limped down the hall at almost three o' clock. He grunted a greeting and went for the fridge.

As Barbason ate his breakfast (if it was stilled called "breakfast" this late in the afternoon), Will asked about MacDonald. He mumbled agreement through a mouthful of cereal.

"Have 'em over whenever," Barbason said. "I got calls to make myself, gettin' ye into school and all. Got up early to get 'em done."

If this was early, Will couldn't imagine his great-uncle sleeping in.

"Just keep in mind, kid, we got another funeral to get to tomorrow," Barbason reminded him.

Will completely forgot. Tomorrow, he would have to face the hardest funeral of a death-filled winter. He didn't comment, but made a note to get his parents' will taken care of early.

True to his word, Barbason spent the next hour on the phone. He sounded confused and disgruntled throughout.

"How am I s'posed to know this stuff anyhow?" he

Chapter 2

said in between calls. "I ain't never had a kid."

Will called MacDonald back. He said he'd stop by the next morning. Will said that sounded great. And with a sigh of relief, Barbason said his school transfer was sorted out. Will would be starting on Monday.

Sleep did not come easy that night. For the first time since the accident, the nightmares were back. The shapeless shadow lurked just outside Will's field of vision, stalking his every move. Only those fluorescent yellow eyes were clear, and somehow they were even more terrifying than the unseen monster. These eyes could chill your blood with a glance, and drive you mad by their scrutiny. Will couldn't stop himself from staring; that petrifying gaze immobilized him better than any shackles. Something about the eyes was especially unnerving, but Will couldn't place it. Then, with the senseless surety that only seems logical in dreams, he realized the most horrific thing about them.

They are human eyes!

Will woke up choking back a scream. His pillow was drenched in cold sweat, and he felt clammy. It was still too early to get up, but Will refused to go back to sleep. In his dreams he was vulnerable, but while awake Will could explain this bogeyman away. He laid in bed, reminding himself that the monster with those eyes probably never existed outside of his mind.

As Will got up and went through another quiet morning, that chill lingered. He took a shower as fast as he could, and only got blasted with cold water near the end.

By the time MacDonald arrived, the start of one last heavy snowfall began. Will took MacDonald's coat, and they each took a seat on the couch. The tired old springs squeaked below them.

Welcome Home

MacDonald sifted through his briefcase and pulled out a file. "I'd like to go over your parents' Last Will and Testament. Are you up for it?"

"Yes," said Will. He felt queasy, as if reading their will would make their deaths official.

"Very well." MacDonald put on his reading glasses, and skimmed through the document. "In essence, their will is fairly simple. They listed each other as the primary benefactor. In the case of both of their deaths, they leave their entire estate to you."

Will expected as much. He couldn't think of anyone else they would have left it to. Both of his parents worked, and were comfortably in the middle class. Will didn't know how much money they had, but he figured he'd have enough to get by.

"Now, this is where it gets a little more complicated. First of all, as a minor you do not have full access to their assets. Most of it will be kept until you are 18, but you are allowed a percentage of it each month for personal expenses.

"Aside from money is the issue of your parents' belongings. The largest asset is, of course, their house. But they each had a car as well, not to mention a household full of personal belongings.

"Your parents also had decent life insurance plans. They were covered for $125,000 each, once again leaving you as the sole benefactor."

This was starting to sound like a much higher number than Will expected. "How much have I actually inherited, Mr. MacDonald?" he asked directly.

MacDonald thumbed through the file. "Based on the information I have, I estimate you would be entitled to at least $450,000. Assuming you sold the house and their belongings, that is."

Will almost choked. When you're fifteen years old,

Chapter 2

$450,000 sounds like an unfathomable amount of money. "Wow..."

"However, that doesn't take recent income into account," said MacDonald. When Will gave him a puzzled look, he continued. "As I understand it, your grandfather lived very comfortably. I don't have all the information about his will yet, but it appears he left the majority of his estate to your mother. Which means everything she inherited, you inherited.

This time Will did actually choke a little. Grandpa Connor was very, very well off. If Will inherited almost half a million dollars from his parents, he couldn't imagine what his grandfather had left him.

"Mind you, it does not sound like Dr. Amon kept all his funds to himself," MacDonald clarified. "A quick search shows that he's made considerable donations to Elkhorn's library, police department, hospital and school district. But based on the value of his house, possessions and life insurance policy you could assume at least as much from him as from your parents."

It was unreal. Just last night Will was hunting in the fridge to find something that wasn't expired. Today, he discovered he's inheriting close to a million dollars.

MacDonald must have noticed the money-glazed look in Will's eyes, because he said "Remember, you only have full access to your full inheritance after you turn 18. Until then you are given a monthly allowance to cover expenses."

That was fine, as far as Will was concerned. He certainly didn't *need* that much money. Still... It was nice knowing it was there. "Thanks, Mr. MacDonald," Will said.

MacDonald nodded as he gathered his things. "We'll keep in touch."

Will watched him drive away. The snow was getting

Welcome Home

heavier now, frosting the streets with a half-inch blanket of whiteness. He wondered how bad it would be by this afternoon. John and Cassandra Lewis would find their final resting place beneath the same snow that covered them on their death day. It was cruel irony.

The thought of this impending funeral, so quickly after the reading of their will, was too much to bear. Will fell to his knees on the dirty doormat, and cried from the bottom of his heart. This horrible winter could take Grandma Eleanor. It could have Grandpa Connor. But it couldn't steal Will's parents from him. That was just... Too much.

I can't take this, Will thought as his emotional defenses broke down. *I'm not strong enough to do this alone. I don't care how much money they left me; I would trade all of it to have my parents back!*

He couldn't calm down. When it's your heart that's broken, you bleed through your eyes. And even when you think the sorrow is at bay, it takes just the slightest thing to rupture the tears, the hurt, and the heartache all over again. Some pain heals with time, vanishing like a forgotten cut or bruise. But losing someone so close to you is different. That kind of loss is like a severed limb; even if the wound closes and the bleeding stops, your life will never be the same without them.

Will didn't notice his great-uncle's approaching footsteps. He jumped when he felt a rough, calloused hand on his shoulder.

"Hey kid," Barbason said.

Will sniffed, trying to hide his tears. "I'm sorry," he said.

Barbason raised an eyebrow. "For what?"

"For... for..." Will didn't know how to say it. "For being an inconvenience. It's not fair for you to take me in. I bet the last thing you need is a teenage kid you barely know living here. I'll... I'll leave. I can spend a couple years in an orphanage. I'll be okay after that."

Barbason stared, kneeling on the floor next to him.

"This isn't your problem," Will sighed. The tears finally stopped, but his heart was still heavy with grief. "It's not your fault my parents died."

Silence was only broken by an occasional sniffle. Will was just about to get up and re-pack his things when the old man's grip tightened.

"Listen kid," said Barbason. His head was hung low, almost in shame. "I know this place ain't much. And I know I ain't no good with kids. But I'm tryin'. So as long as ye'd like this place more than some orphanage, ye have a home here. I owe ye that much, at least."

The good intentions behind Barbason's words made up for their lack of grace. Although still hurting, Will certainly felt better. "Thank you, Uncle Barbason."

Barbason pulled himself into a standing position, using his cane for support. His bones creaked with each move. "Ye know kid... Ye don't have to go stand 'round listenin' to other peoples' grief. Ye can honor yer parents from right here, if ye want. But ye don't have to put on a show for nobody."

Will thought about it. He had resigned himself to going out of obligation; the last thing he wanted was a repeat of Connor's grave-side service. He didn't think he had a choice in the matter. But if he did...

"Thanks," Will finally said. He stood up and wiped the last remaining tears from his cheeks. "If that's alright with you, I think I've had enough funerals for one year."

So Will held his own memorial service. In the solitude of his room, he went through photo albums. Took out a few pictures. Said all the things he wished he could say. There was more crying, but these were good tears. In his own way and

Welcome Home

in his own words, he was putting them to rest.

"Rest in peace, John Lewis," he said, his broken voice barely a whisper. "Rest in peace, Cassandra Lewis." Will stared at a family portrait through watery eyes.

"Mom, dad... I'll miss you."

Chapter 3:

Elkhorn Area High School

By the time Monday morning rolled around, Will was anxious for school.

Despite letting Will live there, Barbason was still not a kid person. With his nocturnal sleep pattern, they barely saw each other anyway (Will caught his great-uncle sleeping in until 5 o' clock on Friday). But the old man did make an effort; one morning Will noticed the fridge stocked with an assortment of vegetables. It looked like they were picked at random, perhaps because Barbason had never bought much in the way of produce. Although Will's diet involved more than celery, artichokes, and eggplants, he appreciated the gesture.

Without schoolwork or friends to keep him busy, Will forced himself to constantly read or fill out Sudoku puzzles. Letting his mind wander would do him no good. So he spent the weekend journeying with Captain Nemo in *Twenty Thousand Leagues Under the Sea,* and conducting mad experiments with the morally-questionable doctor in

Frankenstein. They made for good distractions, but by Sunday night he was growing bored with rereading his favorites.

Still, Will couldn't help feeling nervous as he got his backpack ready early Monday morning. He never had a problem with school; in fact Will found several topics genuinely interesting. But he was going to be the "new kid," showing up in the middle of the school year. Will liked the lack of attention he got at Beloit Memorial High School. He could go through his day without being bothered by anyone but his few friends. It would take awhile before he could walk unnoticed here.

Who knows, Will mused as he strapped on his backpack. *Maybe a fresh start won't be so bad after all.*

Since Will didn't know exactly where the bus would stop, he decided to head outside a couple minutes early. His hope was to catch another student and follow their lead. After only a few minutes waiting by the curb, he heard the sound of a door and a familiar voice call out "Bye Mom!"

Will's pulse skipped a beat. He turned around, thinking he must be imagining it... But sure enough, the girl from Connor's funeral was descending the hill from the house next door. No longer dressed for mourning, the girl was wearing a vibrant, flowery shirt and jeans with the name *ELIZA* embroidered along the side. Their eyes met, and she seemed to recognize Will as well.

"Hey!" she said, walking up to him. "You're Dr. Amon's grandson! Will, right?"

"Yeah," said Will. He was mentally stunned; he never expected to see her again, and felt his ability to speak coherently fading. "Hi Eliza." He would have remembered her name even if it wasn't stitched to her pants.

Eliza smiled. "I heard a rumor you were living with Barbason Amon." She winked. "Looks like we'll be neighbors!"

Chapter 3

He hated to use such a cheesy metaphor, but Will really did feel like a flock of butterflies took flight in his stomach. "I guess so," he said. He attempted a smile, feeling dopey and awkward.

"Oh..." Her tone softened. "I heard about your parents too... That's just awful. Are you holding up okay?"

Will was torn; he wanted to appear strong in front of Eliza, but the idea of being comforted by her didn't sound so bad either. He settled for the generic (and boring) response; "Yeah."

"That's good. If you need a hand getting situated, feel free to ask!" Eliza was back to her upbeat attitude again. "I've been here forever. I know who's helpful and who to stay away from."

"Thanks," he said. Will thought he might like school with Eliza as his tour guide.

She smiled that pretty, knee-weakening smile. "No problem. The school's not far from here. The bus just makes one stop after us, so we get a few extra minutes of sleep." Eliza laughed.

How opposite the two of them would look to passers-by; Eliza's casual grace shined, while Will's social klutziness couldn't even glint. Still, he was glad she was there. Being around Eliza made Will nervous, but her company was worth the awkwardness. Even the subtle scent of her perfume both relaxed and weakened his muscles. The bus finally appeared, and Eliza sat with a friend of hers. Will sighed as he found an empty seat near the back. Another chance to talk to Eliza and he thought he did pretty good.

The bus drove down Bray Road, picked up another student, then finished its course to Elkhorn Area High School. Eliza was right; it was only a few blocks from the end of Bray. Easily within biking distance, if Will ever felt so motivated (or overslept and missed the bus).

Elkhorn Area High School

The sound of a dozen muffled conversations coursed through the air. Will moved as one with the mass of students. So far, no one noticed someone new in their midst.

Will's day started out about how he expected. The Math teacher's voice droned on endlessly. History was clearly a "free period," where texting and hushed conversations ruled while the teacher meekly attempted to educate. Will tried to like Science (his favorite subject), but Mrs. Penbrook failed to inspire him like his old Science teacher could. It didn't help that each teacher introduced "our new student," which tore away what little anonymity Will had. It was beginning to look like things would be about the same here as they were in Beloit.

When lunch hour approached, Will realized he had a problem. While trying to remember all of his school supplies this morning, he forgot to bring any money for lunch. His stomach chose that moment to growl. Will followed the other students towards the cafeteria, wondering what he would do to keep his mind off food.

As the number of students in the hall thinned, Will was startled by a hand on his shoulder.

"So, you must be the new kid," a voice from well over Will's head spoke. There was a snickering sound closer to his height a moment later.

"Yeah." Will didn't want his voice to show how nervous he was. Remembering this was his fresh start, he continued. "My name's Will."

"Will Lewis," said the voice. "Yeah, yeah, I know."

Will turned around, finding himself facing two people. The first one was the owner of the hand, who stood a full head taller than Will. He was athletically-built, had short blond hair, and wore a cocky grin.

Chapter 3

The other person was shorter than Will, his eyes obscured by large round glasses and layers of greasy black hair. His nose was big and he stood with a hunch. He reminded Will distinctly of a mouse.

"You know me?" Will asked, caught off guard.

"Mason makes it his business to know when someone comes into *his* school!" the mouse said, talking fast with a voice as oily as his hair.

"That's enough, Frankie," said Mason. "But it is true; I like to know when something happens around here. And you just so happened to happen."

Only a few stragglers were still in the hall. "I'm new," Will blurted out, realizing how obvious that was. "It's nice to meet you… Mason?"

"Oh yes, excuse my manners." He cleared his throat. "I'm Mason McCree, quarterback of the Elkhorn Elks. This is Frankie, my associate and personal assistant."

Frankie grinned proudly, puffing out his scrawny chest.

"I should probably get to lunch," said Will, a completely empty excuse. He didn't like where this seemed to be going, so he made to turn down the hall.

"Do you see this, Frankie?" Mason raised his voice slightly. It didn't matter if he was loud; the hall was now empty aside from the three of them. "Do you see what's happening here?"

"Looks like he's disrespectin' ya, boss," Frankie squeaked.

"That it does, that it does." Mason cracked his knuckles. "I'm not done talking to you, Lewis. You see, you're new here, so I can't expect you to know. But we have a little… Tradition, shall we call it? And as a new student, it would only be right of you to participate."

Slowly, Will turned back to them. "What's the

tradition?" he asked, wishing he didn't have to.

"You see, in a small town like this, we take our football very seriously. In a sense, the whole school—no, excuse me, the whole town—depends on its team to play at their best. It gives us something to be proud of, something that unites us.

"So, as the star player of the Elkhorn Elks, a great deal of that weight falls on my shoulders. It would be a terrible tragedy if I was poorly taken care of, and slacked off in the game. But here's where you can contribute to your new school." Mason grinned as Frankie let out a shrill laugh. "The *Keep Mason Fed* fund is a way for newcomers to take part in the pride of Elkhorn. And I just *know* you wouldn't want to disappoint everyone, would you?"

Will had to admit, he was impressed. In Beloit, bullies would simply demand your lunch money, or they'll beat you into a pulp. But in Elkhorn, you get to donate to the *Keep Mason Fed* fund. It all meant the same thing, of course. But Will suspected Mason McCree was as dangerous with his mind as he was with his muscles.

If he had it, Will would have given him the money to avoid trouble. Unfortunately it looked like an empty stomach wouldn't be the only reason to regret his mistake.

"I don't have any money. I'm sorry," he responded honestly.

"Ha!" Frankie jumped in. "Like anyone doesn't bring money to school! Unless your mommy packed you lunch."

"I… Forgot." Mentioning his mother hurt more than Frankie could have known.

"Hmm," Mason considered this. "Frankie, you do seem to have a point. This is an unlikely story, Lewis. You know what I think?"

Will thought Mason was addressing him, but it was Frankie who responded. "What d'ya think, boss?"

Chapter 3

"I think Lewis here is holding out on us. And, in a way, he's holding out on the whole town." Mason smirked, stepping towards Will. "And we can't have that, now can we?"

"I'm not lying, I really did forget…" Will repeated, not expected any better luck this time.

"Isn't that a shame…" Another step closer. "I'm going to teach you something, Lewis. Something you'd best not forget…" Mason was right in front of him now. Will craned his neck to keep eye contact. "*Never disrespect Mason McCree!*"

Mason cracked his knuckles. Will gulped. A hand grasped the collar of Will's shirt, and he felt his feet leave the ground. He was suspended an inch above the ground, expecting pain any moment.

"Giving the new guy a lift, McCree?"

The voice came from behind Will, and try as he might he couldn't turn his head enough to see who it was. But Mason could see the interruption. He screwed up his face like he drank sour milk.

"What do you want, Scott? Don't you have anything better to waste your time on?" Mason said.

The voice chuckled. "Better than screwin' with you? Never."

"We're in the middle of something, *Scott-rot!* Go run off and play with some trash!" Frankie burst out, shaking his fist.

"Already am," the voice said casually. An irritated vein started throbbing on Frankie's forehead.

"Let me ask you again, Scott," Mason spoke less smoothly than before. "What do you want?"

Footsteps echoed behind Will. "Always wanted a dartboard with your face on it, actually. Shame the lens cracks every time they take the picture."

Mason tossed Will into the wall. He thundered past

him, towards a kid dressed in all black. In a matter of moments this Scott character was being held by the collar, much as Will was a second ago. Mason could only lifted the kid slightly, as the difference in height was less pronounced.

"I've had just about enough of your wisecracks," Mason's cool composure was faltering. "I should put you in your place right now."

"Oh yeah? You mean like last time, right?" Scott grinned, locking eyes with Mason. Will couldn't believe this kid's guts. He was facing Mason without breaking a sweat. "Remember how that turned out? We got some matching black eyes and bruises, and you got suspended from the football team. This time, I'd bet you'd be out for most of next season."

Frankie was shaking like a lit firecracker, while Mason and Scott remained motionless.

"It'd be your word against mine," Mason whispered.

"Don't forget your pet rat over there and the new guy. I'm sure you trained that weasel to lie on command, but who knows what that kid's gonna say."

Once again Will's stomach lurched as he was brought back into the equation. He much preferred being on the sidelines of their scuffle.

"If he knows what's good for him, he wouldn't talk."

"So basically, it's a gamble," Scott pressed on, still standing with his feet raised and his chest pulled forward from Mason's grip. "If you hit me right now, your hand is dealt, and it's crap. You gotta bluff it out and hope nobody's got the guts to call you for the lying prick you are. The odds are against ya, McCree, and your prized spot on the team is at stake. Should you lose, well… You wouldn't want to let the *whole of Elkhorn* down, now would you?"

Will couldn't believe what he was seeing. This stranger not only had the nerve to stand up to Mason with a smirk on his face, but he possessed the wit to turn Mason's own words against him!

Defeated, Mason loosened his hold, and let Scott go. The triumphant smile on the dark kid's face further agitated Mason.

"This isn't over. I'll let you off easy, *this time*," Mason glared at Scott, then turned his attention back to Will. "And you, Lewis… Watch your back, and remember what I told you about disrespect."

"Mason! Mason! You aren't serious, right?" Frankie was in shock. "C'mon! You can't let *Scott* get the better of you! He's just a—"

"Shut up," Mason cut in. Frankie gave Scott an irritated glance before following Mason down the hall.

"You okay?"

Will straightened himself up. "Yeah," he said. "Thanks for that. You got me out of some big trouble."

"Big trouble?" the kid laughed. "I wouldn't take *McCrybaby* that seriously. He's used to getting his way because nobody calls him out. He's all talk."

"Well still, thanks." Will offered his hand, immediately feeling too formal. "I'm Will."

He shook Will's hand with a lazy grip. "The name's Travis Scott."

Now that the ruckus was over, Will got a better look at him. Travis had a long face, framed by stringy black hair that nearly touched his shoulders. He was wearing all black, from the beanie on his head to his baggy pants covered in zippers, studs, and deep pockets. *Tripp pants*, they were called.

"I guess I should get to lunch," Will told him.

Travis waited until Will was leaving. "I thought you didn't have any money," he called out.

Elkhorn Area High School

In all the commotion, Will forgot the cause of it. He hesitated, but Travis didn't wait for a response. "Here, I've got it covered today. I know a place we can get some cheap eats."

"Thanks," Will said. "But I couldn't ask that of you."

"And you ain't asking, I'm offering."

It didn't feel right to accept Travis' invitation, but Will's stomach wouldn't let him refuse. Travis led him down a few hallways and out of the building.

"Can we leave school during lunch?" Will had to ask.

Travis shrugged. "See anything stop us?"

They crossed the school grounds, towards a run-down shack by the road. This was Papi's; an open-air burger joint that looked like it belonged on the side of a beach. The round, jovial Polynesian man behind the counter only added to the tropical ambiance.

"'Ey, Travis! How you doin', bra?" the man said with an island accent. "Stayin' outta trouble?"

"You know me, Papi," Travis said as he approached the counter.

"That's why I'm askin'!" Papi gave a hearty laugh. "What'll it be, boys?"

"Two burgers, and as many fries I can muscle out of ya for two bucks." Travis was clearly a regular here, judging from his casual demeanor.

"Actually, just one burger is fine," said Will. When Travis gave him a look, he added "I'm vegetarian."

Travis didn't look any more familiar with the concept than Barbason, but brushed it off. "Whatever does it for you."

In a few moments Will and Travis were taking a seat at one of the old picnic tables outside with a burger and a brown bag of french fries.

"You have to try these," Travis held out the opened

Chapter 3

bag. "Papi's fries are the best in town."

Will stuck a reluctant hand into the bag and pulled out a dark, greasy french fry. As he chewed his first bite over, he wondered if these possibly werethe best fries in town. It was truly a frightening thought.

"So, what's the story?" asked Travis. He promptly jammed a fistful of fries into his mouth. Will looked perplexed, so he continued with his mouth half full. "Why you starting school so late? There's gotta be a story there."

"Oh…" He didn't want to relive the details yet, so Will settled for the short (but true) explanation. "I moved here from Beloit."

"I see…" Travis swallowed the load of fries. "Not much of an upgrade, I'm sure. There's a whole lot of nothing in Elkhorn."

They ate without much talking. It was a comfortable silence, like they already knew each other well enough to be out of things to say. A peaceful change of pace from feeling like "the new kid" at every class.

Will glanced at his watch, and did a double-take. "Travis, I need to get back to school. I have class in five minutes!"

Travis paused before biting a single, dangling fry. "So?"

Will sighed. "Let's just go, I'm pretty sure we're not supposed to be out here anyway."

Travis folded the bag to save the remaining fries and got to his feet. "Of course not. That's what makes it fun" he said with a smirk, leading the way back to school.

Travis escorted Will to his class, arriving only a few minutes late. Since they both had English after lunch, Travis reluctantly came along.

Elkhorn Area High School

"Mr. Scott," said the teacher as they entered. "How nice of you to join us today. Might I ask where you were yesterday?"

He glanced at Will and grinned. "Feeding the hungry, Mrs. Baker."

Baker... Will knew that name, but couldn't place where he heard it before. But when he saw her, he remembered exactly where; Grandpa Connor's funeral. Will found himself staring at his mom's childhood friend.

"Hello Will," Mrs. Baker said. Their eyes met, and he felt a bond of grief between them. They had both lost someone dear to them in that accident. But Mrs. Baker didn't break from her role as teacher, and instructed them both to take a seat. She spared him another public introduction.

Will saw another familiar face as he took a seat next to Travis. Sitting in the row ahead was Eliza. Will smiled at her, but only got a disapproving glare in return. He got the impression Eliza didn't like the company he arrived in.

Learning was the clear objective in Mrs. Baker's class. She kept the disruptive students in line, while keeping the environment engaging and interesting to those who let it be. Will loved it.

For the rest of the school day, Will found himself worrying less about studying and more about avoiding Mason. Thankfully Mason left him alone on the few occasions their paths crossed. He seemed to be taking Travis' warning, but Will didn't expect this ceasefire to last. He saw Eliza from time to time, always at the center of a flock of girls.

Travis didn't make another appearance until after school. Will was looking for his bus when he felt a tap on his shoulder.

"Yo, Will!" Travis said. "Hey, want to hang out for awhile? I know a great spot."

Chapter 3

He glanced back at the buses. "I don't know. My bus is leaving."

Travis studied the bus Will looked at. "If that's your bus, you can't live too far from here. I'll give you a ride home later."

Although Will didn't want Barbason to worry, he was in no hurry to go back. Boring as school had been, it sure beat wandering around at B.R. Amon. "Where is this spot?"

Travis grinned. "C'mon, I'll show ya."

"Alright, alright. But I can't stay long," Will told him.

So Travis led Will away from the homeward-bound students, and down the back side of school.

The parking lot of Elkhorn Area High School wrapped around the school. There were enough parking spots to accommodate all the soccer-moms and football-junkies in the area, with gates opening into a wide selection of sports fields. But behind the school there was another gate, concealed from the view of the highway. It led out of the parking lot and down a road lined with barns and other unidentified buildings. It was to this closed gate they were headed.

"Where are we going?" Will asked.

"The fairgrounds," Travis explained as he reached the gate. "Every summer this place sees some action for the County Fair, but it's pretty empty most of the time. Well, except when they set up that cheesy haunted house at Halloween."

Without hesitation he stepped onto the fence's railing, swung a leg over, and stepped off to the other side.

"Can we go in there if it's closed?"

With a careless smirk, Travis said "See anything stopping us?"

Will didn't like breaking rules. But as much as he hated to admit it, Travis captured his curiosity. So he too climbed over the gate (although with much less grace) and followed behind Travis.

They walked down a road lined with white, open-air barns. When the season was right they could house all sorts of farm animals, but now sat barren. Just beyond the barns was a red, octagonal building maybe a hundred feet wide. The sign above the closed garage door called this place the "Wiswell Center." Travis dropped his backpack at the door and approached one of the nearby barns. With the same practiced ease he had while jumping the gate, he stepped up onto the railing and began to climb onto the roof.

"Travis!" exclaimed Will. "What are you doing?"

From a young age, Will understood that some things were acceptable and some things were not. His father made the distinction clear, and Will never had trouble avoiding unacceptable behavior. Although climbing roofs wasn't covered, Will had a good idea what his father would have considered it.

"Just wait," said Travis, as if the good part was about to begin.

After a moment of sizing up the distance, Travis made a running leap from the roof of the barn to the slanted shingles of the Wiswell Center's roof.

Will stood in shock as Travis gave him a thumbs up. He strolled up to the raised center of the roof, where he unhinged a loose window and crawled inside. Will's jaw was still hanging open when Travis opened the door and let him in.

The Wiswell Center was empty inside, other than a few bleachers and a clear showroom floor in the middle.

"What's this place used for?" Will asked. While looking around he noticed a rope ladder hanging from one of the windows high above.

"Auctioning animals and stuff, I guess. All I know is, there's not much security here most of the time, so about two years ago I claimed this place as my personal hideout." Travis put his hand on Will's shoulder, surveying the place with pride. "What do you think?"

"I think you're going to get in big trouble when they find out about this," Will remarked instinctively. But despite everything he was raised to believe, he had to admit this was a pretty cool hideout.

Ascending a few rows of bleachers, Travis searched his large pockets and extracted a harmonica. He began to play a tune somewhere between Blues and Jazz. It had the unpracticed charm of a song being made up entirely as he went. Will took a seat at a front bleacher and flipped to a new puzzle in his Sudoku book. Not a word was spoken. Travis' slightly off-key melody calmed Will's mind, relaxing him for the first time all week. Finally Travis brought his harmonica solo to a finish.

"So, what's the story?"

This was the second time he asked that today, and Will wasn't sure if he was any more ready to talk about it now. "I told you at lunch. I just moved here last week."

"Yeah, yeah, but that's not the *story*. That's just trivia." Travis put his feet up on the next row of bleachers. "Why would your parents move to a nowhere town like this, anyhow?"

Will put down his book, wishing he didn't have to answer. "They didn't. They… Died."

Travis was quiet. "I'm sorry, man," he said, and sounded like he meant it.

"Thanks."

"So, where are you staying now?"

Will put his book of puzzles back in his bag. "I'm

living with my great-uncle at B.R. Amon. It's that garage on the end of Bray Road."

Thump.

Startled, Will turned around. Travis had fallen out of his seat.

"You're kidding me," he sounded both shocked and excited. "Your uncle is Old Man Amon?"

Will cocked his head in confusion. "I guess so. Barbason Amon, right? Why do you ask?"

Travis' whole face formed around a mischievous smile. Will knew that look was trouble. "This is too good. You're related to *the* Old Man Amon!"

Will knew Connor Amon was well-known in Elkhorn, but Travis was definitely talking about Dr. Amon's little brother.

"Do you know Uncle Barbason or something?" Will asked.

He laughed. "Know him? Never met the guy, but I know all the stories." When he saw the perplexed look on Will's face, he went on. "Don't you?"

"What stories?"

"The stories of The Beast," said Travis, unable to restrain a grin. "There's something out there, roaming the fields around Elkhorn. Something big. Something... Unnatural. Witnesses keep coming forward, telling their tale of a creature unlike anything they've ever seen. They describe it as a wolf the size of a grown man, that sometimes runs on all fours and sometimes stands on two legs.

"It's been called the 'Beast of Bray Road,' the 'Wisconsin Werewolf,' or simply 'The Beast.' Everyone has been talking about it, and every week there are more sightings. Whatever this thing is, it's sure getting around."

This story was making Will nervous. He kept having flashbacks of the accident, and the unidentified *thing* that attacked the car... "But what does this have to do with my great-uncle?" he asked.

Travis laughed. "It has everything to do with Old Man Amon. He's been acting strange ever since this Beast started showing up. A couple months back, he closed up shop without warning, and has barely been out around town. He's always been a recluse, so no one thought much of it at first. Until, of course, someone saw The Beast lurking right outside his garage. After that, people started to talk..."

He leaned in close so that his face was almost level with Will's. "Hate to break it to you, buddy, but half the town thinks your uncle is a werewolf."

Chapter 4:

Old Man Amon

Will's mind was still reeling as they crossed the school grounds.

They didn't talk much after Travis told the tale of the "Wisconsin Werewolf." For the most part Will sat there thinking while Travis played an upbeat rhythm on his harmonica.

Now that they were back in fresh air, Will could think clearly. Could Barbason really be a—he had a hard even using the word in his thoughts—a *werewolf?* His first thought was *No, of course not.* But was he really so sure? Will didn't know his great-uncle well enough to defend him. And he was, well... Strange.

But, seriously... Werewolves weren't real. Will was no expert on shape-shifters, but he understood basic biology enough to know they belonged purely in the realm of fiction.

So why am I still rattled? he thought.
("There's something out there, roaming the fields around

Chapter 4

Elkhorn.")

Will thought about the night of the accident. He convinced himself what he saw that night was only part of his nightmares... But what if it wasn't?

(*"Something big. Something... Unnatural."*)

What if that was the same thing the locals were talking about? What if Will had been attacked by the infamous Beast of Bray Road?

He shuddered, but tried to put it out of his mind.

Across the street from Elkhorn Area High School was a small trailer park. A dozen mobile homes in various states of deterioration were parked there. Some still looked presentable, while others clearly lacked the maintenance they desperately needed. As they trudged through the fresh snow, Will wondered if Travis lived here. He didn't want to offend him in case he was wrong (for all Will knew he had friends here. Or, more likely, he knew someone who didn't lock up their valuables) so he kept silent.

But they walked right past the trailers. At the far end of the park was tiny Quonset hut with a door, window and even a little driveway.

"Do you live here?" Will had to ask.

Travis looked less than enthusiastic. "Quite the palace, ain't it?"

He unchained his bike and wheeled it to the road, where the snow was plowed. Will stepped onto the pegs, held Travis' shoulders, and they rode towards the highway.

"Here it is," said Travis dramatically when they turned off the county road. "Bray Road. Home of the Beast."

Before, this stretch of land felt enchanting. But now Will found himself holding his breath around every curve or hill. It was a relief to see B.R. Amon come into view up

Old Man Amon

ahead.

"Dude, you have to introduce me," Travis said as Will dismounted.

Will could not imagine that meeting going well. "Maybe," he said, hoping to avoid the situation if at all possible.

They said their goodbyes, and Travis rode off. Now Will had to face his great-uncle with the seed of suspicion planted in his mind. Will promised himself he wouldn't let Travis' story affect what he thought of Barbason.

He couldn't keep that promise.

It was nearly five o' clock when Will got home, and Barbason only just woke up. Although he was used to the old man's sleep pattern by now, Will had to admit it was unusual.

Will kept reminding himself that his great-uncle was a good guy. He opened his home to a kid he barely knew. Sure he's a little odd, but there's no reason to think he was dangerous.

Well, except for that one time at Connor's funeral…

("Yer father ain't no saint, Cass!")

Yes, there was that.

After putting his school supplies away, Will searched the fridge for some dinner. He was reminded just how much meat there was… It looked like pork chops, chicken breasts, something that might have been ground beef, and a few more exotic (and disgusting) pieces. Having been vegetarian for so long, Will couldn't identify it all with much certainty.

(Could be human, for all I know.)

Will tried not to assume the worst. So what if he likes meat? Plenty of people do. Just like plenty of people sleep during the day. These were ordinary, mundane things. But still…

Chapter 4

He got some food together and joined Barbason at the table. He was having an evening breakfast of barbecue ribs. Will tried to eat his own sandwich without watching his great-uncle tear meat from bones.

"So..." Barbason said in between bites. "How was school?"

You would think talking would get easier between them. But after almost a week, it felt just as forced as the day he moved in.

"It was fine." Will left out the topic of werewolves. Might not be the best dinner conversation.

Barbason chomped into another rib. He appeared to be racking his brain for something to say. "Make any friends?"

Mason's welcoming committee came to mind. "A few."

The rest of dinner was quiet and awkward. Will knew he was being irrational. But try as he might, he couldn't keep his mind off the possibility that his great-uncle could be a werewolf.

The next morning, Will went through the same routine to get ready for school. But this time, he remembered to bring money for lunch. Unless Mason tried the same stunt twice, Will figured he would be able to eat today. He loaded up his backpack, and went outside to wait for the bus.

Eliza was already waiting by the curb. They exchanged greetings, although she was missing her usual smile.

"What's the deal with you and Travis?" she asked.

Even Will wasn't quite sure of the answer. Calling Travis a friend might be stretching it. "He helped me out, that's all."

Old Man Amon

She looked disapproving. "You don't want help from Travis Scott. He only brings trouble."

Will didn't have a chance to say otherwise, because the bus chose that moment to pull up. Eliza gave Will a cold shoulder as they found their seats. Watching the passing scenery, Will wondered if she was right.

To his relief, Will made it through the first half of his day without trouble. Eliza kept to her flock of friends. Mason didn't confront him, but when they locked eyes in the hallway Will knew the score wasn't settled. Travis didn't even make an appearance until English Class, where he strolled in barely on time.

After class, Mrs. Baker pulled Will aside.

"May I speak with you, Will?" she asked.

"Sure," he said.

Travis looked a little offended as he left, as if Will had gotten into trouble without him.

Mrs. Baker closed the door as the last students left. She took her time searching for the right words.

"How have you been? Since the accident, I mean," she asked carefully.

He wanted to say "fine," but the words just wouldn't come out. He stared at his feet without response.

She placed a gentle hand on Will's shoulder. "I am so very sorry. There has been too much tragedy in your family."

Will forced himself to nod. He couldn't bring himself to talk about his parents. Not again, so soon after going over it with Travis.

"Where are you staying now?"

The last time he answered this question, Will got more than he hoped for. He hoped that this time would be less dramatic. "With my Uncle Barbason."

Mrs. Baker looked a little wary. "I hope he's treating you well."

Chapter 4

"He is."

"Well, if you ever need anything," she said, grabbing a business card from her desk. "Anything at all, don't hesitate to call. I'm here for you."

Will felt he could trust Mrs. Baker; she was perhaps the only person who truly shared his grief.

"Thanks, Mrs. Baker."

She smiled. "Please, call me Julie."

Now Will returned the smile. "Okay, Julie."

Will turned to leave, but as his hand reached the doorknob another question came to mind.

"Mrs. Ba—I mean, Julie?"

She looked up. "Yes?"

He had to think of the best way to say it. "Do you believe in werewolves?"

Mrs. Baker was clearly caught off guard. She first looked confused, but slowly appeared to understand.

"I don't believe you have anything to worry about here," she finally said.

"You didn't answer my question."

She looked at the clock. "I think you should be getting to class."

After a quick goodbye, Will left her classroom.

(*I don't believe you have anything to worry about here.*)

Will was wrong; she did answer his question. If she thought the idea of werewolves was absurd, she could easily have said so. No, it seemed that Mrs. Baker believed it was possible.

To Will, that meant it was worth looking into.

"Yo, Will!" Travis called out as Will approached his bus. "Want to go chill at the hideout?"

"Not today, Travis. I really need to get caught up on

homework," he said. It was all too true; coming into the school year so late meant he had his work cut out for him.

Travis looked disappointed. "That's lame."

"But this weekend, I could use your help. Do you think you could take me to the library? I want to look into…" Will lowered his voice. "That thing we talked about yesterday."

Travis' eyes lit up. "*That* thing? You know it, man."

"Great. See you tomorrow."

Will got on the bus and went home. When he got off the bus at B.R. Amon, Will was pulled aside by Eliza.

"You and Travis are up to something," Eliza said, not bothering with hellos.

"We aren't up to anything…" Will tried to sound convincing. Unfortunately he still couldn't keep his voice from faltering around her.

She put her hands on her hips and raised an eyebrow. "Really? Then what are you and Travis looking up at the library?"

Will's first thought was *How could she know that?* But then he remembered they took the same bus. She could easily have been within earshot of that conversation.

"Oh... That."

He was at a loss for words. She wouldn't believe it if he said the real reason, but Will knew he lacked the ability to lie to her. His mind went back to something his dad used to say; *when in doubt, tell the truth.*

He made it sound so easy.

"Well?" Eliza was getting impatient.

With no better options, Will blurted out "We're researching werewolves."

Eliza didn't react in the way he thought she would. No exasperated sigh or roll of the eyes. She just stared at Will, her face unreadable.

Chapter 4

"Werewolves?"

Will nodded.

Then the shock passed, and her original attitude returned. "That's ridiculous," she said. "Werewolves are make-believe! It's stupid to waste your time researching them."

"Well, I mean... With all the stuff going on, don't you think it's worth looking into? Just to see what there is to see." Will had a hard time justifying it; he wasn't sure if he believed it himself.

Eliza was heated. "No, I don't!"

Without another word she stormed up the hill to her house, leaving Will in a daze.

Barbason kept trying to be a good guardian. He attempted to make dinner, although vegetarianism stilled boggled his mind. He tried to make conversation, awkward as it was.

Will found himself wondering why. Barbason lived alone, quit his job, and kept mostly to himself. Why would he care about his brother's grandson? It's not like there weren't other options; he could easily have left Will in an orphanage. And, really, who could blame him? Will appreciated the hospitality, even if he didn't understand the motive.

That Friday, Will had a strange thought while drifting off in Math class. What does Barbason *do* all night? He slept until around five o' clock, and was in bed before Will got up at six thirty. There was a large gap there, and with an inconsistent TV and a lack of books, Will couldn't help but wonder how he passes the time.

(Prowling the cornfields, perhaps?)

Those thoughts kept popping up, no matter how much Will tried to ignore them. So that night, Will decided to ask about his hobbies.

"Hobbies?" Barbason mumbled while eating. "What'dya mean?"

"Like, you know… Hobbies," Will tried to explain. "Like reading, solitaire, Sudoku, things like that."

He swallowed a bite of steak, looking confused. "What's Sudoku?"

"It's a number game," Will said. "You have to get a unique number on each row and column without any duplicates. It's fun."

Barbason's face was blank. "Oh."

"So, what kind of stuff do you like to do? I mean, when everyone else is asleep."

A dark looked flashed across his face, and vanished just as suddenly. "Carve, mostly. Sometimes I play solitaire when the TV ain't behavin', but I ain't no good at it."

Will's curiosity flared. "You carve? What do you carve, and what from?"

Barbason took another bite. "Carve from wood. Got plenty of planks leftover from the shop."

"Can I see?" Will had no idea his great-uncle did anything cool like that.

Reluctantly, Barbason gave a little nod as he took another bite.

Once they finished eating, Barbason took Will down the narrow hallway, and they stepped through the door to B.R. Amon's garage.

Will never saw this place before. This single room was bigger than the rest of the house. Tools, planks of wood, and intimidating construction equipment loomed all around.

"Sorry it's such a mess in here," Barbason said. "I'd like to say it's 'cause the shop closed, but it got messy long before then. Anyway, here's what we came for."

One corner was dedicated to the old man's hobby.

Chapter 4

Wooden statues were scattered across the floor and table, near a pile of the planks they were born from. Barbason handed one to Will.

"This one's most recent."

Will's heart stopped.

"He makes *what?*"

Travis nearly lost control of the bike. They were on their way to the library when Will recounted what his great-uncle showed him.

"Wolf carvings," Will repeated, trying not to sound as disturbed as he was. "Almost every one. He carved a wolf's skull, a claw, a complete miniature sculpture... Even one of a man with a wolf's head."

"Seriously? Man, this is awesome!" Travis peddled faster. "Old Man Amon is our werewolf, alright. No doubt about that."

But Will did have doubts. "This doesn't prove anything, Travis."

Travis rolled his eyes. "You're kidding me. On top of what I've already told you, the guy was showing off his collection of werewolf souvenirs. How else can you explain that? He just so happens to be an enthusiast?"

As much as Will hated to admit it, Travis had a point. This was stretching coincidence a little too far.

"Let's just wait to make any judgments until we know more," he said. "A little research should give us a better idea."

"Suit yourself," said Travis.

They rode through downtown Elkhorn. The busy section of Elkhorn had the perfect combination of small-town charm and historic elegance. You could easily walk or bike to any number of small stores, each adding to the quaint atmosphere. At night, Will could imagine warm lights flickering through the windows, and the scene (with a light blanket of snow just like this) would make a perfect Christmas postcard. The town square was full of snow-covered trees, with many stone paths leading to the county clerk's office in the center.

Beyond the town square was the Mathesone Memorial Library.

It was an imposing building, with tall stone pillars at either end of the two-story glass entryway. Will was impressed. They entered the antechamber, a room with a tall ceiling, windows to a half-story floor of the library, and a grand piano sitting regally in a corner. On their way to the main library, they passed a group of small compartments in the wall, that looked a little like a wall of post office boxes.

Will recognized the compartments. *It's a card catalog!* he thought. Before digital catalogs became the norm, people used card catalogs to search through the library's collection. He doubted it was in use anymore, but it added a feeling of antiquity.

The library itself did not disappoint. Shelves and shelves of books were categorized, organized, and alphabetized. They went to the large round desk, asked directions to the non-fiction section, and climbed up a set of circular stairs.

The non-fiction section was a world of its own. Over a dozen computers were clustered together on their left, and to the right shelves of books were waiting to be read.

Will and Travis wasted no time.

Unfortunately, this was Will's first time to the library (mostly likely Travis' as well), so it took awhile to get familiar with their surroundings. They started skimming through the shelves, picking books that appeared useful and piling them on a table in the corner.

Once they had a sizable stack of books, they settled

Chapter 4

into the table. It was hidden away behind the bookshelves, and the window looked out on the piano in the antechamber.

The difference in their choices of reading material was amazing, even when on the same subject. Among Will's choices were *Fact or Fiction; an investigation of misconceived truths about the Supernatural, The Werewolf Trials, A History of Shape-Shifters,* and *Clinical Lycanthropy; the real-world Werewolves.* Travis, on the other hand, contributed *A Werewolf ate my homework* (a fictional comedy), *The Beast Within* (a werewolf horror novel), several trashy tabloids, and the DVD of *An American Werewolf in London.* How he thought a movie would help was a mystery to Will.

"Hey, it showed the transformation in great detail," Travis explained. "Thought we should see how it works."

Will rolled his eyes as he read the dust jacket of *A History of Shape-Shifters.* "You know that movie isn't even based off a true story, right?"

He shrugged, indifferent.

Will split the books into two piles, and they started reading.

First Will cracked open *Clinical Lycanthropy; the real-world Werewolves.* He never heard of such a thing, and attaching the word "clinical" made the concept more plausible. It sounded promising at first; a rare delusion that the victim is a wolf, or can turn into a wolf. They become feral, often violent, and even exhibit "superhuman strength" (due mainly to increased adrenaline). It all made sense to Will's logical mind, until he realized that it didn't match the encounters at all. People were seeing a *creature,* not a delusional old man.

The next book up was *A History of Shape-Shifters.* It was organized chronologically, covering stories and folklore of people who could turn into animals. Will knew werewolves weren't a new concept, but he had no idea just how broad the topic was. Almost every culture around the world had some werewolf equivalent, although the type of animal varied to match the region. Most of the werewolf action seemed to be in Europe, but the Native Americans had their *Skin-Walkers*. As the stories go, Skin-Walkers could transform into any animal they desired, but had to wear the pelt of that animal. Will decided the book was definitely worth further research, and set it in a pile of books to borrow.

The Werewolf Trials proved to be an interesting read as well. It had many famous cases of werewolf convictions during the 15thto 17thcenturies. It must have been a big deal; in some country called Estonia, 29 women and 26 men were executed for using sorcery, much of it involving the transformation into a wolf. In one case, a shepherd kissed the hand of a "black horseman," turning him into a werewolf and a soldier of Satan. And in another case...

"Travis," Will said as his eyes darted across the page. "This sounds a little too familiar."

Travis perked up. He had been lazily flipping through *The New Encyclopedia of the Occult* without much interest. "About time! What'd you find, buddy?"

Will read the page again, trying to summarize it for Travis. "This was the case of Gilles Garnier, or "the Hermit of St. Bonnet" as the locals called him."

"Hermit of St. Bonnet?" Travis laughed. "I can see why that reminded you of Old Man Amon, alright."

"It gets worse." He read on. "It says Garnier had trouble getting enough food for himself and his new wife, so he would go hunting. While he was out, a spirit came to him, and offered him a magical ointment that would turn him into a wolf. After that... Children went missing. No one suspected The Hermit until he was caught attacking a child. Some witnesses claim to have seen a wolf, but others... They say it

Chapter 4

was Garnier."

The thrilled look on Travis' face was a little unnerving. "What happened to the guy?"

Will gulped. "He was convicted of being a werewolf, and burned at the stake."

Travis was more interested than ever. "We're sure getting a case together here. Before long we'll be able to prove it."

Suddenly, Will lost his taste for the topic. He pictured his great-uncle, tied-up and burning alive, while a crowd chanted *Werewolf! Werewolf!*

It was not a pleasant sight.

He was about to suggest they call it a day, when Eliza unexpectedly appeared.

"What nonsense have you been telling him?" Eliza said scornfully to Travis.

Scowling, Travis said "All I did was give him the facts."

"Facts? You call gossip 'facts' now?"

"Like you can talk, oh queen of the grapevine."

"At least I have reliable sources."

"If your call your airhead girlfriends and brainless jocks 'reliable,' then sure."

"Compared to what? Don't you get your information from TV shows like *The X-Files* and *Monsters of America?*"

Listening to them bicker was dizzying. Will threw up his hands and said "Enough, both of you!" a little louder than he hoped. The librarian cast them a reproachful look from across the room.

"Look," said Will, whispering again. "Travis didn't convince me of anything. He just told me some rumors going around."

Eliza was not pleased. "So why did you bother coming here? You can't really believe these stories, do you?"

Old Man Amon

"I don't know," Will answered truthfully. "I guess that's why I'm here; to figure out if I believe it or not."

Eliza's eyes were hard, but her voice was almost pleading. "But why does it matter?"

Will hesitated, working up the courage to speak. When he did, he looked her straight in the eye, with clarity he didn't know he had.

"It matters because I saw it."

By the time they left the library, the sun was already hidden behind the horizon.

Eliza was quite a hindrance to their research. She fell dead silent once Will admitted his sighting, then returned to resisting the concept with fresh zeal. Her defensiveness didn't make sense; if she thought it was stupid, why didn't she just stay out of it? They weren't exactly close friends.

When they finally called it a day, Will suggested Travis hold onto the books. It would be hard to explain to Barbason why a book like *The Werewolf Trials* was lying around. Neither of them had a library card, so they waited while the librarian (a large, trollish woman ironically named Mrs. Flower) scoffed at their choice of books.

"Rubbish," Mrs. Flower grumbled. "Pure rubbish."

Now, they were riding up Bray Road under the purple-orange sky of sunset. Maybe it was the winter chill, but Will had goosebumps as they approached B.R. Amon. He kept looking over his shoulder, expecting to see something

(Those eyes—Human Eyes)

Watching him. But there was nothing more than snow drifting in the breeze. At this time of twilight, everything seemed creepy; the farm houses looked deserted, the woods were foreboding, and every hill in the road promised danger.

Chapter 4

But they peddled into B.R. Amon's parking lot without trouble, so Will let himself breathe again. He stepped off the pegs, said goodbye, and watched Travis ride back down Bray.

Alone, the uneasiness got worse. Goosebumps tickled across his whole body. Someone was here, someone was watching him. He could almost feel their breath on the back of his neck. He raced for the door, panicked.

Before he reached the handle, the door opened.

Will gasped, but it was only his great-uncle. He was leaning on the door frame, breathing heavily.

"Sit," Barbason instructed.

Will did as he was told, taking off his coat and taking a seat on the couch.

Barbason plopped into his easy chair. "We need to have... A little talk." His words were raspy and strained.

"About what?" Will said. The ominous feeling that followed him home was just as strong now. Stronger, in fact.

"This be the country, kid... When it gets dark, all sorts o' critters come out," said Barbason.

"I'm sorry, Uncle Barbason. I'll try to be home earlier next time."

The old man sat there, silent aside from the wheezing. After a long pause, Will got up, and went towards his room.

"Kid."

He looked back.

"When the sun sets... Don't be out there... You might get hurt."

There was something in Barbason's eyes Will hadn't seen since the funeral. There was darkness behind those pupils, a hungry void trying to pull you in. Will had seen that intensity once before, the day of the funeral.

A wave of fear splashed across Will like cold water. Something stoked a fire in Barbason, and the last time he saw

Old Man Amon

it two people died. The words echoed in his mind the rest of night.

("You might get hurt.")

Chapter 5:

Tales of the Beast

There was not a sound in the house, aside from the scratching of pencil on paper and the distant snores from Barbason's room.

It was five o' clock in the morning and Will was awake, filling out puzzle after puzzle from his Sudoku book. It was another night of little sleep, as most have been the last few weeks. Will didn't enlighten Travis about Barbason's warning, partly because he felt Travis might think it was worth calling a witch hunt. But there was another reason he didn't feel comfortable mentioning it; ever since that night, Will had the disturbing feeling of being followed whenever he left the house. More than likely he just had a case of the jitters, but he kept that encounter to himself all the same.

"A six here, which means I can put a two... Here," Will whispered to his quiet room. He took another look at the nine-by-nine grid and noticed something was wrong. One column just needed a four, but there was already a four on the only open row. Somewhere, probably near the beginning,

Will made a mistake, and had been going down the wrong track ever since. Will drew a large X over the puzzle, admitting defeat.

Could the same be happening in real life?

Restlessly, Will wondered. Something wasn't adding up with this whole werewolf business. Clearly, *something* was strange in Elkhorn. But there was still the simple fact that werewolves weren't real. Physically, it was impossible; a body can't restructure itself so dramatically in such a short amount of time. Maybe there was no transformation after all, and this "Beast" was just a large wolf out of its habitat.

Then how would you explain Barbason's behavior?

Will closed his puzzle book and gave up on the topic. He suspected there was a missing piece, that once found would force him to reshuffle all of his theories. Until then, he would escape into the land of fiction with a good book.

Hours later, it was finally time for school. It was now halfway through March, and the snow was almost all gone. Will waited at the curb in a light jacket, preferring the fresh air to the dusty and quiet house.

Eliza strolled down to wait with him. Although she settled down since she found them at the library, she also kept her distance. Will wanted to talk to her about it all week, but never had the guts. This morning he finally held his nerves, and asked her.

"Are you okay, Eliza? You've been quiet lately."

She looked mildly indignant. "I have not. Maybe you've just been too busy monster hunting with Travis to have a conversation."

That was unfair. Will had scarcely spent time with Travis since the library, despite his frequent nagging to take investigation "on the field." Whatever that meant.

"Why are you so upset about this?" Will asked.

"I'm not," she replied sharply. "I just think you're

Chapter 5

wasting time. There is no 'Wisconsin Werewolf.' And the sooner you realize that, the better."

Will wanted her to understand, but didn't have the strength to argue with her. They boarded the bus without another word.

Something was different at school. At first, it was just a feeling; that nameless suspicion that things are not quite right. But when the feeling didn't go away, Will took a closer look around.

People were staring at him. Lots of people. Almost every set of eyes followed him as he passed. The expressions varied; some were pointing, others slowly backing away. But most just glanced at Will from the corner of their eyes, as if they didn't want to be caught looking.

This behavior continued to puzzle Will, until someone finally approached him after History Class.

"So, is it true?" said a kid Will shared the class with. He wasn't sure, but he thought the kid's name was Jimmy. "Your grandpa is Old Man Amon?"

Whoa. Will didn't know what he expected, but this wasn't it. "Well, more like a great-uncle, actually," he corrected.

The atmosphere in the hall changed. Passing students paused, and the background noise of mingled conversations died off. Now all ears as well as eyes were on Will.

"Isn't he a werewolf?" a ninth-grade girl chimed in.

"A werewolf?" someone said from the middle of the crowd. "Don't be stupid. Werewolves aren't real."

"Then how do you explain that Beast of Bray Road?" Jimmy responded, talking over the crowd. "My neighbor just saw it last week!"

A blond-haired girl tugged on Will's sleeve. "Have

you ever seen him change?"

"I, well—no, not really." Will was fumbling his words. He had no idea how to respond to all of this attention. He felt very self-conscious, and needed to get away. He turned to make a break for it, and walked right into a rock-solid torso.

"What's the hurry, Lewis?"

Will looked up. Towering over him was none other than Mason. "Not now, Mason. Please."

Mason sneered down at him. "And let you miss out on your fifteen minutes of fame? I don't think so."

When Will saw the satisfied look in Mason's eyes, he came to a horrible realization. "You did this, didn't you? You spread rumors about where I live and who I'm related to."

Mason's smirk was filled with malice. "They're only rumors if they aren't true. Please, feel free to deny it if I'm mistaken."

Will was appalled. "Why would you do this?"

Even with all the commotion, Will could hear each word Mason whispered. "I warned you, Lewis. Never disrespect Mason McCree. Consider this your second warning. Next time, I won't go so easy on you."

The need to escape was overwhelming. Will felt betrayed. He had never intended to aggravate Mason, yet here he was going out of his way to make Will's life miserable. Without another word he turned from Mason and broke through the crowd, unmindful of the stream of questions. If it wasn't for the bell, he might have kept running until he reached the end of school.

During Science Class, Will spent very little time on the subject. His mind kept running in circles, from anger to hurt to confusion and back. But the question that wouldn't go away was... How? How did Mason find out about his connection to Barbason? They didn't share a name. Will hoped they didn't look alike. And he hadn't exactly made it public knowledge. Only a handful of people knew of the relation, and none of them seemed likely to share the news with Mason.

Oh well. Will supposed it was only a matter of time, anyway. He once heard a saying: *There are no secrets in a small town.* There was some truth to that, alright.

As Will left class, someone grabbed his arm. He shuddered, expecting to see Mason or another student harassing him about werewolves. To his relief, it was only Travis.

"Hey man, want to have lunch at Papi's?" Travis asked.

Typically Will avoiding doing this, but the thought of another audience forming in the cafeteria was reason enough to bend his rule. "That would be great, thanks."

They made the trek across the school grounds to the shack lovingly called Papi's. Will offered to pay, and Travis gladly accepted. The big islander behind the counter was beginning to recognize Will, although he referred to him as "the little vegetarian brah" in his most jovial tone.

"Figured you'd like to get outta that place," Travis said once they were settled on their rickety table. "I got wind of today's gossip headline."

That wasn't surprising. Travis was unnaturally attuned to that school. He knew hallways and routes to avoid attention, and was always up to date on what went on.

"Thanks," said Will, examining a charred french fry with unwarranted attention. "What bothers me is how Mason found out in the first place. You didn't tell him, did you?"

Travis laughed. "Nah, wasn't me. Although I like the idea of threatening to sic the Beast on him next time he gets in the way. See how tough he is then!"

Tales of the Beast

Will flung a fry at him. "That's not funny. Seriously, do you have any idea how he could have heard?"

"Hmm..." He chewed a mouthful of Papi's finest grease sponges. "Who all knew about it before today?"

"Other than us?" Will made a mental count. "Well, Uncle Barbason of course. Mrs. Baker, Eliza..."

Travis almost choked. "Eliza? You mean to tell me *she* knows your Old Man Amon's brother's grandkid?" He was spewing bits of food as he spoke.

It took a moment to translate Travis' wording. "Yeah, she's my neighbor. She sees me come from his house every morning."

"Well sound the sirens, we have a winner ladies and gentleman!" he exclaimed bitterly. "She spilled the beans to McCrybaby. No doubt about that."

"You don't know that," said Will. If that was true, it could possibly be the only thing that could make his day any worse. "Anyone else on my bus might have figured it out. Uncle Barbason's house is one of the last stops. Just because you two don't get along doesn't mean she's all bad."

Travis swallowed the mouthful of fries he was working on. "I'm not saying this because she's a shallow stuck-up priss, bro."

"Then why are you saying it?" Will sighed.

Reaching his hand into the grease-stained bag of fries, Travis continued. "I'm saying this because she's a shallow stuck-up priss who McCrybaby hangs around like a dog to a fire hydrant."

Will's heart sank as he understood what Travis was saying. "You mean Mason and Eliza are, well... Dating?"

"Don't know, mate. But if they ain't, McCrybaby would sure like to change that." Travis wiped his hands on his baggy Tripp pants. "Why do you care, anyhow? You got a thing for Little Miss Priss?"

Chapter 5

He said it jokingly, but when he saw the color drain from Will's face his mood changed.

"Oh *hell* nah! You *do* have the hots for her!"

What was the point of denying it? Will absentmindedly took the last fry, his silence confirming Travis' fear.

"Man, I hate to tell you but she has got to be one of the worst girls you could be crushing on," Travis said. They got up and headed back to school. "She's way out of your league, a total prep, and you'd have the biggest lowlife in town competing for face time with her. You don't exactly seem fond of his tactics so far, I might add."

"Okay, okay, I get it." Will didn't want to hear it anymore. He just wanted this day to be over—or better yet, to have never happened in the first place.

The news of Mason's interest in Eliza cast a shadow over Will's day. Not that he ever really thought he had a chance, of course. But in her smile or her playful wink, there seemed to be a glimmer of hope. Now he didn't even have that. He was so distracted that he hardly noticed as students asked him stupid questions about his great-uncle.

Eliza and Will both seemed to avoid each other. They didn't meet eyes in English Class. They stayed away in the halls. And when the bus dropped them off, they went straight to their own homes without saying a word.

As the week went on, Barbason's behavior was getting stranger (which truly was saying something.) He was quieter at dinner, without his usual forced attempts at conversation. Sometimes he would barely eat, instead just staring blankly into nothing. But other times, his appetite would be voracious; so much so that Will had to shield himself from bits of flying food!

Tales of the Beast

Most alarming of all, sometimes Will heard his great-uncle leave in the middle of the night. He would return an hour or two later, gasping for breath and limping heavily.

As if that wasn't enough, things were getting worse at school. Throughout the week it seemed the "Beast of Bray Road" was making its rounds; three more people came forward with sightings by Friday. Travis (who Will had reluctantly told about Barbason's strange activity) insisted they take their research on-location, since they weren't finding any answers at the library. Will didn't like the idea, but agreed they could take a look around Saturday.

In preparation, they spent Friday afternoon at the hideout, pouring over their borrowed werewolf literature. Will brought a spiral notebook, and began taking notes on anything that could relate to their investigation. Travis got bored reading, and proceeded to add background music with his harmonica.

"Looks like we'll want to bring something silver. A cross, preferably," Will said while copying notes from *Fact or Fiction*. "I figured that was all Hollywood, but I guess there's some truth to it."

Travis wore a proud smile. "See? The movies know what they're talking about. Now if we could just get our hands on some silvers bullets, we'd be all set."

"That wouldn't be a good idea," Will said.

"Why's that? Are werewolves bulletproof?" Travis perked up at the thought.

Although some of the *Werewolf Trials* did mention immunity to injury, Will was thinking along more practical lines. "No. But somehow I think carrying a rifle loaded with silver bullets might attract the wrong kind of attention."

Travis considered this. He didn't look entirely convinced. "Alright, fine... What about a BB gun?"

Will hid his face behind a book, sighing.

Chapter 5

The next morning, it was Saturday. This turned out to be one of Barbason's "sleep like the dead" days, which was fine by Will. His great-uncle never asked many questions when Will was out, but he was grateful to avoid the topic entirely. All the same, he thought leaving a note was a good idea. He tore a piece of paper out of his notebook and wrote.

Uncle Barbason,

Went with Travis (Friend from school). Be back this afternoon.
— Will

He thought about adding "back before dark, don't worry," but didn't want to bring up that night again.

Travis arrived early right on time, contrary to his nature. Much to Will's relief he didn't appear armed.

"So what are we packin'?" Travis asked.

"Not much," Will confessed. "I didn't have a cross or anything, but I did find some old silverware that belonged to Uncle Barbason's dad."

Travis laughed. "Great, we're hunting a werewolf with a silver butter knife."

"I know, I know. But it's all we've got."

He shrugged. "We could still pick up that BB."

Will just shook his head.

It was a wet, dreary March day. No rain yet, but the air tasted moist and the clouds promised showers anytime now. It wasn't late enough in the season for the cornfields or soybeans to be grown, but already you could see life sprouting in the fields.

Travis peddled down the road a ways, until B.R. Amon was out of sight.

"One of the first sightings happened right up here," he explained. "It was on Halloween."

Will was skeptical. "Halloween, huh? Sounds like a prank to me."

"Yeah, a lot of people thought that, too. It wasn't until more people came forward anyone took her seriously." He brought his bike to a stop as the road made a gentle curve. "It happened right around here. This lady was driving home late at night, and as she came around the bend she saw something by the side of the road. When it came into view of her headlights, she was greeted by a pair of glowing eyes."

A shiver threatened to creep down Will's spine. "Eye shine. Lots of animals have eyes that reflect in headlights."

"That ain't all she saw. Those eyes belonged to a big hairy creature. Whatever it was, she said it was kneeling by the road. It had its claws held up, holding something. She wasn't sure, but the lady said it looked like it was holding roadkill."

"What happened?" Will's interest was piqued.

"Nothing," said Travis. "It just watched as she drove by. But you know what unnerved her the most?"

"I'm sure you're going to tell me."

Travis cracked a grin. "Those eyes weren't canine. She would swear on a bible that the eyes watching her belonged to something more human than animal."

Will's heart started racing. This was reminding him too much of the accident. Of the creature. And of nightmares plagued by terribly human eyes.

"Let's... Keep going," Will said. If he was this spooked already, he wasn't sure he could handle the rest of the day.

Chapter 5

They continued down the lonely road. Travis kept a constant narrative of sightings, some that happened in the area and some from other parts of town. Will wondered how much of these stories were embellished in their retelling.

"Somewhere along here, Louie Enders—he's this mechanic bloke from the trailer park—actually hit the Beast! He was in his project car, this crappy little Geo Tracker that's half black, half rust. Anyway, Louie was speeding along, putting his recent tune up to the test, when something ran across the road. He slammed the breaks, but not fast enough. Now, I've ridden in that Tracker, and you could feel the bump when it runs over a penny. So when it hit this thing, Louie and his little Cheap Jeep went sailing!

"Once he got control of the car and pull off to the curb, Louie went to see what he hit. He's a decent guy, Louie. Thought it might have been someone's dog, and wanted to check for a collar. So he gets out, and Louie gets one hell of a surprise. It was so huge he first thought it was a bear, but it's body was built more like a dog... Or a wolf.

"The thing he hit didn't stay down long. It was up and growling in seconds, and that's when Louie decided to high-tail it outta there. He slammed his door shut and peeled out of there, but not before the Beast slashed up his Tracker!"

Disturbingly human eyes. Car collisions. This was a little too familiar. "Was he hurt?"

"Louie? Nah. I bet he had to change his pants afterward, but he's fine. His car got pretty messed up though. I saw the claw marks myself."

Will wanted to see them, too. Maybe later they would pay a visit to Louie Enders.

"And for our next stop on the Werewolf Safari," Travis continued. He was alight with humor and excitement; Travis must have spent many bored years in Elkhorn before he had the Beast to talk about. "We are turning off of Bray

Tales of the Beast

Road, and down a little stretch I like to call Hospital Road."

As narrated, they left Bray Road and went south. Hospital Road was flatter than Bray, but out in the farmlands they all looked pretty similar; fields, woods, and a few houses scattered about like an afterthought.

"That farm house over there belongs to Crazy Borys Kava and his family. This guy is like, one hundred twenty percent Polish, and always rambling about the freaky foreign crap he cooks."

"And that's enough to be called crazy?" Will asked.

Travis scratched his chin. "Nah, it ain't because of that. He's just crazy."

It wasn't hard to believe why Barbason was nominated as the town werewolf. It didn't take much to earn a reputation around here.

"But that's beside the point," Travis said. "Crazy Borys started waking the neighbors at the crack of dawn, shouting a bunch of stuff that was only half English. Apparently, some 'hooligans' were messing around in his barn. This story is pretty well-known, because Crazy Borys likes to stop random people around town and complain about stuff. He kept hearing commotion during the night, and each morning his barn was ransacked and his cows were spooked. Some were getting sick, and Crazy Borys was *convinced* kids were poisoning the cow food. He started buying fancy imported stuff, and bought bigger locks for the barn."

They stopped in front of "Crazy" Borys Kava's home. Travis let down the kickstand and continued.

"So anyways, a couple days before you showed up, Crazy Borys heard that noise again, but this time he wouldn't wait until morning. He put on his snow boots, grabbed his shotgun, and went out to greet whoever was hanging around his barn."

"Wait a second," Will interrupted. "You mean the

whole town calls this guy crazy, and he's still allowed to own a gun?"

Travis shrugged. "Dude, this is Wisconsin."

He had a point.

"Besides, I don't think Crazy Borys planned on shooting the culprit," said Travis. "Just scare them halfway back to Poland. But boy, was he in for a surprise.

"There was a huge, dark shape scratching away at the locks. Crazy Borys stood and watched it for awhile. Maybe trying to decide if he could make it into some funky Polish stew or something, I don't know. But eventually he raised his weapon, and yelled at it to shoo. Well, the Beast stopped alright, and faced Crazy Borys. The sight of it made the guy more hysterical than usual. He said he was staring at the Devil himself, and would berate anyone who tried tell him otherwise. So he said a little Polish prayer, aimed, and fired."

"I take it he missed?" Will said. "Otherwise there wouldn't be much of a Beast left to look for."

Travis laughed. "Try tell Crazy Borys that. He swears he hit it square in the face. The Beast howled... And was gone. No body, no blood. Nothing."

"That... *Is* interesting." In his heart, Will still suspected the Beast was nothing more than a wolf. A really big wolf, maybe, but an animal all the same. But disappearing into thin air was certainly not normal behavior for wolves, no matter how big.

Travis got off his bike. "Let's go check it out."

"Wait, what?" said Will. "That's private property, we can't go down there!"

"See anything stopping us?"

"Travis," Will hoped if he spoke slowly, logic might sink in. "You call Mr. Kava crazy, and just told me he wanted to scare kids off with a shotgun. You can't really be thinking about trespassing!"

Tales of the Beast

But he was more than thinking it. Travis was halfway across the lawn by the time Will finished talking.

"Last one there's a wimpy wolf!" Travis yelled back.

Will couldn't believe it. He chased after Travis, hoping to catch him and drag him back to the road. But Travis was much faster, and Will didn't catch up until they were both standing in front of the barn.

"Here you are; Werewolf Exhibit A!" Travis proclaimed, gesturing at the barn door like a game show host.

Now that he was here, Will thought he might as well look (and *then* hurry back to safety). There was no doubt that *something* happened here. There were large cuts in the wood, in some places deep enough to see light on the other side. And you couldn't miss the impact of "Crazy" Borys Kava's shotgun. A dozen bullet holes covered the barn door, where the buckshot scattered. If a person (or animal) was on the receiving end, they would be in bad shape. Will touched the door, imagining the conflict that took place.

("She would swear on a bible that the eyes watching her belonged to something more human than animal.")

("It was so huge he first thought it was a bear.")

("He said he was staring at the Devil himself.")

"What *is* this Beast?" Will wondered out loud.

The sky, which had threatened to rain all day, finally gave in. A few drops sprinkled over the countryside. There was a brisk, moist breeze, and Will felt his bones go cold.

They were being watched.

He didn't know how he knew, but Will was certain of it. The air was heavy with someone—or something's—gaze. Will jumped as he heard rustling in the woods.

"Something's out there," Will said.

Travis must have heard it too, because he grinned from ear to ear. "Looks like the star of the show is making a grand entrance!"

Chapter 5

Fear was creeping into Will's every muscle. It was the same nightmarish fear that haunted his dreams. *This* was the feeling he had when he first saw those eyes in the darkness, the eyes that swallowed up his parents and nearly took him with. He was so sure that any minute, that devil with human eyes would come out from the cover of trees, and finish the job it started a month ago.

"Can I help you boys?"

Will tensed up so suddenly, he could have turned to stone. The voice didn't come from the trees; it came from right behind them.

Travis turned around, sighed, and put his arms in the air. Will expected to see a rambling Polish farmer with a shotgun. His stomach tightened painfully when he saw who the voice belonged to.

Standing behind them was the Walworth County Sheriff.

They were in big trouble now.

Chapter 6:

The Beast of Bray Road

I knew this was a bad idea, I knew this was a bad idea...

Will thought it over and over until his brain hurt. "I can explain, officer."

The sheriff didn't look angry, but he didn't have to. The badge on his stetson hat and the gun in his holster was intimidation enough.

"I'm sure you were just leaving," said the sheriff. "Am I right, Mr. Scott?"

"I swear, I don't even know how we got here," Travis said. "My legs must have a mind of their own!"

The sheriff shook his head. "You should have that looked at. In the meantime, how about I escort you boys home?" He gave them a stern look. "Where you will keep to your own property."

"I call shotgun!" Travis yelled.

Will couldn't believe Travis' mockery. He acted like this was just some teacher scolding him for his antics. But this was the *Walworth County Sheriff,* and they could be in for

Chapter 6

much worse than detention. As he took his first ride in the back seat of a squad car, Will remembered something Eliza once said.

(*"You don't want help from Travis Scott. He only brings trouble."*)

Maybe she was right.

The drizzle was full-fledged rain when they reached the trailer park. It was no surprise that the sheriff knew where Travis lived. This was clearly not their first encounter, and not likely to be their last. But it was surprising that he turned back up Bray Road without asking for directions.

"The name's Stan Fillmore," said the sheriff as they drove.

Will's mouth was so dry, he could barely talk. "I'm Will, sir. Will Lewis."

"I figured," he said. "There aren't many new faces around here. I heard you'd be around this age."

It wasn't comforting to know the sheriff already heard of him.

"I was a friend of Connor Amon. Barbason, too." The addition of Barbason sounded like an afterthought. "Seems you've had a run of bad luck. I'm sorry."

"Thanks," Will said.

Sheriff Fillmore glanced over at him. His thick red mustache formed a perpetually serious look, although his eyes were soft. "You might find that luck continue if you spend your days with Travis Scott. He's not a bad kid, as much as he'd like you to think so. But he gets into all kinds of mischief. I don't want you to get dragged down with him."

"I understand, sir," said Will. "And I appreciate the ride, but I don't want to inconvenience you."

The sheriff laughed as they pulled into B.R. Amon. "Trust me, it's no problem. We're neighbors, after all."

He cocked a thumb at the house next to Barbason's.

The Beast of Bray Road

Eliza's house.

Will's stomach tightened.

Will was still dazed as he came inside. But he snapped out of it the moment he saw his great-uncle.

Barbason was sprawled out on the kitchen floor, gasping for breath.

Dropping his backpack, Will rushed across the room. He was at his great-uncle's side in no time.

"Uncle Barbason! Uncle Barbason!" he frantically called.

His eyes fell on Will, but they looked through him with glassy indifference.

Will panicked. "I'll be right back Uncle Barbason. I'm going to call an ambulance." But as he stood up, a hand seized him firmly by the arm.

"*Nooo...*" Barbason wheezed.

"But—you need a doctor. You're hurt," Will pleaded. Will was powerless to help his parents; but maybe he could save his great-uncle.

"I need..." Each word was broken by a deep breath. "My... Cane."

Will nodded. The hand-carved cane was sitting lopsided next to Barbason. Slowly, with the support of his cane and his nephew, Barbason made it to the couch. Will fetched him a glass of water, which the old man downed in two hearty gulps.

"Uncle Barbason, what happened?" Will asked.

He hesitated. "Lost... My balance." Barbason was still out of breath.

That wasn't the whole truth. Will didn't buy it for a moment. "We need to get you to the hospital."

"No!" he snapped back. "I—I'm fine. Just need...

Chapter 6

Rest."

He thought he needed a whole lot more than rest, but Will didn't fight him about it. They made their way slowly down the hall, and Barbason went to bed.

Something was definitely wrong with him. Will knew he had to keep a closer eye on his great-uncle from now on.

Barbason spent most of the week in bed. Not that he went very far before, but now he was reduced to hobbling through the house at a cripple's pace, putting almost all his weight on his cane. Will didn't know what was wrong. Barbason was exhausted all of the time, and his muscles were weak. But those were the only symptoms. Will kept insisting they go to the hospital, but he refused.

"I'm just gettin' old, kid," Barbason would say. "Ain't nothing to it but that."

But Barbason wasn't even in his seventies. Grandpa Connor was older, and in considerably better shape. He shouldn't have this much trouble moving around. Not unless there was a medical reason, of course.

So Will didn't wander far, and stayed home in the afternoon instead of visiting Travis. He kept busy with his homework, which proved difficult. Every time he sat down to work on it, his mind drifted to the topic of werewolves.

Still, he forced himself through it, if only *because* his thoughts kept going there. There might be some Beast in Elkhorn. Who knows—it could even be a genuine werewolf. But a large part of Will resisted the idea. He never liked *maybe* or *possibly*. Will much preferred facts that could be proven, measured or calculated.

And the fact was, he needed no proof of how much homework there was to be measured.

The Beast of Bray Road

When Saturday rolled around, Will was in for a surprise. He was going over his math textbook when a knock echoed through the room.

In over a month of living there, the only visitor at B.R. Amon was Mr. MacDonald, the attorney. Since then, knocking at the front door became a foreign sound. But the real surprise was who was there when Will opened the door.

It was Eliza.

"Oh, uh... Hi," Will said. She was the last person he expected to find at his doorstep.

Eliza smiled, but it lacked her trademark confidence. "Hey Will. I was hoping you were home. Can we talk?"

Stunned, Will nodded. "Sure. Uncle Barbason's sleeping, so we have the place to ourselves." After saying it, Will realized how suggestive that might sound. "Or, I mean—we could talk somewhere else, too."

"Inside is fine," Eliza said.

Feeling foolish, Will led her inside and took a seat on the old couch. She sat next to him, only a few inches apart, and his heart started pounding.

"So, what did you want to talk about?" Will asked, trying to keep his voice steady.

For once, it was Eliza who looked nervous. "I heard you met my dad last week," she said.

"Oh, that..." Will certainly remembered. "Look, I can explain."

"You don't have to," Eliza said. "You and Travis were looking for the Beast."

Will thought about denying it, but cast the idea aside. "I know you don't believe in it, Eliza. To tell the truth, I wouldn't either if it wasn't for what I saw."

"And what *did* you see, Will?" She looked him right in the eye. "I never asked because, well... That was the night

Chapter 6

your parents died. I didn't want to upset you."

He slumped back on the couch. Will tried not to think about that night; those memories had a way of coming back with stark clarity. His throat dried out like sand paper, but he talked. He started out vague, but as the moment of the crash approached he was retelling every detail.

The silhouette.

Those eyes.

The feeling of the wind rushing at him.

That claw.

And, finally, the climactic sensation of ramming headfirst into another vehicle.

Eliza didn't interrupt once. Will told his tale, reliving each breath. He was nearly trembling by the time he finished. Eliza took his hand, and Will's stomach didn't succumb to nerves. It was comforting.

"That was the last time I saw them," said Will. He was struggling to hold back tears. "I don't know what happened that night. I don't know if it's connected to this 'Beast' or not. And that's the part I can't stand—not knowing. I'm not looking for a werewolf, not really. What I'm looking for are answers."

Eliza squeezed his hand. "I understand, Will."

When their eyes met, Will was surprised by what he saw; she was just as scared as he was.

"So, why the change of heart?" Will asked. "You've always fought us when we mention the Beast of Bray Road. *Werewolves are make-believe,*'remember?"

She let go of his hand, and looked away. It was bizarre seeing Eliza, the social queen, at a loss for words. "I went trick-or-treating this Halloween. Call it stupid, but me, Penny and Angela still like to dress up and go door to door. We might be a little old for it, but we have fun. Sometimes we mock other kids' costumes, sometimes we just gossip and get wired off all the sugar.

"We made our rounds through town, and my dad brought us back to our houses. Living out in the country, you can't really walk all the way back. After dropping the girls off, there was still time before trick-or-treating hours were over, so I went to a few houses nearby." She smiled. "Barbason wasn't expecting anyone. But he found some Little Debbie oatmeal cream pies in his cupboard, and insisted I take them."

Will raised an eyebrow. "You went trick-or-treating *here?* Weren't you scared of my great-uncle?"

"This was back when he was working. Before things got... Strange," she explained. "We've been neighbors my whole life. I always thought he was nice."

"I see," Will said. It was hard to imagine Barbason was just another one of the townsfolk a short five months ago.

Eliza shuffled her feet uneasily. "I went farther down the road, to visit the Zimmerman's. They always have those big Twix bars, and if you come late they usually give you a bunch.

"I was on my way home when I saw it."

Will did a double take. "Saw what?"

With a gulp, Eliza continued. "At first, it was just a feeling. Like I was being watched, you know? Then I heard something behind the trees next to the road. I quickly turned to look, and I almost screamed.

"At the side of the road, there was a monster staring at me.

"I couldn't yell. I couldn't move. I could barely breathe. This terrible, terrible *thing* petrified me. I took in every detail; its silvery-white fur, its dog-like face... And these eyes. They were awful. I could feel them analyzing me. There was so much intelligence in that gaze.

Chapter 6

"Intelligence... And malice."

Eliza was as rattled as Will. She looked pale, like the memory itself was draining the color right out of her.

"What happened?" Will asked.

"Nothing," said Eliza. "It just stared at me, and after a few moments it vanished. Vanished! Like it was never even there!" She laughed a small, humorless laugh. "So that's what I told myself; that it never happened. I haven't told anyone what I saw, until now."

It made sense now why Eliza kept trying to convince Will and Travis that the Beast wasn't real.

She was trying to convince herself.

"So, what do you and Travis plan to do next?" Eliza asked.

Travis? Will almost forgot about him. "I don't know. We've seen about all there is to see at the library, and I'm not about to go looking through anyone's yard again."

She stood up. "Because I was thinking... What if we talked to other people who have seen it? I've got some connections. Hearing more first-hand accounts would be more reliable than Travis' version of the truth."

Will also got up. "We could even cross-reference the descriptions, like the police do with criminals. If we take enough notes, we could get an accurate picture of the Beast; how it acts, where it's seen... Stuff like that."

"That's perfect!" Eliza smiled. "I should head home and make some calls, then. Promise to keep me in the loop from now on?"

"Of course," said Will. He knew Travis wasn't going to like it, but he wasn't about to turn down Eliza Fillmore.

She gave him a hug, and Will's stomach did another round of somersaults. When Eliza left B.R. Amon, she left Will in the best mood he's had since living there.

The Beast of Bray Road

This time, Monday meant more than another week of school. It meant telling Travis that Eliza would be joining them. As expected, his reaction was not favorable.

"Absolutely not," Travis insisted.

They were having lunch at Papi's when Will shared the news. The big islander started stocking tofu burgers for his "little vegetarian brah," on the condition that they stop eating the flavorless gruel at the cafeteria. Will appreciated it, despite the teasing he got from Travis.

"She knows people who've seen the Beast," Will explained. "We'll get further with her help."

Travis flicked a fry at Will. "Hey, I know people too. Remember Louie Enders and his Cheap Jeep?"

After dodging the fry, Will nodded. "Yeah, but we'll need more than that. If she can get even one witness to sit down and talk with us, it would be worth it."

Travis rolled his eyes. "Use your head, man. Her old man's the sheriff, she's got this 'reputation' to uphold, and *McCrybaby* has his sights set on making her his next trophy girlfriend. Not to mention you're so head-over-heels for this girl you'd throw yourself in front of a train if she said 'please and thank you.'"

He had a point, and Will knew it. But he refused to think his judgment was slipping on account of his feelings for Eliza. "Well, she set up an interview with someone tomorrow after school. I'm going. If you don't want to, that's fine."

"Oh *hell* nah," Travis said. "I ain't going to let you try this alone, not with *her*. You'll never get any decent answers if your mind is on Miss Priss the whole time. I'll be there."

Despite his attitude, Will was glad Travis was coming. Love him or hate him, Travis said what was on his mind. That could prove to be very useful.

<h1 style="text-align:center">Chapter 6</h1>

By Tuesday, Spring was in full bloom. Everything was obnoxiously green, and the smell of pollen and freshly-cut grass was strong in the air. But March wasn't over yet, and the breeze was a chilly reminder of the Winter left behind.

On that bright Spring day, Will, Travis and Eliza became a team.

They biked into town to visit Clint South. His daughter, Lori, was in Eliza's extended circle of friends. Lori became the center of attention when her father had a very strange encounter. When Eliza asked if they could talk to him about it, she set up a meeting.

Clint's sighting was brief, but intriguing. "I was headed home one night, coming up Highway 11. I work in Delavan, you see," he told them.

Will interrupted to ask what day this happened.

"Oh golly," said Clint. "It was a little over a month ago now. February twenty-fifth, twenty-sixth maybe... Something like that.

"I was just getting near town when something ran right in front of my car! I only saw it for a few seconds, but I won't never forget it."

The trio leaned in closer.

"What was it?" Eliza asked.

"Don't rightfully know," said Clint. "It definitely had the physique of a wolf. I've seen 'em before while camping. Big critters, them wolves. But this was much bigger. Its shoulders were higher than the hood of my car. If I'd have to guess, I'd put it at around five feet tall, running on all fours.

"Its body was thin and sleek, almost to the point of bony. It must have had some muscle, though, because it cleared the road faster than any animal I've seen!"

"Can you describe the fur?" asked Will, writing down

every detail.

Clint thought it over. "Well, it was pretty dark, but I'd say it was kind of brown and gray. It was long and matted, more unkempt than most wolves or dogs keep their fur."

They thanked Clint for his story, and left. He didn't seem like the brightest guy in town, but Clint had an honest face. Will believed his tale.

"Besides, I don't think he had the brain-power to make that up!" Travis added.

The next day they visited Louie Enders at the trailer park. Will had Louie repeat the sighting. His description matched Travis' version of events, except Louie showed more affection for his poor little car. The scratches on that Geo Tracker were convincing; deep gashes tore right through the rusted frame, much like the marks on Crazy Borys' barn.

Louie offered the group a ride home... But after that story they opted for their bikes instead.

By Friday Eliza arranged another werewolf interview. Josh Royden, a kid from school, let slip that his dad saw the infamous Beast. Eliza worked her charm, but Josh couldn't convince his dad to talk to a group of "wannabe investigators." Finally, Josh agreed to sit down and tell them everything he heard about the sighting.

Mark Royden worked for the Elkhorn Police Department. He had the night shift on Christmas Eve, sometimes referred to as "Santa Watch" at the station. Mark was on the west side of town, patrolling around the elementary school, when a noise caught his attention. It was a howl, more haunting and intense than anything he ever heard.

He followed the sound to Hazel Ridge Cemetery. Eventually Mark found the source of the howling. There was a large, dark figure kneeling beside a grave. Josh said his father heard it "scratching at the ground, wailing like an

Chapter 6

injured animal."

Mark radioed the station for backup, but hoped he could scare the creature off before it did any damage. He turned on the high beams of his patrol car, and got his first good look at it.

The creature was definitely kneeling (much like one of the first sightings, Will noted), with fur as white as the snow and bright, reflective eyes. It turned to stare at Mark. Josh explained that his father wasn't particularly religious, but said that he "felt a real, palpable evil in that thing." Then the Beast stood on its hind legs, towering higher than any man, and let loose a blood-curdling growl.

A strong breeze blew through, and the Beast ran off.

Will found this story particularly unsettling. He asked Josh what grave the creature was kneeling by.

"No idea," said Josh. "Dad never told me. They did go back the next day, but there weren't any foot prints. Probably all smoothed out in the wind."

They thanked Josh for helping, and went on their way.

On Sunday Eliza took them to her best friend's house. Penny Peterson lived on Plank Road, one of the little routes between Bray and Highway 11. Once, her house might have been a lavish farm, but it passed its prime many decades ago.

Penny greeted Eliza with hugs and smiles, but shot a reproachful glance at the boys. "Theseare the friends you're bringing? Travis the Troublemaker and Wolf-Blood Will?"

"Penny!" Eliza snapped. "Don't say that! Will is my friend."

"Uh huh, sure," said Penny. Her opinion didn't change.

The Peterson house felt like a zoo of kids. Between Mrs. Peterson's home daycare and their foster children, there always seemed to be a kid racing through one door and out the other. Penny led them upstairs, to the room she shares with her little sister Shayla. She was only about thirteen, but that made her the oldest in the jungle of children.

Shayla told them what she saw. It was nearly dark, and she was playing in the back yard with the kids from daycare. Six year-old Tommy came to her crying, saying a monster was eating the neighbor's cow. She followed him to the fence, and saw the monster for herself.

"It was scary," Shayla said. "It was as big as the cow, but way skinnier. Its fur was all wild and dirty, and it was stalking the cows from the tall grass. Then, I watched it leap out and attack! It knocked the cow over, and I heard biting and crunching and I couldn't watch anymore!"

Shayla was quivering at the memory.

"I ran to get my mom, but by the time we got back the monster was gone."

Travis scoffed. "And what did your mom think of the mutilated cow?"

"Well..." Shayla shuffled her feet. "The cow didn't get eaten up. When we got there it didn't have any bites or nothing."

Travis rolled his eyes, but Will looked intrigued. "So, the cow was fine?" he asked.

She shook her head. "Nope. It got real sick. It died the next morning and no one knew why."

Will, Travis and Eliza exchanged a nervous glance. Will took notes at breakneck speed.

Monday after school, the troop agreed to meet at the library to go over their findings. They settled into their favorite table in the non-fiction section, the one hidden behind bookshelves with a view of the piano.

Chapter 6

Will emptied his backpack onto the table. He spread out his notebook, a printed map of Elkhorn, and a calendar. All had his handwriting scribbled throughout.

"Wow, you've been busy!" said Eliza.

Will blushed. "I'll be paying for it when our History homework is due."

"So what did you find?" Travis asked, leaning in across the table.

"Well, none of this is new to you guys," Will explained. "All I did was compare notes from each witness, find common trends, make up a map and calendar of sightings."

Eliza smiled at him. "This is amazing, Will! I can't believe you did all this."

Will turned a brighter shade of red. "It's nothing, really."

"Can we save the flirting for later?" Travis interrupted, looking slightly annoyed. Eliza glared at him.

"Right," Will forced himself to focus. "So, as far as I can tell the first sightings happened on Halloween, and have continued ever since. That was just over five months ago. Does that sound right to you two?"

Travis and Eliza nodded.

"Here," Will slid the map across the table. "I marked the location of each sighting we've cataloged. They aren't all exact, but you get the idea. It's been spotted all across town, but definitely most often in the country around Bray Road."

"Hence the name," Travis added.

Will nodded, and continued. "The Beast also appears to be nocturnal. Almost every sighting is either after dark or at dusk. It was late afternoon when Louie hit it, he said around four o' clock, and that's the earliest so far.

"It's always described as being big. The most accurate guess at size was by Clint South, who put it at a shoulder height of five feet. I looked it up, and the biggest wolves barely reach three feet. So whatever the Beast is, it's definitely not a common wolf.

"Fur color is inconsistent. Sometimes it's solid white, other times it's kind of brown and gray. I did find a pattern, though; all of the recent sightings are of the brown and gray fur, but every sighting before the new year had white fur."

"Why would it have different colored fur?" Eliza asked.

Travis lit up with excitement. "Maybe there's more than one Beast!"

Will suppressed a shudder. "I didn't think of that. It's possible, though. I was thinking it might have changed with the seasons. You know, white to blend in with the snow. It's not uncommon."

"That's not nearly as cool," Travis pouted.

Will sifted through his notes. "Now, here's where we run into a problem. The Beast has left limited physical evidence so far. Limited, but convincing. Those claw marks were hard to dispute."

Travis puffed out his chest. "Told you it was worth a look."

"But the strongest proof of the Beast is buried in Hazel Ridge cemetery, right next to my grandpa," Will said. He kept his face composed, but his heart felt like lead. "It's capable of very real danger."

Eliza watched Will, her expression full of sympathy. "So where's this problem you mentioned?"

Will tried to decide how best to put it. "It's left evidence behind, but not nearly enough. Other than a couple of scratches and... And one accident, there's close to nothing. No footprints, no feces, no remains of its prey. Simply put, the Beast can't be real."

The statement hung in the air, leaving nothing but

shocked silence. Everyone wanted to argue, but could not find a logical defense.

"C'mon man, you know better than anybody the Beast is out there!" said Travis, ignoring the need for logic.

"Oh I know," Will agreed. "I never said it isn't out there. I just said it can't be *real.*"

Eliza and Travis looked dumbfounded.

"How, um... Superstitious are you guys?" Will asked.

Travis laughed. "We're huntin' a werewolf, what do *you* think?"

Will couldn't help but join the laughter. "Good point. Then you won't think I'm crazy to suggest this. I don't think we're dealing with a flesh-and-blood creature here. My theory is that the Beast is something intangible, like a... Well, like a ghost."

"I guess that's possible..." said Eliza. "But I've never heard of a ghost that can hurt people."

Will dug a book out from his backpack. "I have," he said. He opened the book, *Haunted America,* to a marked page. "Poltergeists are said to be able to move objects. Bang pots and pans, slam doors, stuff like that. But there's one story of a man getting 'phantom scratches' all over his body, allegedly caused by an angry ghost."

Travis sighed. "Okay then, how do you explain Old Man Amon? He sure ain't no ghost."

"Easy," said Will. "He has nothing to do with it. The only 'evidence' connecting him to these sightings is circumstantial at best."

"*Circumstantial?* The guy carves wolf-men, closed down his business unexpectedly, and has shut himself out from the rest of the world!" Travis argued.

"I admit, Uncle Barbason is strange," Will said. "But there's just nothing concrete tying him into all this."

Travis crossed his arms. "Nothing, huh? How about

the fact that since the Beast has shown up, your whole family suddenly died off?"

Will was stunned. He believed the Beast was responsible for the car accident, and the death of his parents. Grandpa Connor died in a fire... But it wasn't until now Will remembered the controversy over his death, and his theory that his grandpa had been murdered. Grandma Eleanor had *Creutzfeldt–Jakob* Disease. She had been headed toward death for the better part of a year... But *CJD* didn't kill her. She was making a miracle recovery when she died of a heart attack.

Could it all somehow be connected to the Beast?

Sticky with sweat, Will grabbed his calendar of sightings and started writing the dates his family members died. His parents died February 14th, a day he would never forget. Grandpa Connor died a few days earlier, on the 10th. He racked his brain to remember when Grandma Eleanor died, but it finally came to him; December 16th.

It was all after the Beast's first appearance on Halloween. Just maybe, if two of the four deaths were because of the Beast...

"No," Will said, shaking his head. "It's a coincidence. It has to be."

(Because if it isn't... Then I could be next.)

After that, Will didn't want to discuss the Beast anymore. It was getting late anyway, so they decided to call it a day. Travis went through town back to the trailer park, while Will and Eliza took Highway 11 straight home.

"You know, that was really impressive the way you figured all that out," Eliza said as they rode.

He smiled. "I'd wait to be impressed until we find out if my theories are right."

"You see, like that," she said. "You're looking at all of

Chapter 6

this objectively. That can't be easy."

It's like a Sudoku puzzle, Will thought. "I've had practice."

They pulled into the sloped parking lot of B.R. Amon, and just in time; the sky was still orange, but the streets grew dark in the twilight. Eliza hugged Will, the kind of hug that uses your whole body instead of just your arms. Will's stomach knotted up, and he awkwardly returned the hug.

"Goodnight," she said with a smile.

"Goodnight," Will replied, confident his face was turning as red as the sky.

Will watched her run up to her house and go inside. His clothes still carried the faint scent of her perfume, and for a moment he just stood there, relishing the closeness they shared.

A bitter wind picked up, much too cold for early April. Will braced himself against it, then felt something fly out of his backpack. He turned to see his notebook sailing across the street, carried away by the gust. He ran after it, suddenly very anxious to get inside. He chased it to the edge of the field before the wind lightened up. As he grabbed the notebook, he felt a chill course through him that had nothing to do with the breeze.

Something moved in the field.

Will stood completely still, listening for the noise that alarmed him. It was subtle; just the snapping of a twig or unusual ruffling of grass. But a sense of terror threatened to overwhelm him. It was like the all-consuming emotions of nightmares, the fear that suffocates you without a knowable cause.

Another sound.

He wanted to run as fast as he could, but Will had to look. He felt compelled, despite his terror—or perhaps *because* of it. Some sane part of Will's mind said *look, there's nothing to be afraid of.* He wanted to prove his fear was unfounded, but knew in his heart that wasn't going to happen.

Across the field of sprouting soybeans, the tree line was shrouded in darkness. At first Will saw nothing, until a glimmer of light flickered in eyes suspended in midair. Slowly the shape of a huge, dark creature came into focus around them, so disguised among the shadows it would have gone unseen if its eyes didn't betray it.

He was facing his parents' killer, the Beast of Bray Road.

It took a silent step closer. Even from this distance, Will felt the power of that icy stare. He remembered thinking those eyes were human, but feeling that gaze on him again he knew that wasn't true—they were demonic. No human was capable of the evil reflected there.

It's not real, Will told himself. *It's like a ghost.*

That loosened the hold fear had on him. His skin broke out in sweat, and Will made a break for it. He fled across the road, racing towards his great-uncle's house.

It chased him.

Will felt its cold breath on the back of his neck, but could hear only his own footsteps and the thrumming of his frantic heart. As he sprinted up the hill of B.R. Amon's parking lot, Will lost his footing and fell face-first.

It was all over now.

There was no way Will could scramble to his feet and get away. So, laying on the pavement, he turned to face his fate.

The Beast cleared the field and crossed the street in no time. Everything happened so fast, and the sky was already so dark, that Will couldn't get a clear view of it. But he could see the texture of its mangy hair, long and gnarled and flowing in the wind. He could see the outline of its face, every canine feature taking on the most nightmarish quality. And he could see those eyes, like thin lenses filtering the true depths of its unrelenting malevolence.

He couldn't bear it. Will lifted his arm to shield himself, although he knew it was futile. The Beast pounced, crushing Will under its weight.

I was wrong, he thought. *The Beast is as real as I am!*

An enormous jaw opened around Will's arm. He flinched away, unwilling to watch himself be torn to pieces. He heard it bite down, and felt blood splatter across his face.

But the blood was not Will's.

The Beast recoiled, wailing in agony. Will's arm was covered in cold, red blood, but he felt no pain. But the Beast—oh, it was in pain alright. It thrashed around, eventually pausing long enough to glare at Will. That's when he saw where the blood came from; it was gushing openly from the Beast's mouth. One of the teeth that lined the monster's maw was shattered, almost entirely missing.

There was another gust of wind, so strong Will was forced to cover his face. By the time it passed, the Beast was nowhere to be seen.

Will tried to stand, but his legs were jelly. His arm, which was drenched in blood seconds ago, was now dry. The blood, it seemed, disappeared with the Beast. He also noticed his watch—given to him by his mother but never worn until her death—was cracked. Slowly, Will started to suspect his mother just saved him from beyond the grave.

She had, after all, given him a *silver* wristwatch.

Once he found the strength to move, Will hurried home. Inside, he would be safe. Inside, that monster surely couldn't reach him. He locked the door behind him, and stumbled towards his bedroom.

At the end of the hall, Barbason's door opened with a

bang. Will jumped, adrenaline still electrifying his muscles. The old man's silhouette was leaning against the door frame, his body rocking with heavy breaths. His face was concealed in the lack of light.

"Uncle Barbason?" said Will. He could barely speak, and something about his great-uncle's silence made him nervous. "Are you... Okay?"

The outline of Barbason took a labored step forward. Moonlight from the window struck his face, and Will gasped at what he saw.

Barbason's mouth was bleeding. He was missing a tooth.

"No," Barbason said. His voice was so raspy, it was almost a growl. "I'm... Not."

Chapter 7:

Mason's Revenge

Will panicked.

At the sight of his great-uncle, he bolted. Will fled across the living room, almost stumbling in his rush. Barbason called out "Come... Back here!" as he reached the door. He didn't hesitate to unlatch the door and slam it shut behind him.

After a long breath, Will realized he was outside again, in the Beast's territory.

I'm trapped, he thought. *I can't go back inside, but I'm no better off out here.*

He frantically tried to think of a solution; but really, what *could* he do?

My friends, he thought. If there was ever a time Will needed his friends, this was it. Turning to Eliza meant knocking on Sheriff Fillmore's door, asking to see his teenage daughter at night without an explanation. But the alternative was to go to Travis, by crossing Bray Road alone after dark—and that was *not* an option.

Mason's Revenge

Behind the walls, Will heard the crippled footsteps of his great-uncle. There was no time to think; Will had to act, and fast. So he dashed to the house next door, took another deep breath, and knocked. He hoped Eliza would answer, but luck was not on his side tonight. Instead a different kid answered, several years older but unmistakably Eliza's brother.

"May I help you?" he asked, puzzled.

"I'm here to see Eliza," Will said while trying to steady his pulse. "May I please talk to her?"

The kid crossed his arms. "That depends. Who are you?"

Will tried to think of the best way to word it. "Tell her Will needs to see her. Tell her what we talked about earlier is happening right now."

He raised an eyebrow. "Fine. Wait here, okay?"

Will nodded. He was only alone for a few moments, but during that time he kept glancing in every direction, terrified the Beast was lurking just beyond his vision. But if the Beast was there, it didn't strike in time; the door opened, and never was Will more relieved to see Eliza. She took one look at him and knew something was wrong.

"Will! Are you alright?" she asked, pulling him into a hug.

For the first time since she left ten minutes ago (*has it only been that long?* Will wondered), he felt safe.

"We need to get inside," he said.

Eliza let him in and locked the door behind them.

Inside, her brother watched them curiously.

"So Eliza, who's this?"

She sighed. "Nick, this is Will Lewis. Connor Amon's grandson, and our neighbor. Will, this is Nick. Unfortunately, he's my brother."

Nick still looked suspicious. "Uh-huh. So what's all

this about?"

Eliza hesitated. "Will and I really need to *talk* about something," she said, emphasizing on the word *talk*. "Don't tell Mom, okay?"

Nick sighed and shook his head. "If she finds out, she'll tell Dad. Then we're both in for it."

"C'mon bro! You owe me, remember?" she said. A mischievous little smirk crossed her face.

He thought it over, sighed again, then turned to leave. "Fine, fine. But you better not get caught."

"Thanks Nick!" Eliza smiled, hugging her brother's back. He looked less than enthusiastic.

Quietly, she led Will up the stairs and down the hall. There was no mistaking Eliza's room; color and floral patterns were everywhere, from the wallpaper to the bedspread. More than anything, it was the smell Will recognized. He was surrounded by the sweet scent of roses and lavender. It was like Eliza's flirtatious smile, distilled into an aroma.

"What happened?" Eliza asked once the door was closed.

Trembling, Will took a seat on the bed. He wished he could deny it, convince himself this was a dream or a misunderstanding. But he knew better. After going face-to-face with the truth, Will could no longer hide in the comfort of ignorance.

"I was wrong," he admitted. "Uncle Barbason... He really is the Beast. He killed my parents, and tonight he almost killed me."

Eliza sat next to Will, holding his hand tenderly. "Are you sure?"

Will nodded.

"Did he hurt you?" she asked. Her eyes scanned for any sign of injury.

Mason's Revenge

He stared at his watch, its face cracked and its silver glistening. "I think I hurt him more."

Eliza's grip tightened. "Are you going to be alright?" she asked, her voice a whisper.

"I don't know," said Will. "Werewolves aren't real. It's just not possible. Yet tonight, I saw one—and was nearly killed. Everything I believe has turned upside-down, and I'm..." He closed his eyes, feeling crushed under the weight of this nightmare. His voice faltered on the verge of emotional breakdown.

"I'm scared, Eliza."

She pulled him close, wrapping him in her caring embrace. Will clung to her, as if she were the only real thing left in a world of darkness. For once, she didn't make him nervous; Eliza was a comfort he desperately needed.

Then she kissed him.

It was a kiss born of compassion, not romance. As their lips connected, they were lost in each other. For a few blissful moments there was no Beast and no Barbason. There was nothing but the warmth of knowing you're not alone. They kissed, and kissed, and kissed, until finally the fear was at bay. Even then they held each other, not willing to let this moment end.

"I'm so sorry," Eliza breathed into his ear.

Eventually they let go of each other. Will was calm again—at least, as calm as you'd expect after being attacked by a monster.

"What are you going to do now? Eliza asked.

Will shook his head. "No idea. I can't go back to Uncle Barbason, not after this. Maybe I can stay with Travis for awhile, but... I don't think it's safe to be out tonight."

Eliza rested her chin on her palms, thinking. "You're right. Well, you'll just have to stay here tonight."

That brought Will back to reality. It sunk in where he

was—and what they just did! His face felt very hot, undoubtedly turning bright red. "Won't you get in trouble for letting a boy spend the night?"

"Only if my parents find out," said Eliza. "If Nick helps us, I'm sure we'll be fine."

A question from earlier came back to Will. "What did you mean earlier, about him owing you?"

"I've covered for him while he's had a lady over," she said, grinning. Will caught the meaning. "I'll go ask him."

"Eliza," Will stopped her before she left. She looked back, and Will couldn't find the words he wanted to say. There were really only two words to describe what he felt, as simple as they were. "Thank you."

Smiling widely, Eliza said "Anytime."

Nick agreed to help, but on one condition; Will wasn't staying in Eliza's room. Eliza protested but Will thought that was fair, so he spent the night tossing and turning on Nick's floor. What scattered sleep Will managed was filled with horrible nightmares—the worst he's had since his night at the hospital.

Sneaking out in the morning was difficult. Eliza's mom was busy making breakfast, and checking to make sure the kids were awake and ready. But with Nick's help they managed to get Will out the back door undetected.

Before school, Will had a daunting task; retrieving his school supplies from B.R. Amon & Sons, Inc.

Only the knowledge that Barbason usually slept through the morning gave Will the courage to unlock the door. Still, his hands shook as he turned the knob and entered the lair of the Beast. He didn't feel safe, not for one moment; the Beast may sleep, but perhaps with one eye open. Will crammed his backpack with school books, clothes, and his laptop, hoping never to set foot here again.

Eliza was waiting at the bus stop. When Will rushed out of B.R. Amon she gave him a reassuring hug, just as the bus pulled up. They boarded as usual, but to the shock of everyone on board Eliza did not sit with Penny Peterson in the front; she followed Will to the back and joined him.

That's when people started to talk.

"I *told* you, man!"

On their way to Papi's, Will explained to Travis what happened. Of course, he didn't mention kissing Eliza; that part was too private to share, even with his best friend.

As Will expected, Travis gloated.

"Haven't I been saying Old Man Amon is a werewolf all along? Now that we know who the Beast is, we can finally take care of it," Travis said proudly. His boyish grin was bigger than ever when they strolled into the little shack. "Yo Papi! What's free and good today?"

Papi chuckled. "The air on the islands. Everything else is taxed!"

Will froze while Travis placed their order. Once they took a seat on their favorite rickety table, Will said "What do you mean, 'take care of it?'"

Travis casually separated their food. "What do you think we were monster-huntin' for in the first place? To take pictures of its million-dollar smile? We got to put a stop to it the good old-fashioned way."

"What are you suggesting? We kill my great-uncle?" Will couldn't believe what he was hearing. "That's murder!"

Travis shrugged. "If you'd rather tie him up with a bunch of garlic, be my guest."

"That's for vampires," said Will. "I'm pretty sure garlic has no effect on werewolves."

Chapter 7

Travis rolled his eyes. "Whatever."

"You're terrible," Will said, exasperated.

He looked at Will, his expression more severe than ever. "Got a better idea? Look man, it's a dog-eat-dog world. Kill or be killed, survival of the fittest, all that shit. I don't mean to sound crude bro, but you ain't never had to learn that. Not until now."

Often times, Travis' logic made sense in some twisted way. But not this time. Will couldn't accept that Barbason—the man who took him in, clearly suffering from ill-health—had to be hurt, werewolf or not.

"I do have a better idea," he said. "We stay away from him."

"'Stay away from him?' There's a monster living up the street, terrorizing the town and killing off your family one by one, and you're solution is to give the guy some space?" Travis scoffed. "Sorry man, but that ain't going to work. Not for long, anyway. You can crash with me for now but I'm telling you, Old Man Amon isn't done with you. When he shows his teeth again, you'll have to decide if it's him or you that will bite the silver bullet."

Will knew it was true; sooner or later he would have to face the Beast again. And truth be told, he had no idea what he would do when that time came.

Travis made himself scarce the rest of the school day, as usual. On the few occasions Will crossed paths with Eliza, she gave him a warm smile. Will didn't know where he stood with her now; it was quite a kiss last night, but it *was* just for comfort. He wondered if she would turn down a kiss under different circumstances. She probably would. After all, this was still Eliza Fillmore, the most popular girl in school. And, Will thought to himself, he's nothing but the new kid with the crazy relative. Crazy *werewolf* relative. He shouldn't get his hopes up, but he couldn't help it; all day his mind kept drifting to Eliza.

Once school was over, Will's attention was back on practical matters. He was nervous to stay at Travis' home. He was imposing on Travis' father, who he never even met. And what reason could he give? Surely Mr. Scott wouldn't believe their wild tale, true as it may be.

But, as was often the case since moving to Elkhorn, Will was surprised.

Frank Scott was many things. It didn't take long to see that. He was a drinker. A smoker. A couch potato. He was no comedian, but had a bad joke for every occasion and laughed at each one. He ate bags of Doritos by the dozen and smelled of stale pipe tobacco. But there was good in Frank Scott as well. Because despite how broke Travis and him were—and how cramped their quonset hut already was—the only question he asked of Will was "Bears or Packers?"

"Huh?" Will didn't understand.

"You a Bears fan, boy? Or a Packers fan?" Frank repeated.

In truth, Will didn't like football at all. But he knew lots of people followed their team with almost religious zeal. He looked to Travis for a hint, but he only shrugged. "Packers, I guess."

Frank broke into a fit of laughter, his beer belly rippling. "I thought you looked gullible! Don't you worry boy, I'll get you converted by the end o' the week."

"Good luck with that, pops," said Travis. "Will here is so thick he can't see the shit he's walking through!"

Father and son laughed. Even Will grinned, at his own expense.

Travis shoved the mess on his floor into a pile of

Chapter 7

mess against the wall. Will set down his backpack, and felt something he hadn't felt since he lost his parents. Here, on the floor of a little quonset hut full of broke Bears fans, Will was part of a family. More than he ever was at B.R. Amon.

Over the next few weeks, Will grew to love and hate Travis more. He was an only child, after all; living with another kid was a new experience. In the confined space there was little break from Travis' snide remarks and blunt opinions, which were bad enough in small doses. But somewhere between their frequent bickering and annoyance, they became closer friends than ever. In fact, they became more than friends; through this ordeal they came to think of each other as brothers of a sort.

There was plenty to keep Will's mind off of werewolves. Finals were right around the corner, and Will welcomed the distraction. He and Travis made a habit of visiting the hideout after school, so Will could study and Travis could slack off. It was a comfortable routine.

One day, Travis insisted on showing Will one of his old hobbies. He refused to "spoil the surprise" by telling him until they were settled in at the hideout.

"Check this out," Travis said as he dug through his backpack. Will held his breath, and nearly choked when Travis pulled a large knife out from among his school supplies.

"You were carrying that all day?" Will asked. "What if you got caught in school with that thing?"

Travis rolled his eyes. "Okay mommy, I'll be a good boy starting tomorrow, 'kay?"

Will shook his head, but protested no further. After awhile it wasn't worth worrying over every stupid thing Travis did. "This is what you wanted to show me? You could have done this at home, you know."

"The knife's only half of it," said Travis. "Here's the real fun."

Next he pulled out an old dartboard from underneath his books. He hung it from one of the columns, stepped ten paces away, and turned to face it.

"I haven't done this in awhile. Let's see if I still got it," said Travis. He held the knife and carefully eyed the target. He pulled back his arm, and sent the knife whirling through the air. The blade struck the outer rim of the dartboard, making Travis punch the air in triumph.

They spent hours at the hideout that night. Travis practiced his throw, while Will practiced ignoring him. He kept nagging Will to give it a try. Finally, he gave in; an hour of Travis' persistence has a way of changing your mind, even if just to shut him up. The knife flew to the right of the dartboard, making an anticlimactic *thud* as it hit the floor. That was enough for Will to call it a night.

"C'mon man, there's a werewolf running around! You never know when this stuff could come in handy," Travis insisted.

In the back of his mind, Will suspected Travis might be right.

During the weeks away from B.R. Amon, Will became closer to Eliza as well. She wasn't shy about stopping to talk as they passed each other in the halls. She asked how he was doing, reminded him daily to be careful around Travis, and asked in a whisper if there's been any sign of the Beast. It was small talk, mostly, but Will got the jitters each time. It was the smell. Now when he caught a whiff of her perfume, it reminded him of her room... And those intimate moments they shared.

To Will's surprise, Barbason didn't try to contact him. And he had no more close encounters with the Beast. Once or twice he thought he was being watched, but the feeling passed as quickly as it came.

Times were peaceful again. Will only wished it could last.

It was the last week of April, and that meant the last week of class. When that bell rang on Friday, the students rejoiced. They had finals next week, then an entire summer of freedom. Will wasn't so excited; he was finally comfortable at Elkhorn Area High School, and was going to miss his daily routine.

But Will wasn't free to leave just yet.

A hand picked Will from the crowd and dragged him to an empty hallway. He knew who it was before he saw them; the firm grip and snickering laugh gave it away.

It was Mason and Frankie.

Once out of sight he slammed Will hard against the lockers. Will's breath escaped him, and his back flared with pain.

"W—what?" Will tried to speak, but could barely make a sound.

Mason backhanded him. The blow struck Will's temple and knocked his head into the lockers. Warm blood trickled down the back of Will's neck.

"What she sees in a wimp like you is beyond me," said Mason. His face was the very image of scorn. "Must be pity."

Will tried to catch his breath. "I don't... Know what you're talking about," he said in a breathless voice.

"Don't you give me that, Lewis." Mason lifted Will by the collar until they were eye level. "Maybe I didn't lay down the rules well enough last time, so let me make myself unmistakably clear; Eliza Fillmore is off-limits to you. In fact, she's off limits to anybody but me."

It seemed that nothing good could happen without a catch. Eliza finally paid attention to Will. But with the gossip mill at school, he should have known it wouldn't be long before Mason found out.

"Show that twit what happens with you mess with us, Mason!" Frankie cheered.

Mason grinned, as if he could picture sweet, sweet revenge in the future. "Oh, I will. I will teach you what you forgot so easily before, Lewis. If you cross Mason McCree, you will regret it. This..." He slammed Will back into the lockers. "Is just the beginning. Mark my words, these kids will have something new to talk about this summer."

Frankie snorted with laughter.

"See you around, Lewis," Mason said. They left Will sliding to the floor, his back aching and his head scrambled.

Whatever they were planning, Mason and Frankie thought it was hilarious. And that meant bad news for Will.

Travis took one look at Will after school and said "McCree."

Will nodded.

"What's wrenched up his ass now?" Travis asked.

"I guess he noticed Eliza spending more time with me," Will said while rubbing the back of his head. It felt like razors were jammed into his skull.

Travis spat. "So beating you up is supposed to win her heart? Man, and people think *I'm* an idiot!"

"It didn't sound like this was the last of it, either," said Will. He held onto the wall for balance. "Let's get to the hideout. I need to lie down."

They made their daily jaunt over the fence and into the fairgrounds, Travis muttering profanities about Mason the whole way. He jumped from rooftop to rooftop with his usual ease, sneaking down to unlock the door of the Wiswell Center. Travis was more disgruntled than normal, pulling out the dartboard and knife immediately. Will stretched out on one of the bleachers, using his backpack as a pillow. He tried to distract himself with Sudoku, but it wasn't enough to keep him from worrying.

("I will teach you what you forgot so easily before, Lewis.")

It made Will uneasy. He didn't know to what lengths Mason would go for revenge, but clearly bodily harm was no concern for him.

Will laid there, puzzling over round after round of Sudoku, completing them slowly. Once Travis mellowed out he let the poor dartboard recover and played his harmonica. The music soothed Will until the throbbing dulled. Somewhere in the middle of filling in a square, Will dozed off. He was deeper into sleep with each passing minute.

He woke up with shivers running down his spine. Will sat bolt upright, sweating.

Travis stopped playing. "Whoa, what's the matter with you?"

Will looked up to see a dark sky through the high windows. "But that's impossible," he muttered. "It can't be dark yet, it's only—" Will checked his watch and froze.

It was almost seven thirty.

Will grabbed his backpack and sprang to his feet. "We need to get home, now!"

"Okay, okay," Travis said. "Chill out, dude."

"Travis," Will looked him in the eye. "I think *it* might be out there..."

It took a moment for Travis to understand. When he did, his face lit up with childish excitement. "Alright! Looks like tonight's the big night!"

"No, it's not," Will said sternly. "We're getting out of

here and going straight to your place. We're not playing heroes."

It was too late. Travis had his knife out again. "Who said anything about heroes? Monster-killing vigilantes maybe, but 'hero' is open for interpretation."

"Don't be stupid, Travis!" Will yelled. "You don't know what you're dealing with! You've never seen it!"

But Travis was already headed for the door. He looked back over his shoulder, grinning from ear to ear. "Not yet."

Will chased him out of the hideout, into the dark and deserted fairgrounds. Out in the open, the sense of foreboding was unmistakable. Travis must have felt it too; he kept looking over his shoulder, his grin lost. Now that their eyes adjusted, they could see the shapes of barns and buildings around them, but there wasn't enough light to make out any details. Something could be lurking around any corner, and they wouldn't see it until it was too late.

When Travis looked back at the hideout, Will saw a new expression on his face; Travis Scott was afraid. Will turned, dreading he knew exactly what was there.

A pair of luminous yellow eyes watched them from atop the hideout.

Will slowly backed up. The eyes crept down the roof of the Wiswell Center, the body only visible as a slightly darker patch of night. Will was on the verge of panic. Travis, who had never experienced real terror before, let fear get the best of him. He sprinted for the gates.

Sure enough, the eyes vanished at the first sign of a chase. Will couldn't tell if they disappeared or moved too fast to see, but he wasn't waiting to find out. He ran after Travis.

"Holy shit!" Travis skidded to a halt.

The Beast was right in front of them.

At this distance they could see it in detail. It was

Chapter 7

huge; on all fours it was nearly as tall as Will! But despite its size, the Beast looked starved. You could count the ribs in its emaciated chest, and the hard features of its face were haggard. Will noticed with some pride that one tooth was still shattered.

It took a step towards the boys, who were rooted to the spot. The panicky voice in Will's head started screaming. *I'm going to die I'm going to die it's going to kill me and eat me and oh god I'M GOING TO DIE!* Yet there was nothing he could do. The Beast took another step. In those yellow eyes, Will thought he could see his great-uncle. There was something sad about those eyes, almost tortured.

Then the Beast froze. It looked over its shoulder, ears perked.

It noticed something, Will thought.

A strong breeze came and something very strange happened. The body of the Beast, real and dangerous as it was, dissolved into a dark mist and blew away with the wind. The fear was lifted as the Beast vanished, but something was still wrong. Why did the Beast leave?

"Holy shit!" Travis repeated, his enthusiasm returning. "Did you see that? That was *it,* man. That was the *Beast!*" He could hardly contain his excitement.

"Travis, go get your bike," Will said.

He looked puzzled. "Why?"

Will's voice quivered. "Because we need to get to B.R. Amon, and fast."

Bray Road was not the same. It was still dark and eerie, but without the sense of foreboding. It was as if the presence that usually guarded these roads had its gaze elsewhere.

"So remind me again why you suddenly *want* to go

back there?" Travis asked as they neared the end of the road.

It was hard to explain. "I think Uncle Barbason is in trouble," Will said.

Travis laughed. "I'm pretty sure he can take care of himself!"

Will wasn't even sure himself why they were doing this. If Barbason was the Beast, wasn't he responsible for killing his parents?

"Looks like we have company," Travis said as they came around the final bend.

Two figures were running down the hill from B.R. Amon. Bright graffiti covered the garage door, the words *HOME OF THE BEAST* standing out in the darkness.

Travis pulled up next to a yellow sports car parked on the side of the road, right where the vandals were headed. Will recognized their shapes; it was Mason and Frankie. They looked winded and more than a little edgy.

Mason greeted them with an angry glare. "What kind of trick are you trying to pull?" he barked.

"The hell are you talking about?" asked Travis. "We just got here and found you dingbats redecorating over there."

Frankie huffed and puffed. "Don't try that with us! We know you're trying to freak us out—how *else* do you explain that growling?"

Will and Travis exchanged glances.

"Shit," Travis muttered.

Mason grabbed Will by the collar. "You think this is funny, Lewis? Think you can toy with us?"

"No," said Will. The feeling of being watched was returning. "This isn't a game. This is real, and we really need to get out of here."

Mason pushed Will until he was pinned to the hood of the car. "Like hell we do! What are you going to do, call

Chapter 7

the cops? Get Eliza's daddy to bail you out? Face it, it's just us out here and there's nothing you can do about it!"

Then there was a loud *thud* above Will's head, followed by a deep growl.

No one moved. Slowly Mason's eyes drifted up, and his anger was gone in a flash. Frankie let loose a wild shriek. Travis stumbled backwards. Everyone saw what was on top of the car except for Will, who already knew what was there. Mason let go of Will and backed up. The car shook as the Beast pounced, within seconds pinning Mason to the ground. Frankie ran for dear life, screaming the whole way. The Beast watched him run, but kept its attention on Mason.

Travis grabbed Will and pulled him to his feet. "C'mon, let's get out of here!"

While being dragged away, Will watched the Beast crouch down over Mason. He was unconscious, either from a head injury or sheer fear. Will couldn't bear to watch as the Beast bore its mismatched teeth.

When he closed his eyes, Will saw his parents.

Will couldn't leave anyone to die, not even Mason McCree. He yanked his arm out from Travis' grip and did the only thing he could think of—he quickly unlatched his watch and hurled it at the Beast. His aim wasn't perfect, but it was good enough. The Beast cried out as the watch struck it in the shoulder. Its body dissolved into a dark cloud and disappeared.

"What the hell, man?" Travis shouted.

"We can't leave him," Will insisted. He went to check on Mason, who wouldn't wake up but otherwise seemed fine.

Travis stood over them impatiently. "Sure we can. I'll gladly show you how. We use McCrybaby here as bait, hop on that bike, and get a head start before Beastie shows up again. Easy."

Will tried to hold Mason up, but couldn't. Mason was

much too heavy and Will wasn't exactly the strongest kid in class. "Just give me a hand, alright?"

Sighing, Travis took one arm and hoisted Mason to his feet. "You're going to get us killed over this jackass."

"I thought you weren't afraid of danger," Will pointed out.

"I'm not," Travis explained. "I'm just more interested in my survival than his."

Will didn't argue further. He was too worried about what they would do now. They had to find safety, but where could they go dragging Mason along? Will remembered the yellow car, the name *MUSTANG* etched into the door. An idea came to him. "Travis, do you know how to drive?"

"Sure," said Travis.

Although Will doubted "know how to drive" and "have my license" were the same thing to Travis, they didn't have a lot of options. "Okay, then help me find his keys."

They searched Mason's pockets for his keys, then unceremoniously threw him in the back of the car. That was no easy task—there were only two doors, so they had to figure out how to move the front seat then toss him in back. Travis hopped in the driver's seat, revving the engine. The Mustang shot forward, making a wide U-turn, then sped back down Bray Road. Will watched the speedometer climb from 35 to 45 to 55 to 65, and wondered if he would have been safer with the Beast than in a car with Travis.

Houses flew by as they drove. A strong wind rocked the car, making Will and Travis uneasy. They came around another hill, and were greeted by a pair of yellow eyes.

"Shit, shit, shit!" Travis yelled. Will said nothing, but in his mind repeated Travis' statement.

The Beast ran towards them. Travis made an abrupt turn down Hospital Road, barely making it without flipping the car. Will held on for dear life, listening to Mason banging

Chapter 7

around in the back of his own car. They kept gaining speed, passing 80 miles per hour. Will's heart was beating so fast, he thought he might have a heart attack. Travis, on the other hand, looked like he was having fun.

Trees blew as the wind itself seemed to follow them. No matter how fast they went, they could feel an icy breath right behind them. Then with a *bang* the car shook and fishtailed. Travis regained control, but was losing speed.

"Great, I think it just burst a tire," Travis said, punching the wheel. He used what momentum they had to coast into a derelict barn at the side of the road. The barn doors burst open while the car skidded to a halt inside.

Travis stopped the engine. "Quick, grab sleeping beauty and haul his ass out of here!" Together they pulled Mason out of the back, and hid behind a large pile of hay.

It was quiet.

Will expected the Beast to be right behind them, and the fact that it wasn't made him edgy. He looked at Travis, who kept his knife at the ready. They held their breath, but nothing happened. Will didn't dare move, but after ten minutes he thought it might be safe to relax.

Then a breeze rattled through the barn.

In the silence, every step the Beast took was loud and clear. He could hear its nostrils flare as it sniffed around the car. Will was sweating bullets. There was no way they could hide here, not from *that*. To wait was like suicide, but his other options didn't sound any better.

Still, he had to try.

Shaking, Will stood up from behind the haystack. Travis was shocked, but kept his head down. The Beast seemed even bigger in the confined space. It saw Will, and they locked eyes. It did not snarl or growl. The Beast simply stared, and Will could do nothing but stare back.

"Uncle Barbason?" Will said.

It didn't move.

"Don't... Don't kill him." He struggled to keep his voice even. "Don't kill me.

It continued to gaze into him.

"I... I want to help you, Uncle Barbason."

Slowly the Beast raised itself onto its hind legs, looking down at Will from a great height.

"Let me help," Will begged.

It paused. Then the Beast's violent howl filled the barn, shaking the walls and the shingles. As the building trembled, the Beast's body became a wisp again, swirling away into the blackness of the night.

A few moments later, Barbason came limping in through the open doors. He was half dressed and seemed to age ten years since the last time Will saw him.

"Kid... We gotta talk," he said. Barbason sounded awful; his voice was hoarse and weak. He looked at Will with pleading eyes. Exhausted eyes. *Dying* eyes. "Hear an old man out?"

Will glanced at Travis, then cautiously stepped out from behind the haystack.

"Fine," Will said. "Start by telling me what the hell is going on."

Interlude:
Monsters of America

While the Beast chased Will and Travis, thousands across the country were watching *Monsters of America.*

The screen panned over a shot of the full moon, clouds rolling by in accelerated motion. A low voice, fitting for a radio personality, narrated the scene.

"Werewolves. Countless books and movies have filled our imagination with these half-man, half-wolf creatures. But what if they weren't fiction? What if these stories were based on something real?

"Uncover the mysteries, here on *Monsters of America.*"

The title appears, followed by tonight's episode name, *The Tale of the Wisconsin Werewolf.*

Scenes play of driving through farmlands and cornfields. "Something's strange in the small town of Elkhorn, Wisconsin. Something that no one seems able to explain."

A man in a badge and stetson hat appeared on screen. "I'd say we get two, maybe three calls a week about it." The name at the bottom said *Stan Fillmore, Walworth County Sheriff.*

The clip changed to an interview with *Michele Vernes, Werewolf Witness.* "There was growling and fighting in the backyard. By the time I got there our dog was dead. We still don't know what attacked her."

"It was Devil," said *Borys Kava, Werewolf Witness* in a thick accent. He was a pudgy old man with a few strands of curly white hair and a gargoyle-like face. "No doubt of dat. It was evil in de eyes. It was Devil, very very evil."

Country roads flash across the screen. "It's been called 'The Beast of Bray Road' and 'The Wisconsin Werewolf.' But the people of Elkhorn have only one real question; what is out there? To find the answer, we've sent Natalie Elwin, *Monsters of America* investigator, to the scene."

A pretty woman appeared, with light bronze skin and a long black braid of hair. She walked along the wilderness at the side of the road.

"What people don't realize is that werewolves aren't an isolated phenomenon," says *Natalie Elwin, Paranormal Investigator.* "We're used to hearing about them in English folklore, but shape-shifters are part of almost every culture's history."

The screen transitions through old werewolf wood carvings. "It's true. Native American legends tell of *Skin-Walkers,* people who can turn themselves into an animal by wearing its skin. In old Norse tales, *Berserkers* wore the hide of a bear, and fought with inhuman strength. In ancient Greek writings, King Lycaon was turned into a wolf as punishment for trying to trick Zeus. But the wolf was a symbol of honor to the Turkic people, who claimed their greatest shamans could transform into the humanoid *Kurtadam,* literally meaning 'Wolf-Man.'"

"The first thing to do in Elkhorn is determine what sort of paranormal event is happening," said Natalie. "If it's a cryptid, or currently unknown animal, we need to treat it like one. If it's some kind of natural phenomenon or illusion, we have to explain it."

Then, with a background image of the full moon, the narrator asks "But what if Elkhorn has a true half-man, half-wolf monster? Could a person in this small town really become a werewolf by night?"

"It's possible," Natalie says confidently. "I've researched dozens of werewolf accounts, and there are signs of a legitimate man-to-wolf transformation in Elkhorn."

Sound effects cue for a howling wolf. "Despite the number of witnesses, there are still too many unanswered questions," says the narrator. "*Monsters of America* will continue its investigation. If you or someone you know has information regarding the 'Wisconsin Werewolf,' call the number on your screen.

"Join us next time to follow Natalie's discoveries. We may not know who or what the 'Beast' is, but you can count on one thing; the truth will be revealed, here on *Monsters of America.*"

Chapter 8:

Barbason's Tale

The ride back to B.R. Amon was awkward, to say the least.

Barbason instructed Travis to take Mason and his car back to the school, then go straight home. Then he led Will to his old pickup truck, and drove in complete silence.

When they finally arrived, Barbason limped to the front door. Will noticed the old man's back (where a certain watch struck the Beast) was bleeding through his shirt. They got inside and Barbason collapsed into his easy chair. In the light it was clear that Barbason was very sick—he lost weight, his skin was pale, and in his face had all the signs of a dying man. He sounded worse than he looked. You could hear the pain each breath cost him.

"I'm... Sorry, kid," Barbason said.

Will didn't respond. What can you say to something like that?

"I wish I could tell ye this wasn't my fault. That the reason yer life's gotten so screwed up ain't because o' me."

Chapter 8

He paused to steady his breath. "But... I ain't a liar."

"Then it's true," Will said in a hushed voice. "You really are the Beast?"

It was Barbason's turn for silence.

"You're a... A werewolf?" Will had come to believe it over time, but having this conversation to his great-uncle's face made it seem impossible.

Barbason took a deep breath. "Yeah. I guess I am."

The words finally confirmed his suspicions, which opened a floodgate of questions. "How did this happen to you? When did it happen? How do you change?"

He chuckled weakly. "Kid, do me a favor? Forget everything ye think ye know about this. It ain't what ye're expectin',"

There was a pause. "Then tell me everything," Will pleaded.

Barbason looked at him, his eyes full of sorrow. "I never told nobody the story. Ain't particularly fun to relive. But ye deserve to know." He leaned back in his chair. "After everything ye've been through, ye've earned that much."

Will sat on the edge of his chair, his attention piqued. "I want to know, Uncle Barbason. I want to know all of it."

"Fine," Barbason said. He cleared his throat and thought over how to begin.

"I guess it all started when yer grandma Eleanor got sick," said Barbason.

Will remembered. " Creutzfeldt–Jakob Disease."

The old man nodded. "Yeah, that. She started actin' different and havin' these strange delusions. Soon after, she lost control o' her motor skills. Connor was real worried, being one o' them neurologists and all, so he brought her to a colleague and she was diagnosed with CJD. Connor was devastated. Ye gotta understand kid, Connor and Eleanor were soul-mates if there ever was such a thing. Fell in love in high school and never fell out of it, not after fifty years. There ain't no cure for CJD, and he knew it; all ye can do is watch the love o' yer life degenerate until she finally passes on."

"Were you a werewolf back then?" Will asked.

"Kid," Barbason sighed. "Don't interrupt. And like I said, I'd bet the building this ain't gonna play out how ye think"

Will tried to stay quiet after that.

"Anyway, Connor refused to accept it. He started talkin' to all sorts o' specialists, all across the country. Visited research facilities. Did more studyin' on his own. But he kept comin' up empty handed. Everyone agreed there ain't no cure, but that didn't stop Connor; he started lookin' overseas. Now mind ye, all the while poor Eleanor kept getting worse. I swear it broke my brother's heart when he went to visit her and she didn't even recognize him. I ain't never seen a man so miserable in me life.

"In time, he got wind o' this Dr. Jacques DuPuis. I guess he was known for unconventional treatments, and was pretty successful. Connor was sort of vague on the matter, but he flew out to France to meet with him. Before he left he says to me 'Barbason, take care of my girl while I'm gone.' And I did. It wasn't easy, let me tell ye, but I did it. She was less herself every day, and I thought my big brother was crazy for thinkin' there was a fix for this."

"But, she did get better, didn't she?" said Will. "I mean, she made such a miracle recovery."

"Yer gettin' ahead o' the story, kid," Barbason said. "So Connor spent a couple o' weeks in France. Didn't call much, just on occasion to check how Eleanor was doing. It got real strange when he came back; I asked if this Dr.

DuPuis had any treatment for her, and he just looked me in the eye, spooked as could be, and said it was taken care of. Wouldn't say no more than that, and didn't keep up his search for a cure. In fact, he became a real shut-in. He hardly spoke to nobody, and rarely left his wife's side.

"As it turns out, that's right about when people started talkin' about a Beast."

Will's excitement rose. "I get it! So Grandpa Connor must have become a werewolf while in France, then bit you or something?"

Barbason stared at him impatiently. Will made a zipping motion across his lips. "Sorry," he said. "Go on."

"Like I said, people started seeing somethin' out o' the ordinary. But that ain't the real strange part. The real shocker was that Eleanor started getting better. Not overnight o' course, but not far off. Every day she was actin' more like her old self, and she wasn't getting no treatment at all."

"I bet grandpa was thrilled," Will commented.

Barbason gave a cynical grin. "Ye'd think. But instead he was all down in the dumps and sullen. Soon he came to me, and he said 'Brother, I need to tell ye somethin', but ye got to promise it stays between us. No matter how ill ye think o' me, ye can't speak o' this.' Well o' course I agreed, and I haven't told a soul since. Not 'til tonight.

"He told me that, in France, he found somethin'. Somethin' that could save his Eleanor, but at a steep price."

"What was it?" Will asked.

"A book," said Barbason. "A horrible, horrible book."

Will was captivated; he leaned forward in his seat as if the story was physically drawing him in.

"This book belonged to some forgotten cult. They worshipped Moyset, the 'Devil's Messenger,' and claimed this deity could grant all sorts o' miracles. But these gifts weren't free; only those loyal to Moyset get its blessin'."

"Where did Grandpa Connor get this book?" Will asked. It didn't sound like the sort of medical textbook his grandfather was searching for.

"Dun' know," Barbason admitted. "I asked that, too. Thought maybe that Dr. DuPuis might have given it to him, but Connor wouldn't say a word on the matter.

"Now this book had all kinds o' terrible things in it, including a ritual to summon Moyset. Connor ain't never been religious or even superstitious, but at this point he was desperate. He performed the summoning ritual, expectin' another dead end like all the rest he'd run into.

"Well... It worked." Barbason paused. "That might not be all that surprisin' now, after what ye've already seen. But remember, this was Connor; a man o' science who ain't never had reason to suspect dark things like that existed. Quite frankly, neither had I.

"Connor said his encounter with Moyset was the most terrifying thing he ever experienced. He was shakin' from head to toe the whole time he was tellin' me. He wouldn't describe it any more than sayin' it was a demon, and o' that he was sure. So Moyset made him a deal; Eleanor would be cured in exchange for Connor's soul. Well Connor wasn't no fool, so he asked what exactly that meant. The demon explained that, through him, it could give itself shape. Create a body of its own, which I guess demons don't have. And with that body, it could grow stronger in our world.

"Well he hated the bargain, but Connor was blinded by love. He agreed, and came back to Wisconsin with that *thing* latched onto him. Moyset kept its word, as ye know. Eleanor got better alright, but that's how the Beast found its way to little ol' Elkhorn after centuries of sleepin' and waitin'."

Will was astonished. "Wow, so Grandpa Connor sold

his soul to the Devil to save his wife? That was so brave of him..."

Barbason spat. "It was foolish and ignorant. I ain't never been religious either, but I do know that evil has a way o' trickin' people into thinkin' it's good, and I told him that. And now that it was too late, Connor agreed. He wanted out of his bargain, but didn't know how."

After so much talking, Barbason had to take a breather. Will saw anger rising in his great-uncle's eyes. It reminded him of Grandpa Connor's funeral.

(*"Yer father ain't no saint, Cass!"*)

Barbason's reaction that day was beginning to make more sense.

"And then I... I told 'em that..." The old man's eyes flickered open and closed.

"You need sleep," Will suggested. He didn't want the tale to end, but Barbason was clearly exhausted in more ways than one.

He let his eyes rest for a moment. Then Barbason sat upright with a start. "No! No I can't... Can't sleep yet. Too... Dangerous."

"Why" Will asked.

Barbason slapped himself in the face. "Easier for the Beast to take over when I'm sleeping. And it be a night creature, so falling asleep after dark is just invitin' it to come out and play. If I'm awake I can at least fight it, for all the good it does."

Will was beginning to understand. "So that's why you're always sleeping during the day?"

Barbason nodded.

"But, how do you actually transform? What's it like?"

He thought it over. "Ye ever have dreams, kid?

"Sometimes," said Will. He thought it was an odd question.

Barbason's Tale

"Well, it feels like that when the change comes. You still see and feel everythin', but it ain't like when you're awake. You aren't really in control, and ye ain't thinkin' like yerself. I s'pose dreamin' is what it is, too, since my body stays put every time."

Will raised an eyebrow.

Barbason shrugged. "My body don't change, kid. It's somethin' else. Maybe my soul, maybe somethin' that we don't got a name for. When the change comes my body gets all weak and sleepy, but at the same time I feel like I'm being pulled out o' myself. And when it's over, I'm right where I was when it started, wishin' the stuff I did really was just a dream. So to answer yer questions, I don't know how or even what happens. It just does."

One thing about that didn't make sense to Will. "Wait a second. If your body doesn't move, how did you get to the barn tonight?"

"Well, while the Beast was chasin' ye, I was chasing it," Barbason explained. "If I try really hard, I can still move about a little while it's out. But I'm really weak. I was fightin' for control the whole time, and barely made it there in time."

"I see," said Will. "So… How did *you* become a werewolf? Grandpa Connor's the one who went to France, and you said you know better than to deal with the Devil, right?"

"Kid," said Barbason. "Evil don't just punish people who deserve it, and one man's mistake can cost others just as deeply."

"Then what happened?" Will urged.

Barbason cleared his throat. "Can't hide much from Moyset. That demon found out Connor was trying to back out, and wasn't too happy 'bout it. Now the Beast wasn't as strong then as it is now, but it was still plenty capable o' ruinin' Connor's life. So it took control, and paid Eleanor a visit while she slept... It took all the energy the Beast had, but it—and by extension, Connor—murdered her."

"Wait," Will interrupted. "I thought Grandma Eleanor died of a heart attack."

Barbason thought it over. "She did and she didn't. Ye don't really understand how this whole thing works, kid. But she didn't die o' no natural causes, that's for sure. You see, Moyset promised she would be cured of CJD, but said nothing about her surviving long after that. It was a loophole, ye see. And Connor had to watch it all, from the eyes of her killer."

"That's awful..." Will muttered.

"Connor went mad with grief. I ain't never seen him so hysterical, so unhinged. I didn't know how to console him."

Barbason was struggling to continue. He took a deep, rattling breath and let it out in a sigh.

"One night, I was just getting home from a job—this was before I closed down shop, mind ye—and was putting away my tools in the garage. Then I heard a growling behind me, and just about jumped out o' my skin! I ain't never seen this Beast before, only heard Connor talk about it, and I was scared witless. It looked rabid, eyes wide and mouth foaming. Knowin' what I know now, I don't think there was nothing o' Connor in it that night; it was a Beast o' pure, insane fury. I tried to run, but I never stood a chance."

With great effort, Barbason slipped his shirt off. To Will's surprise his body was a maze of scars, crisscrossing his chest, back and stomach.

"Also crushed me leg, which is why I have this godforsaken limp," Barbason mumbled.

"How did you survive?" Will said in amazement. Even a person in their prime would likely die from injuries like these, and Barbason was far past his prime.

Barbason's Tale

"Shouldn't have," he said as he put his shirt back on. "Passed out in a pool o' me own blood. Even unconscious, I was afraid. I didn't want to die, kid. Not that I had much going for me in life, but when ye're looking down that long tunnel ye tend to get scared. So when I heard a little voice whispering that I could survive… I trusted it. I was also delusional from the blood loss, so I wasn't in a frame of mind to wonder if this voice was my imagination, or something worse. It told me if I let it in, I would live…"

"Oh no…" Will put a hand to his mouth. "Moyset?"

Barbason gulped, then nodded. "Ay, Moyset. I had horrible nightmares after that. Unspeakable, they were. But eventually, I woke up. I was still hurt and still drenched in blood, but I was well enough to clean myself up and dress my wounds. I felt funny, but I just figured it was because o' the loss o' blood. Once I was cleaned up, I dug out my ol' shotgun and kept it by the bed. I don't think I could've shot it if the Beast came back, though, not knowin' it was me brother, but without it I ain't never would've slept.

"As soon as I got up in the morning, I knew somethin' was wrong. I could smell everythin' in the house, see the specks o' dust on the floor, hear the damn mice stompin' around in the attic."

Will raised an eyebrow. "We have mice in the attic? I never heard them."

Barbason managed to laugh. "I hope ye never do, kid. And all those cuts were well on their way to healed! Not perfect, o' course, but better than they should've been after one night.

"Connor shows up later, more hysterical than ever. He was babblin' all sorts o' nonsense, and I couldn't get a word in edgewise. I kept shakin' him and tellin' him to calm down, but he wouldn't have it. Then I heard him mutter something about Moyset, and that he 'should never have

135

made another deal'… I froze. I think he sensed my anger, 'cause he quieted up too. I looked at him and I says 'Connor, ye tell me now and ye tell me honest… What have ye done this time?'

"He gets all nervous, but starts talkin' after a good hearty shake. He admits he went pleadin' back to Moyset, desperate like he ain't never been before, and begged to have his Eleanor back. Said he'd do anything—*anything*—to see her again. Well Moyset, that bastard, says there is a way. But at the cost of an innocent life.

The old man grumbled. "He broke into tears as he was tellin' me. Then all he could do was yell 'I didn't know! I didn't know it would be ye!' over and over. I stopped listening. I was angry like I never knew I could be. I practically threw Connor out the door. It felt like my body was on fire, I was so mad."

"So, Moyset lied?" asked Will. "I mean, Grandma Eleanor didn't come back, did she?"

"Nope. But I'd say that demon kept its word alright; my brother was with his wife again before long."

Will's eyes widened with realization. "It was you…" he whispered. "It wasn't an accident at all. You… You killed Grandpa Connor."

Barbason was silent.

"That's why you were so distant at his funeral," Will said. Then he remembered something else from that day. "Why were you and my dad arguing?"

"Yer dad didn't trust me. He saw the way Connor and I spoke in hushed voices at Eleanor's funeral, so o' course he suspected I knew more than I was lettin' on. Which I did. Yer dad was sharp, I'll give him that."

Will's heart sank. "So he blamed you for Connor's death, and you got mad… Really mad. That's why…"

He couldn't finish, but didn't have to. They both

knew the painful truth; Barbason lost his temper, and murdered Will's parents.

"The rest is history, I guess," said Barbason. He looked at Will, his eyes filled with remorse. "Kid, I ain't never wanted to hurt nobody. What I really wanted to say tonight is, well… I'm sorry. I don't expect ye to forgive me or nothin'. I couldn't ask that of ye. But I needed ye to know I never wanted none o' this to happen. Especially not to you."

Will put a hand on Barbason shoulder. "Uncle Barbason, I understand. This wasn't your fault any more than it was mine. I forgive you."

The old man's face was blank as he processed his forgiveness. Will pulled him into a tight hug. Barbason held him close, crying in dry sobs. Will knew that whatever happened next, they were in it together. Because now, Will knew the *real* killer of his parents and his grandparents. He knew who was responsible for tearing his life apart.

Moyset.

The next day Will woke up to pounding at the front door. Before he could crawl out of bed to answer, he heard Travis yelling.

"I know you have him in there! C'mon out before I break in and get him myself!"

Will opened the door, and was speechless. The sight was so comical, he almost laughed. Travis was covered in camo paint, with chains (possibly intended to be silver, but more likely simple steel) wrapped around his chest. One hand held his knife, the other paused mid-knock in the air.

"There you are!" Travis shouted. He grabbed Will with his free hand and pulled him outside. "Good to see you made it out alive, man. Did you slay the Beast, or do we have to go back in and take care of it?"

Chapter 8

Will frantically waved his hands. "Travis, relax," he said. "We're fine right now, don't worry."

He looked Will up and down. "He didn't bite you, did he? You're not one of them now, are you?" Travis asked, pointing the knife at Will.

Before Will could respond, Eliza came jogging down from her house. "What on earth are you doing with that knife?" She said accusingly.

"Stay out of this, I'm interrogating a suspected werewolf," Travis told her.

Eliza rolled her eyes. "Put that knife away before my dad sees it."

Travis looked suspiciously between the two of them, knife still raised.

"I'm not a werewolf," Will confessed.

Finally he put the knife down. "Alright, so what did I miss last night?"

This caught Eliza's attention. "Last night?" She noticed how exhausted and bruised Will was. "What *did* happen last night?"

Will wondered if he should tell them or not. He couldn't see any harm in it, and at this point he could use all the help he could get. "Alright, let's take a walk and I'll explain."

"Alright," Travis agreed.

"Sure," said Eliza. "And Travis… What is all over your face?"

It looked like Travis forgot. "Oh yeah. Camouflage. That way the Beast couldn't see me."

Eliza laughed. "Funny. I always thought people covered in mud stand out more in a crowd."

Travis mock-laughed at her.

They strolled down Bray Road. Travis and Eliza were hesitant, but Will assured them it would be fine. As they walked past fields and woods, Will retold the events of last night. Much of it was new to Eliza, who missed out on Mason and Frankie's vandalism and the close encounter with the Beast. When he got to Barbason's tale, they were both as caught up in the story as Will was.

When he finished, Travis paused. "Wait a minute, so you mean all along I was right about Old Man Amon being a werewolf, *you* were right about him being innocent, and we were *both* wrong about what the Beast actually is?" He slapped his forehead. "Aw man, could this get any more complicated?"

"It could," said Will. "Because now we have to ask ourselves; what do we do about it?"

"What do you mean?" Eliza asked.

Still walking, Will explained. "Think about it. Silver hurts the Beast, but it hurts Barbason just as much. Remember when I threw my watch last night? He has an open wound where it hit."

"But I thought his body wasn't there," said Eliza. "I mean, didn't you say it was more like a dream?"

"That's the frightening part," Will said. The scenic spring view did nothing to ease his tension. "His body wasn't there. It was laying on his living room floor. But when silver hit the Beast, the wound burst open on his back. We can't hurt the Beast without hurting Uncle Barbason."

"Dude, you're not still stuck on this whole pacifism thing?" said Travis.

Will was getting irritated. "Uncle Barbason did nothing wrong."

"This isn't about justice. Sounds like Moyset dealt the last of that after he tricked your gramps not once, but twice. No offense bro, but he's the one to blame. He brought it to Wisconsin, and now he's paid the price. Which sounds all fair and dandy, except we've still got a Beast running around getting stronger every night."

"So what do you suggest?" Eliza said. "If we kill the Beast, then…"

Eliza couldn't finish, but Travis could. "Then an innocent man dies, yeah I get it. But I have a news flash for you kids; that's already happened. Connor killed his brother when he condemned him to this. Call it a terminal illness or a death sentence. He's breathing, but his days are numbered. And while he rots away, more people die. More people like your parents, Will."

It was a stab at Will's heart, but Travis was getting his point across.

"The Beast is deadly," he continued. "If we wait, more kids will be orphans. Or maybe next time, we'll have to watch parents bury their children."

No one argued. The trio turned around, and Will thought about what Travis said. He was right; if someone else died, the blood would be on their hands as well.

(*"Kid, I ain't never wanted to hurt nobody."*)

There *had* to be another way. Barbason couldn't be a lost cause, not after all he's been through.

"There is another solution," Will said at last. "We go straight to the source of the problem. We find a way to stop Moyset, once and for all."

Eliza smiled. "That's perfect!" she said. "I mean, that's the real cause, not Mr. Amon."

Travis, on the other hand, was still skeptical. "Sounds great. So enlighten me, O brilliant savior of murderous old men, how do you suggest we fight this 'Moyset?' Or even what the hell it really is."

"It claims to be a demon," said Will. "That gives us a place to start looking."

Travis laughed. "Okay, sure, let me grab my phone book and find an old priest and a young priest. Little Miss

Priss here can go shopping for some crosses—wooden, not silver. Don't want to hurt the guy, after all—and some holy water. And Will, you just keep a bible handy. You know, just in case."

"Stop being a smart-ass, Travis," Eliza said hotly. "You're not helping."

"No, I am helping. You just don't like the sound of the truth."

Will put up his hands. "Guys, calm down. Either way, we need time to research. Travis might be right, but I'm not giving up on Uncle Barbason until we've tried."

Eliza and Travis were poised to keep up the argument, but agreed to the ceasefire. They walked back to B.R. Amon without another word.

Will, Travis and Eliza decided to continue their research once finals were over. They would be too busy with last-minute studies to make any progress, anyway. Until then, Will suggested they wait. He reminded them that desperate decisions are what brought the Beast here in the first place.

"Later guys," Travis said as he mounted his bike. "Hope no one dies while we're cramming for a math final."

"Goodbye, Travis," said Will sternly. "Tell Pops I said hi."

Travis waved and rode off.

Will and Eliza walked up the hill to their houses. After everything that happened last night, Will forgot all about the graffiti; but he couldn't mistake the words *HOME OF THE BEAST*, written in bold lettering across the garage door.

"I guess I better clean that up," he said. "Not exactly the message we want to send."

Eliza smiled. "I guess not. How are you going to get

Chapter 8

it off?"

"No idea," Will confessed. "But Uncle Barbason keeps all sorts of equipment in the garage. I'll figure something out."

"You wouldn't want a hand with that… Would you?" Eliza asked coyly, her hands held behind her back. She looked adorable. "And in exchange, you help me study for my science final? I'm drowning in that class!"

Will's stomach was knotting up, but in contrast to the seriousness of the last 24 hours it was a welcomed feeling. "That would be great," he said. "If you don't mind, that is."

"It'll be fun!" she said. "I'll just change into something I can get dirty, and be right back."

She ran off while Will looked for something to clean with. Around the corner of the building he found a water spigot he could use, and inside he uncovered an old pressure washer. By the time he dragged it outside Eliza was back, dressed in simple jeans and a T-shirt. It was a rare sight to see Eliza in "plain" clothing, and Will thought she still looked amazing.

Getting the pressure washer up and running was, in theory, a simple task. But with their combined lack of mechanical skills, it became an adventure in and of itself. First, they lost control of the hose once the water was on, realizing too late they didn't screw it in tight enough. Then Will forgot to plug it into an electric outlet, leaving him dumbfounded as to what was wrong. Finally they discovered just how much pressure it had, as the first spray knocked Will to the floor! By the time it was up and running, Will and Eliza were already drenched.

By taking turns scrubbing and spraying, they made considerable progress de-vandalizing B.R. Amon. It was slow work, but the sun was shining and the water kept them cool. Hardly a minute went by without laughter and smiling. It was a long time since Will felt this at peace, and he would have stayed out there all day if he had the strength. But by mid afternoon, they decided they did enough for now. All that remained of the message was a faint outline.

Eliza sat down, leaning against the wall. "Not bad for a day's work," she said, catching her breath.

Will plopped down next to her. "Not bad at all. Thanks for all your help, Eliza. It would have taken twice as long without you."

She giggled. "It would've taken longer than that just to get that pressure washer running!"

"Hey! I would have figured it out… Eventually," he replied, although she was probably right.

They laughed together. Eliza scooted over until she was right next to Will.

"So, did Mason really do all of this because of me?" Eliza asked, shifting in place.

Will's throbbing head reminded him of the beating he got yesterday. It seemed like such a long time ago now. "I guess you could say that. He thought we were, well… Dating."

"Oh…" She looked embarrassed. "I owe you an apology, then. I never would have played along with his flirting if I thought he would get this defensive."

"It's fine," Will said. In his opinion, spending time with her was worth getting beaten up and vandalized. "He'll think what he thinks. And it's not like it's true, anyway."

More laughter. This time, it sounded fake from both ends.

Will gulped. With all the courage he could muster, he asked "Is it?"

She hesitated. Just when Will thought he was wrong to ask, she surprised him by turning the question around. "I don't know, Will. Is it true?"

Chapter 8

"Well…" Will didn't know what to say. "Would you, um… Like it to be true?"

Eliza didn't answer. Instead she stared off into the fields, the wind gently blowing her hair. After a long silence she said "I've only had one boyfriend before."

Will was shocked. "Really? I figured you had plenty. I mean, as popular and pretty as you are."

She blushed at being called pretty. "Last year I dated a boy named Justin. He was everything I thought I wanted; smart, funny, good-looking, but after dating for six months, I found out he was cheating on me."

"That's terrible," said Will.

Eliza tried to smile. "So we broke up, and I haven't dated since. Every boy who's interested is so superficial, just like Justin. I promised myself I wouldn't let myself be used like that again."

Will hesitantly put a hand on her knee for comfort. "I'm sorry," he said.

Eliza took his hand in hers, then gave him a light kiss on the lips. "I like you, Will. You're different."

"I like you, too," Will confessed. His face was turning red, which had nothing to do with the sun. "And, if it's alright with you… I'd like Mason to have a real reason to hit me next time."

They locked eyes. Then, spontaneously, they laughed. Laughter turned to kissing, which turned to cuddling and smiling in the shade of B.R. Amon's garage.

For the first time since moving to Elkhorn, Will was truly happy.

It wouldn't last long.

Chapter 9:
The Werewolf Trials

Considering he was nearly killed and proved his great-uncle was a werewolf, Will's weekend turned out alright.

Once they finished with the graffiti, Will and his girlfriend (a term he repeated constantly to himself) went to her house to study. Beast or no Beast, this was their last chance to prepare for finals, and they couldn't put it off. He was introduced to Eliza's mother, and pretended to meet her brother Nick for the first time. Mrs. Fillmore was surprised to see her daughter dating again, and seemed to appraise Will throughout the evening. Before long she warmed up, judging Will as an appropriately well-mannered and quiet young man. By dinner time she was treating him like part of the family, insisting on a second helping of spaghetti.

After dinner was what Will worried about. That was when Eliza's dad—the Walworth County Sheriff—came home from work. Eliza gave him a big hug, and introduced Will as her boyfriend.

"Boyfriend, is it?" Sheriff Fillmore said, looking Will

Chapter 9

up and down. "When did this happen?"

Eliza beamed. "Just today."

The sheriff crossed his arms. "I see. Staying out of trouble, Will?"

Will felt his nerves tremble under his stare. Neither of them forgot their one and only meeting. Trespassing with Travis Scott was not an ideal first impression. "Yes sir," he said with an eager nod.

"How's Barbason doing? Haven't seen him around town much." The sheriff's small talk did nothing to lighten the mood.

"He's been sick," said Will.

Sheriff Fillmore went into the kitchen, returning moments later with a plate of leftovers. "Doesn't surprise me. Everybody's in a funk right now. I mean, people always act strange around a full moon, but it's been going on for weeks now." He laughed. "At the station we're calling it a full moon month!"

Will was nervous. Eliza managed a strained giggle.

"What's been happening?" Eliza asked.

"Mostly people are just antsy," he explained. "Arguments with cashiers turning into serious threats, a bad case of road rage causing a fender-bender. You know Jerry Smage down the street? Guess he threatened his wife with a carving knife because she put walnuts in the salad. He didn't do anything, but she was worried enough to give us a call anyway. Then there's all this 'Wisconsin Werewolf' crap."

"Wisconsin Werewolf?" Eliza showed interest, hiding her own knowledge on the subject. "I've heard people talking about that at school. What's it about?"

Sheriff Fillmore grunted. "Nothing but a bunch of bored folks looking for something to talk about. I'm sure some of them saw something—a wolf or coyote from up north is my guess—but half are just making things up now.

The Werewolf Trials

The stories are getting ridiculous."

They casually agreed, not pressing their luck any further.

When it finally got dark, Will said his goodbyes to Eliza and went home. Barbason's health worried him; he kept losing weight, and struggled to maneuver around the small house. They didn't discuss the Beast. Bringing it up seemed distasteful. But the air was finally clear between them, and they could talk freely like they never could before.

Sunday meant more studying, although this time Will and Eliza spent the day at B.R. Amon. Barbason was sleeping the day away, which gave them the house to themselves.

Neither of them could concentrate.

"So Will," said Eliza, putting down her stack of notes. "How *do* you think we can save Mr. Amon?"

Will fiddled with his pencil. "Honestly, I have no idea. But there isn't much time. He's sick, Eliza. I think he's dying. We're going to lose him before long." He looked into her eyes. "He's the only family I have left. Moyset has taken everyone else. I won't let him take my great-uncle too."

Eliza squeezed his hand. "We'll think of something. I know it."

"It's like a puzzle," Will said. It was his favorite analogy. "We're so close to solving it, but the last few pieces have us stumped."

They didn't discuss it after that, but for the rest of the day Will couldn't focus on school. His mind was on demons, werewolves, and Uncle Barbason. One idea crossed his mind, a way to buy them time they desperately needed.

It was a thought Will didn't dare speak aloud, even to himself.

That night, Barbason was worse than ever.

Chapter 9

Normally he was watching TV or carving away in the garage by the time Will went to sleep. But he only saw his great-uncle leave his room once to use the bathroom. Worried, Will knocked gently on his door.

A groggy voice responded. "Yeah?"

"Uncle Barbason, it's Will. Can I come in?" he asked through the door.

He grunted. "It's open, kid."

Will entered to find Barbason lying in bed, wheezing with every breath. He took a tentative step closer. "Are you alright, Uncle Barbason?"

He coughed, given a rough nod in the middle. "Fine," he muttered.

Standing over his great-uncle, Will could hardly believe what he saw. Barbason looked decades older than he was; his mane of straggly hair thinning to wisps, his pale skin hanging loosely from a bony frame. Even his eyes took on a hollowness, like they already caught a glimpse or two of the light at the end of the tunnel.

Emotions welled up in Will. The sight alone nearly brought tears to his eyes. "What is that monster doing to you?"

Barbason's face was surprisingly calm. "It's… Winnin', kid. Simple as that. We been fightin' each other for months now, and it finally be winnin'." He looked at Will. "I'm holdin' it back best I can, but there ain't much I can do now. It's been takin' over all day, just a minute or two at a time. Patrollin' its turf, I suspect. Tonight'll be hell."

Will felt Barbason's forehead. He had a slight fever and was clammy to the touch. "What happens if you, well… If you get worse? What happens to the Beast?"

"Dunno," said Barbason. "I s'pose there's a chance it'll go with me, and I we could all rest in peace. But I ain't bettin' on it. Knowin' Moyset, it'll find another way to torment us."

Will didn't speak. He knew Barbason was right; it wouldn't be that easy. But seeing his great-uncle on his deathbed was unbearable. "You need a doctor," he finally said.

Barbason grunted, which turned into a fit of phlegmy coughs. "And tell 'em what? That I got a bad cause o' demonic possession? They can't help me, kid. Besides, if one o' them prods me the wrong way, who's to say the Beast won't pick 'em as the next target? I ain't gonna be responsible for that again, not if I can help it."

At last, the tears Will tried to restrain broke through. "I don't want you to die, Uncle Barbason."

Barbason was speechless. As the tears kept coming, the old man pulled Will into a tight, bony hug. Will let himself sob into his great-uncle's shoulder. He didn't care if it was weak of him; he had lost enough people he cared about. Despite everything, Barbason gave him a home and tried his best to take care of him. It might have been because of guilt, but he still did it. Barbason was the only family Will had left, and now that they were close he couldn't stand the thought of losing him.

"It'll be alright, kid," said Barbason, patting him on the back.

But it wouldn't be, and they both knew it.

Monday meant two things. For one, it was the beginning of finals; three today, two tomorrow, and then school was out for summer. But it also meant the masses would find out Will and Eliza were dating (because, as Will learned, Elkhorn Area High School prided itself in its gossip mill).

Travis confronted him before their first exam.

Chapter 9

"So you tied yourself down to her, eh?" he asked.

Will blushed. "I guess so."

Shaking his head, Travis said "Bad call, man. Bad call."

"You're just saying that because you don't like her," Will said.

"True," he confessed. "But that doesn't mean I'm wrong. This will draw a lot of unwanted attention from McCrybaby, and his little dog too. Don't you think he'll be mad enough after the other night?"

He had a point. Will wondered what Mason thought of *his* face-to-face encounter with the Beast. Now on top of that, Will was dating the girl he's been after all year.

There was definitely reason to worry.

To Will's surprise, Mason didn't confront him. They crossed paths on occasion, and there was no mistaking the contempt in Mason's glare, but for now at least he kept to himself. He only saw Frankie once, but he hurried down the hall as soon as he saw Will.

"Maybe they think I'll send the Beast on them again," Will said to Eliza on their way to the next exam. She laughed.

There was another reason school was unbearable. Friday night (coincidentally the same night the Beast attacked Mason) a show called *Monsters of America* did a special on the Wisconsin Werewolf.

Everyone's excitement was renewed. Once again the whole school could talk of nothing but the Beast. Will heard his name come up more than he liked, and knew the rumors about his involvement were far from gone. And during the weekend, the Beast must have been busy; over a dozen new witnesses came forward. The sightings ranged from brief encounters to corpses of livestock mauled by an unknown predator.

The Werewolf Trials

None of it surprised Will.

("Tonight'll be hell.")

It did concern him, however. Media recognition was the last thing they needed. Will didn't think convicted werewolves were still burned at the stake, but he wasn't comfortable with how close people were to the truth.

As if Will didn't have enough to worry about, something else was becoming painfully clear; he was not doing well in his exams.

He was a bright student, but his lack of concentration since transferring to Elkhorn finally caught up with him. Will knew he was only guessing at most of the answers, and felt his anxiety grow by the hour.

During his English exam, Mrs. Baker watched Will closely. She pulled him aside once the exam was over.

"Will, I could use a hand cleaning up," she said. "Would you mind?"

Hoping it might improve his grade, he said "Sure, Mrs. Baker."

"Just Julie, remember?"

"Sorry. Julie."

The class cleared out. Will gathered stray pencils and straightened chairs. He didn't say much, his mind still far from class.

"How was the exam?" Mrs. Baker asked while tidying her desk.

"Hard," Will replied. It was no exaggeration.

She gave him a serious look. "Yes. It would require your full attention. But I couldn't help noticing you looked distracted."

Will hung his head. He didn't want to disappointed Mrs. Baker. Not just because she was his teacher, but she was his mom's friend. "I'm sorry, Julie."

"Care to let me know what's bothering you?" She

leaned against her desk, her mannerisms unprofessional. She wasn't in "Teacher-Mode." Mrs. Baker was just Julie, and Will sensed she was genuinely concerned for him.

"I…" He didn't know where to begin. Or for that matter, how much he could tell her. "I've had a lot on my mind."

"I can tell."

She waited for him to say more, but Will was quiet. He wanted to confide in her. Tell her everything from start to finish. But she couldn't possibly believe him. Who could?

Mrs. Baker stood up. "I'll let you enjoy your summer, then. But before you go…" She took a piece of paper, wrote on it, and held it out to Will. "Take this. If you need anything at all, even just someone to talk to, give me a call or stop by. We don't live very far from each other."

Will accepted it reluctantly. "Thanks, Mrs. Ba—Julie."

"Anytime, Will." She walked him to the door. "Have a good summer."

"You too."

Will folded the paper with her address and phone number, stuffing it into his pocket. He wished it made him feel better, but the fact that Mrs. Baker could tell he was struggling reminded him how poorly he must have done in her exam.

I can always catch up with school, he tried to assure himself. *Lives are at stake here. That's more important than stupid grades.*

But it was no comfort. The hopelessness of his academic career only made him feel more lost. He was only guessing at answers to save his great-uncle, too, but if he was wrong he couldn't try again. One solution, risky as it may be, kept nagging at his mind. Will pushed away the thought.

The library, he told himself. *We'll find a way there. And if not…*

The Werewolf Trials

If not, then I'll do what I have to do.

For better or worse, the school year was over.

Students exploded out of the school, rejoicing at three months of freedom. Will felt like the only kid who wasn't jumping for joy. He knew he was going to war with Moyset, and he had the sinking feeling there would be great sacrifices before the first leaves of autumn fell.

Wasting no time, they went to the library that afternoon,

Will, Travis, and Eliza had the place nearly to themselves. None of their classmates were likely to spend their vacation browsing bookshelves at the library. The solitude was perfect; they could roam freely without as many prying eyes.

"So, what exactly are we looking for?" Travis asked.

"Demon lore, demonology, anything along those lines," Will explained. "Of course, look for anything that mentions Moyset or werewolves. We should probably grab some of the books we looked at before, too. They might make more sense with what we know now."

They split up, stacking any books of interest at their favorite table. They could only find one book on demonology, *Encyclopedia of the Demonic,* but Eliza found several religious texts that discuss exorcism and holy rites to repel evil. Travis picked up some of their past favorites; *A History of Shape-Shifters* and *The Werewolf Trials,* among others. Will suggested someone run down to the adult fiction section and pick up *The Exorcist.*

Travis was indignant. "Now wait a minute. You gave me hell for looking up movies and stuff, and now you're going to start quoting fiction? Hypocrite."

"It's not as hypocritical as you think," said Will. "I

Chapter 9

read once that William Peter Blatty's novel was inspired by a true story of demonic possession. It might help us."

He shrugged and wandered off.

They split the books up between them. Skimming *The Exorcist* was Eliza's job, and although fascinating it wasn't enough like Barbason's case to be of any real use. Travis looked up demon names in the *Encyclopedia of the Demonic*, finding no mention of Moyset. Will was rereading books from their last visit, spending extra time on *The Werewolf Trials*. The theme of devil-worship and witchcraft felt even more real now. He was seeing history in a whole new light, where what once sounded crazy now seemed more plausible than ever.

They searched and searched, coming up with nothing but dead ends. Then suddenly, Will's eyes lit up. "Whoa, hold on guys! I think I found something!"

Eliza dropped her book immediately. Travis snapped out of the nap he was taking behind his.

"What did you find?" Eliza asked.

"Listen to this," said Will, finding his place on the page. "It's from the trial of Pierre Bourgot. There was a terrible storm, and his sheep scattered. *'In vain did I labour, in company with other peasants, to find the sheep and bring them together. I went everywhere in search of them,'* he told the judge."

Travis rolled his eyes. "Get to the good part!"

"Fine, fine." Will's excitement was rising. "He said three black horsemen rode up to him. One said to him *'whither away? you seem to be in trouble?'* Pierre told him about his sheep, and the horseman promised Pierre that his master would protect his flock. He said that soon he would find his sheep, and in five days he would return to make him another deal, this time for great sums of money and protection.

"The horseman returned, right on schedule. Pierre learned this horseman was the servant of the Devil, and he forswore God and Christianity to pledge his loyalty to Satan. He kissed the horseman's left hand, which was *'black and ice-cold as that of a corpse.'"*

"You think this horseman is the same demon that came to Connor?" Eliza asked.

Will nodded. "Oh, I'm pretty sure alright. *'And for two years I never entered a church, according to the desire of my master, whose name I afterwards learned was Moyset.'*

Deafening silence filled the already still library. Eliza seemed frightened. Travis looked excited. Will was a combination of both.

"Well tie a tail to my ass and call me a hound, we have ourselves the culprit!" Travis exclaimed.

Mrs. Flower, the librarian, shot them a scornful look.

"What happened next?" said Eliza.

Will skimmed the rest of the article. "His flock was protected, that's for sure. And get this, later he had to perform a ceremonial dance and rub a magic salve all over his body. It says the salve—given to him by Moyset—turned him into a wolf. He attacked, and even killed, women and children from his own village. *'I found that I could now travel with the speed of the wind.'* Sounds just like when the Beast flies away on the breeze to me. Once the transformation was over, Pierre was weak and could barely move." He went through the account one more time. "This sounds exactly like what's happening now!"

Eliza was in awe. "I can't believe it. When was this trial?"

He flipped back a page. "December of 1521," Will read aloud. "But the events happened nineteen years earlier."

"That means…" Eliza looked weary. "Moyset has been terrorizing people for at least five hundred years. Five hundred years, and no one has been able to destroy it."

Will felt nauseous. She was right. This was proof that

Chapter 9

what they were facing was an ancient evil, surviving over half a millennia.

This was worse than they expected. Much, much worse.

Chapter 10:

Summoning

After their discovery, the trio didn't stay long at the library.

They didn't talk much. Will couldn't speak for the others, but he felt disheartened. More than ever the task of stopping Moyset seemed impossible. How could three kids defeat an ageless monstrosity? And even then… Could they do it in time to save Barbason?

At Will's insistence, they spent their entire first week of summer at the library. After only a few days, they exhausted every possible book of use to them, but that didn't stop Will. He brought his laptop, connected to the wifi, and continued his search online. Searching "Moyset" didn't turn up anything new; one website had the same trial of Pierre Bourgot, which reiterated what they already learned of the demon.

He searched for "werewolf," "werewolves," "demon," "demonology," "exorcism" and, at Travis' request, "silver bullet prices." They were getting nowhere.

Chapter 10

Eliza patiently reread *France at a Glance,* but by the weekend Travis was restless.

"We've spent every damn day of summer break at this place," he moaned. "What do we have to show for it? One relevant tale, and a lifetime's supply of Mrs. Flower's creepy glances. Can we give it a rest already?"

Will ignored him. He searched "demons of France" and sifted through the results.

"Maybe he's right," Eliza said. "I mean, if there was anything else to find we would have found it by now. Let's go home."

"Go ahead," said Will absently.

Eliza reluctantly put her book away and got up. "Are you coming?"

He didn't respond.

"Will, you'll drive yourself crazy like this," she put her hand on his shoulder. "Come home. Sleep on it, and tomorrow we'll work on a plan with what we know."

Typing another search term, Will said "Go ahead. I'm going to stay here a little while." He looked up from his monitor and saw the concerned look on her face. "I won't be much longer. Promise."

Eliza hesitated. After some time she gave him a quick kiss. "Okay. I'll see you tomorrow."

"Mmhmm."

"Catch you later, bro!" said Travis. He hopped out of his chair and raced to the door.

Several hours later, trollish Mrs. Flower told Will the library was closing and he better pack up. She had to remind him twice before he left, at which point she had to unplug his computer and urge him from his seat.

Truth is, Will was more desperate than Eliza or Travis could understand. For them, this was hardly more than a game. It wasn't personal.

Summoning

Neither of them lost their parents. And neither of them had another loved one at stake.

Will's determination was fueled by another kind of fear, too. If he couldn't find a solution here, Will knew only one other way to save his great-uncle.

He was desperate to find something, *anything,* else.

Over the weekend, Will, Travis and Eliza sat down to form a plan.

It was Travis' idea to meet at the hideout. It was everything they needed; quiet, isolated, and away from B.R. Amon. Will knew he couldn't think clearly there. His mind would run back to his great-uncle at the end of the hall.

Plus, Travis assured them the atmosphere at the hideout was "totally right" for this kind of thing.

Planning turned out to be as much of a dead end as their research. Travis' suggestions were brutal at best. Eliza tried to help, but her ideas could only slow the problem, not solve it.

Will mostly kept to himself.

"Look," said Travis. It was Sunday afternoon and they had talked in circles for hours. "I know I'm not popular for saying it, but we *do* know something that hurts the Beast. Silver. I say we get ourselves some weapons, track down the big bad wolf, and put a few silver rounds in him. End of story."

"And the end of Mr. Amon," Eliza said. "We aren't murderers, Travis."

"I don't exactly want that blood on my hands, either. But it's getting worse, man. I've been keeping an ear out, and the Beast sightings are more violent by the day. Before long, it'll kill again."

They went home without coming to a decision.

<h1 align="center">Chapter 10</h1>

On Monday, Will went to the library by himself.

He didn't expect to find anything. He wasn't getting his hopes up. But he had to keep searching, if for no other reason than to keep his mind busy.

The walk through the Matheson Memorial Library was now so familiar, Will could walk it blindfolded. Walk in, turn right, go up the half-flight of stairs to the non-fiction section, right again down the rows of bookshelves, right along the window, and there was his favorite table, hidden from view.

The table wasn't empty.

Two people sat there. One was a man with messy black hair and thick glasses. Very bookish. Maybe college aged. The woman was a little older, in her late twenties or early thirties. She was attractive in a strong-willed, determined way. Will couldn't place her ethnicity; she was mixed, but mixed with what? It could have been Mexican, Native American or possibly even Asian.

The woman brightened when she saw Will. It looked like they were waiting for him.

She stood up and extended her hand. "Why hello there!" she said. "I'm Natalie Elwin, *Monsters of America* investigator. And this is Eric, my cameraman."

Eric waved.

"Uh… Hi," said Will. He didn't like the sound of this.

She smiled. "What's your name, sport?"

Reluctantly, he told her. "My name's Will."

Her eyes shined. "Will Lewis, by any chance?"

Oh boy. Will nodded, unable to think of a believable lie.

"That's wonderful!" Natalie clapped her hands. "We've heard so much about you! Eric and I are in town doing a follow-up to our 'Wisconsin Werewolf' episode. Say, you wouldn't be interested in an interview, would you?"

"Well I, uh…" Will tried to think of a way to back out. "I'd love to, but I don't really know anything about werewolves."

Natalie patted him on the back. "We won't take long, will we Eric?"

Eric shook his head.

"What have you got to lose?" Natalie said. There was something wrong with her smile; it was the grin of someone who knows more than they let on. "You're not hiding anything, are you?"

Great. Will didn't want to be on TV talking about the Beast, but if he turned her down it would look suspicious. He figured he might as well bite the bullet and get it over with. At least then he could clear the air. "I guess that'd be alright."

"Perfect!" said Natalie. "Let's step outside, shall we? Fresh air is the best backdrop."

Will followed them into the parking lot, where a *Monsters of America* van waited. Eric spent a few moments setting up his camera equipment, while Natalie skimmed through notes on a clipboard.

Once the cameras were rolling, the questions began.

"Are you sure you don't know anything about the 'Beast of Bray Road,' hun? I mean, you live right in the heart of the Beast sightings, don't you?"

She knows where I live? Will thought. So much for this interview being random. "I've heard a few things at school, but that's it."

"I see," she made a note. "And have you ever had a paranormal experience yourself?"

"Nope," Will lied. He doubted it was very convincing.

"Nothing?" Natalie persisted.

"Never."

Chapter 10

It was beginning to feel more like an interrogation.

"Do you believe in the supernatural? Cryptozoology? UFOs?"

"Not really."

"Do you find the subject interesting?"

"Just in the movies."

"I see," Natalie paused to write. "So, you have no interest in books about, say, old werewolf stories?"

Will was getting nervous. The camera watching his every move didn't help. "I guess not," he said.

Natalie tilted her head, analyzing him. "Ever heard of a book called *The Werewolf Trials,* by chance?"

Shocked, Will couldn't speak. He assumed other interviewees mentioned him, and that's why he was being targeted. But no one at school was aware of his reading choices. "How did you know about that?" he asked.

Immediately Natalie jotted down notes. "Excellent! Are you getting this Eric?"

Eric gave a thumbs up.

"So you have read *The Werewolf Trials?*" she said, more as a statement than a question.

Will's mind was recoiling. "Hold on, I never said that!"

"But you have, haven't you?" Natalie put a hand to the side of her mouth and whispered "You can admit it, kiddo. Your charming librarian already let us peak at your history of books checked out."

Mrs. Flower, of course. She was the only one who knew what they were reading. Not to mention she knew they spent *every day* at that table. It shouldn't have surprised Will she tipped Natalie off.

"I…" he didn't know what to say. The wise words of his father came to mind. *Better to say nothing than something you'll regret.* "I think I should go."

Summoning

As Will turned to leave, Natalie called out "Would you say Barbason Amon, your great-uncle, is out of the ordinary?"

Will did a double take. This woman had no shame. "What is that supposed to mean?"

"A simple *yes* or *no* would do fine, Will," Natalie said politely.

"How is this relevant to your show?" he asked.

She continued adding notes to her clipboard. "Based on what you read in *The Werewolf Trials,* would you say your great-uncle shares traits with people convicted of *lycanthropy* during that era?"

"What—no, he doesn't. And again, what does Uncle Barbason have to do with your show?"

"No, you say?" Natalie had to start a new page of notes. "Would you care to elaborate?"

Taking a deep breath, Will turned around. "Goodbye, Miss Elwin," he said over his shoulder.

Giving it one last shot, Natalie yelled "Be sure to ask Barbason if he'd like an exclusive interview!"

That was the last straw.

Now that Natalie was on their case, it was too risky to be at the library. She would be waiting to pounce again, each time making their efforts all the more public.

There was only one option left.

Once it was dark, Will went to visit his great-uncle.

Barbason's health kept getting worse. He looked more like a skeleton every time Will saw him.

"Hey kid," he said.

"Hey." Will kept the emotion out of his voice. He was determined not to cry this time. "How are you feeling?"

Barbason wheezed. "hangin' in there," he said.

Chapter 10

Will came here with a purpose. Asking the question took more courage than he expected. "Uncle Barbason… What happened to the book? The one that told Connor about Moyset."

He stared at Will, his expression blank. "I took it after he died. Didn't want it fallin' into the wrong hands, ye know. Far too dangerous."

"So you have it?"

"Yeah, why?" Barbason was puzzled.

"We've searched through everything at the library," Will explained. "We haven't come up with much. That book might have some answers. We can't afford not to check it out. Can I borrow it?"

Barbason raised an eyebrow. He looked at Will for a long time, until he thought he would refuse.

"I ain't sure ab—" he coughed. "—'bout this. It's… It…"

The bed shook. Barbason was having convulsions, his head and limbs flailing violently.

"Uncle Barbason!"

Will flung himself on his great-uncle, trying to hold him steady. Barbason's coughs started to resemble growls.

The old man opened his eyes. They were bright yellow.

Will gasped. He stepped back as his great-uncle made a menacing growl. The window flew open with a crack.

Barbason's face was changing; the lines of his face contorted, his lips curled back in a snarl, and his eyes grew more ferocious. Then, the strangest thing happened… Will saw Barbason's face, vicious yet human, but he *also* saw the monstrous visage of the Beast. The wolf's face seemed to overlay the man's, like a hologram.

The Beast's image flickered, only partially visible. But it was rising; slowly Will saw claws, chest, and legs lifting out of his great-uncle's body. The Beast faced Will, who trembled from head to toe.

"*Nnnoooooooo…*"

In a flash, the Beast vanished. Barbason was gasping, his hand clutching his heart. Judging it was now safe, Will returned to his side.

"Sorry kid," he said once he caught his breath. "It's… Getting stronger."

"Uncle Barbason," Will said urgently. "If you have it, give me the book. Before it's too late for you."

Still breathing heavily, Barbason nodded. He opened a drawer on his bedside table, extracted a little black book and handed it to Will.

It was very old, judging from the condition of the leather binding and the color of the pages. There were no words on the front or back, but on the spine he found the title in faded gold letters: *Livre de la Bête*.

"What does it mean?" Will asked.

"I looked it up," said Barbason. "*'Book of the Beast.'* Dun' know if you'll find it very useful, though."

"Why not?" Will asked, but as soon as he opened the book he understood; it was written entirely in French. "… Oh."

When Will looked up, Barbason was fast asleep. He left, closing the door quietly behind him.

In his room, Will sat up in bed with *Livre de la Bête*. He flipped through the pages, hoping sheer determination could cross the language barrier. But aside from a few archaic symbols and diagrams, none of it made sense.

Just when Will was about to give up, he found what he was looking for. His eyes lit up with excitement and terror. His hands were sweating, his eyes scanning the page at breakneck speed.

He knew what had to be done.

Chapter 10

Eliza knocked and knocked, but Will wasn't answering.

Finally he came to the door, still in his pajamas. Will hardly slept; he tossed and turned for hours when he tried. Eventually he surrendered, and watched late night TV in the living room until exhaustion knocked him out.

"Will!" said Eliza. "Were you still sleeping? It's almost noon."

Rubbing his eyes, Will said "Couldn't sleep."

She gave him a kiss. "I'm sorry. I didn't mean to wake you."

"It's fine. Come on in."

They sat down on the old couch.

"I was wondering if you wanted to go back to the library," Eliza asked. "Travis is antsy, but I'll still go with you."

"That wouldn't be a good idea," said Will. He explained what happened there yesterday with Natalie and her silent cameraman, Eric.

Eliza crossed her arms, agitated. "That woman needs to mind her own business."

Will nodded.

"Well… We could always go over plans again," she suggested. "Maybe we'll think of something we missed before."

"That's okay," Will told her. "There's actually one thing I want to look into. It might help."

"Really?" Eliza was surprised. "Well, that's great! Would you like my help?"

"No, that's alright. I'd like to do this by myself, if that's okay." He couldn't make eye contact with her.

Eliza seemed disappointed. "Oh, alright… Well, if

Summoning

that's what you want. Just let me know if I can help, okay?"

"Okay."

That wasn't the real reason he kept Eliza out of it, but it was close.

Really, he didn't want her to talk him out of it.

By nightfall, the preparations were complete.

B.R. Amon's abandoned garage had changed. All equipment and clutter was pushed against the walls, leaving a great clearing in the center. On the ground, a huge circle twenty feet in diameter was drawn in chalk. Within this circle was an elaborate and disquieting symbol. It was the Seal of Moyset, recreated with painstaking detail.

Will stood at the edge of the circle, the Book of the Beast open in his hands. He checked the accuracy of his work one last time, then flipped off the light switch.

Immediately the room fell into darkness. The only

light came from six candles around the circle, giving the impression that the Seal stood suspended in an endless abyss.

"The Seal of the Great One, drawn inside a Circle of Invocation," Will spoke in a whisper. Although he couldn't read French, his grandfather could. On the back of the most important page, Connor left a handwritten translation.

"One basin of water, placed in the center of the Invocation Circle. One athame, *or ritual dagger,"* he said. Unfortunately Will didn't have a basin and certainly didn't have a dagger of any kind, but he hoped a stainless steel pot and cutting knife would do the trick. He glanced at the final steps, playing it over again in his mind. It was committed to memory by now, but it was still safer to imagine than actually do.

Clutching the book like a child might clutch a pillow, Will stepped inside the chalk circle. Other than nerves, he felt no change; no thresholds crossed, no sins yet performed. Maybe, just maybe, it wouldn't work. Will clung to the hope that nothing would happen, that he would walk away feeling foolish but otherwise fine. He wondered if his grandfather held onto the same delusion as he approached the center of the Seal. Will took one last look at the incantation before setting the book aside. He took a deep breath, just in case it was his last.

The time had come.

"Tis night! 'tis night! and the moon shines white," Will recited. All was silent as he spoke the cursed words. *"The shadows stray through burn and brae, and dance in the sparkling rill."*

The candles flickered. The sense of standing in a void intensified. Will swayed in place, as if balancing at the edge of an impossibly high cliff.

> *"'Tis night! 'tis night! and the Devil's light*
> *Casts glimmering beams around*
> *The maras dance, the nisses prance*
> *On the flower-enamelled ground."*

Summoning

As the words echoed back, they took on a strange inflection and timbre completely foreign in Will's voice.

"'Tis night! 'tis night! and the werewolf's might
Makes man and nature shiver.
To the great Moyset, I have this to say;
Thy presence please deliver!
A boon I ask thee, mighty shade,
Within this circle I have made."

Will paused to catch his breath. The words left a putrid taste in his mouth, as if they had been vomited forth instead of spoken.

"Haste, haste, haste, lonely spirit haste!
Here, wan and drear, magic spell making,
Findest thou me - shaking, quaking.
I pray you send hither,
Send hither, send hither,
The great grey shape that makes
men shiver!"

Will took the knife and—before he could hesitate—cut down his wrist. Blood dripped into the water, creating formless shapes that danced as if with intelligence. Eyes watering with pain, Will whispered the final words.

"Shiver, shiver, shiver!
Come! Come! Come!"

The garage was unnaturally quiet. The silence made each noise all the more dramatic—the thrumming of Will's heart, the clatter of the knife when he dropped it, even the trickle of blood through Will's fingers as he held his wound. He waited, looking for a sign of success or failure.

A wintry breeze cut through the room. Not only was it unseasonal, there were no windows to let in a draft. The candles flickered, threatening to go out and leave Will stranded in the abyss.

Out of the darkness came a voice, colder even than

the wind. *"Comme j'étais cité à comparaître, ici je me présente."*

Will turned, squinting to see who spoke. But the void gave no hint of where the being was.

"As I hath been summoned, here I present myself," the voice translated. It was a sound unlike anything Will ever heard; it spoke in hisses, rasps, and rattles, yet each syllable was unmistakably clear. The voice was deeply unsettling, but strangely comforting. *"Speaketh thy boon, childe, or tread here no more."*

He turned and turned, but no matter where Will looked the voice came from right behind him. He could even feel its icy breath on the nape of his neck. The goosebumps covering Will's body were so defined they almost hurt. "I… I want to make a deal," Will said, trying not to tremble.

Silence. Even the candles were still. *"Propose thy bargain,"* said Moyset.

"My great-uncle is dying," Will said. "If something isn't done, he won't last much longer. You're killing him."

"His demise is naught but his own doing. He is human. His nature is wrought with self-mutilation of thy soul and skin." The demon's words were haunting. Will felt increasingly like he was dreaming; between the disembodied voice and the empty darkness there was nothing of reality to cling to. He was living out his darkest nightmare.

"This isn't Uncle Barbason's fault. You tricked my grandfather by promising him miracles," said Will.

"Yes," said the blackness beyond the candles. *"His err was of the heart. That was his folly and through his imprudent actions arose his undoing."* Otherworldly laughter, inhuman and malicious, rang across the room. *"Human nature."*

Will's fear kept rising. Despite the cold, beads of sweat poured down his face. "I want to save my great-uncle. He's the only family I have left."

Eyes out of nowhere watched Will. He could feel

their scrutiny; weighing his soul, dissecting his emotions. He felt naked under its shameless gaze. *"What is thy proposal?"*

"Take me instead," Will said before he could stop himself. "Let him live, and recover from the damage you've done. Take me in his place. If you left my grandfather for Uncle Barbason, you must be able to."

Moyset paused, considering the arrangement. *"And for what reason shall I accommodate?"*

"You need me," Will said, hoping it wasn't just a bluff. "If Uncle Barbason dies, what does that leave you with?"

"Death of the material need not mean death of the spiritual," the demon replied. *"Death comes more than once."*

Not what Will hoped to hear. He was beginning to wish he never called forth this monster. "Then… What is it you want?" Will asked. "You clearly don't want to help people. If you want revenge, I'd say you got it after what you did to Grandpa Connor. And if it's power you want… Then why tie yourself down to a weak old man? Why not have a young, healthy teenager?"

Seconds ticked by in unbearable silence.

"And you would lay down thy life for me? You would imbibe my essence and become my body? You would willingly sign sovereignty of thy existence to me?"

The reality of the decision overwhelmed Will. One wrong move, and countless lives could be destroyed. He was playing with fire, so close to the flames he couldn't tell if he was already burning.

"I'll agree on one condition, Moyset. My body, my life… It's yours. But you can't have my friends or family. No matter what happens, you have to promise not to trick them into a bargain. In exchange, you'll have me, for the rest of my long life."

The demon thought it over. *"Misguided emotions appear*

Chapter 10

to be a familial trait," it said.

"Do you promise?" Will persisted.

"So be it," said the voice from nowhere. *"And do you agree to my terms, childe?"*

Will closed his eyes. He was colder than he thought possible, but it wasn't because of the temperature. It was like a physical manifestation of his overwhelming terror. He hated the deal, but maybe, with time, they could learn how to defeat the demon. Until then he could keep Barbason alive and his friends safe. He took one last breath, shaking from head to toe.

"I agree, Moyset."

The air began to move. It started slow; just enough to gently blow your hair. But quickly it picked up, faster and faster, becoming a tornado with Will at its core. All six candles went out, eliminating the last glimmer of light. Will felt dizzy, lost in complete, blinding darkness.

Faster, faster, the wind gained speed. The vortex tightened around Will until he felt whiplashed by its intensity. Standing upright became a heroic challenge in this abyssal typhoon, and each second Will feared he'd find himself tumbling into infinity.

In the middle of emptiness, a vague shape appeared.

He couldn't discern anything as defined as a silhouette, but Will had no doubt Moyset was here, in front of him. It had a pair of yellow eyes, glowing like planets in a starless sky. The demon charged, knocking Will off his feet.

Will fought, but the threat was now internal. He could feel it crawl under his skin, making his muscles spasm and blood freeze. It ravaged his body, his mind, his very soul. It was ripping him apart. As the monster made a home of his flesh, Will felt chunks of his identity being torn out, littering the ground like the remains of a sloppy meal. He wanted to scream but couldn't. All he could do was thrash about, agony blanketing every inch of him.

When it was over, he was numb with fatigue and pain. He stood up and realized he was no longer Will Lewis, not fully.

Now, he was also *la Bête*. The Beast.

Part
2

Chapter 11:
Cursed

Will tested himself.

His eyes adapted to the low light, giving him just enough vision to navigate the garage. He felt every little muscle as he flexed. Not only did he hear his heart thump, but he could trace the flow of blood as it raced through his veins. He stretched, the sensation completely euphoric.

He was aware of every inch of himself like never before.

In a detached way, Will realized his wrist was still bleeding. Once it had his attention he felt the stinging pain again, but it was distant. He wondered if it had started to heal or, perhaps, he was just less bothered by the pain. It didn't matter either way; his work was done, and now he would to tend to his wounds.

Will crossed the garage, his stride faster than he remembered. Every step sounded thunderous, and—there it was—he finally heard the mice in the attic. The bathroom had a mélange of smells. He detected the scent of bleach and cleaners, long covered by the odors of human waste. Almost comically, cheap air freshener was thrown into the mix. Will smirked at the thought. But when he went to open the mirror cabinet, all humor was lost.

The face staring back at him wasn't his own.

It might have shared the same basic structure, but never had Will seen such menace in his reflection. The features looked angled, almost canine. The lines of his face were defined. And the eyes took on a strangely luminescent yellow.

Whatever he saw, it was gone now. The mirror showed nothing but his shocked expression. Will felt his own face frantically, but all was as it should be.

In the few minutes since his transformation, Will wasn't afraid; in fact, the change in him felt *great*. It wasn't until then, catching a glimpse of his demonic doppelgänger, that he panicked. He quickly wrapped his arm and hurried away from the mirror.

He left the bathroom as the door at the end of the hall opened. Barbason stood in the doorframe, leaning heavily on his cane. He stared at Will in disbelief.

"Kid… Tell me ye didn't," Barbason pleaded. When Will didn't answer, the old man started to cry. "No, no… Tell me ye didn't do it kid! *Tell me ye didn't!*" he yelled. Barbason collapsed to the floor, pounding on it in rhythm with his sobs.

Will ran over and dropped down beside him. "I'm… Sorry, Uncle Barbason," he said. "But now, you are free."

Barbason choked out a laugh. "Free? Yeah, I'm free to watch it do to ye what it did to me! Free to see the kid I'm s'posed to protect get eaten alive from the inside out!"

It was hard to watch Barbason break down. Will knew this was his fault, but what's done is done. This was Will's demon now. He would fight it day-in and day-out, keeping it leashed as long as he could.

"Go to sleep, Uncle Barbason," Will said, putting his arm around him. "Rest, for the first time in months. This isn't your burden anymore."

Their eyes met. "I hope ye know what ye're doing, kid," said Barbason.

In the back of his mind, Will heard unearthly laughter.

"I hope so, too."

Will helped Barbason to his feet, and brought him to bed. As soon as the old man closed his eyes he was out. Finally, his great-uncle could sleep peacefully. But as Will crept into his own room, he knew it was his turn to have sleepless nights and exhausted days.

The torch had been passed. This marked the beginning of Will's battle.

There would be no sleep tonight. To keep his mind occupied, Will tried to dive into one of his favorite books. He grabbed *The Island of Doctor Moreau,* curled up in bed, and tried to slip into the comfort of fiction. But his enhanced senses proved to be a constant distraction. Even if he stared at nothing but the book, soon he would only see the texture of paper and shades of ink. The words had less meaning with each line. Too restless to read, Will got up and paced his room. He wanted to go out for a midnight stroll. The fresh, cool air sounded wonderful, but Will suspected that was the Beast talking.

Unlike Barbason, Will didn't have a nocturnal sleep pattern yet. He would have to adjust, but for now he would have to make due. Will was already getting tired. By three o' clock in the morning, all Will could do was sit at his desk and exert all his energy to staying awake. He wondered how he would break the news to Travis and Eliza. What would they think of him now? Would Eliza still like him? Would Travis

Chapter 11

want to kill him like his great-uncle? He was most concerned about Eliza. He daydreamed about her, wondering where she was now. Fast asleep no doubt. He could picture her, lying under her floral sheets. Will imagined what her aromatic room would smell like to him now. He focused on the vision of her, dressed maybe in silk pajamas, breathing ever so gently.

The image was so real, Will began to forget he was sitting in his room at B.R. Amon. It was almost like he was actually there, watching her through her window…

… Through the window I watch her. The little girl sleeps undisturbed, unaware she has a visitor.

I pass through the glass, silent as a ghost. The pungent taste of chemicals nearly overwhelms me. The room is a mockery of wildlife, laced with artificial images and scents that only resemble true flora and fauna to the most deprived observer. I slide across the room and come to rest over her bed. The defenseless little girl, who sleeps so unguarded. How tragically naïve she is. Her throat is bare, an invitation for any intruder such as myself to cease her breathing with a simple slice. I come closer, sniffing the air around her exposed head. Oh, how she tries to hide her scent with cheap imitations of the world's aromas. They are no less chemical than the oil they feed their metal steeds. But beneath the pleasing toxins is her true scent; a feminine smell intertwined with the pheromones of a maturing young woman, all subtly yet distinctly her own.

She stirs. My bodiless face is only inches from hers. Perhaps she feels my presence, but not with her five simple senses. To those I leave no trace; but as an unmarked sense of foreboding she might come to believe she is not alone. If I wished not to wake her I would retreat, but it does not matter. She could open her eyes and be just as blind to me.

A siren-like noise is going off. It is not her bedside timepiece, however, but something distant. Something in a room only a building

Cursed

away. Beep beep. *The sound comes from another time-keeper.* Beep beep, beep beep. *It's close. Getting closer. Closer…*

The alarm on Will's clock kept chiming. He snapped out of his vivid daydream.

That was no daydream, he realized. Will wasn't just imagining Eliza; he was *seeing* her and *tasting* her. But not with his body. Now he understood what happened.

He just experienced his first "transformation" into the Beast.

Barbason was right. The sensation was very dream-like. Already the details of the short journey were leaving him, like memories from a dream lost after waking. But the *feelings!* Those were strong if not clear, like vibrant colors of paint randomly thrown against an easel.

Will shut off the alarm and rubbed his eyes. Six twenty-five. Normally, he would have just enough time to hit the snooze once before his morning routine.

Now Will was truly glad for summer vacation. It meant he could sleep during the day when needed. If he was expected at school every day, it would have been nearly unbearable.

He set his alarm eight hours ahead, and at long last went to sleep.

Will's phone woke him up.

His dreams were a kaleidoscope of concepts, free of rational thought yet full of brilliant imagery. They were almost primal, like long-forgotten memories of an era when humans were mere animals themselves.

Still half-asleep, Will reached for the phone. "Hello?"

"Hey." It was Eliza. "How's it going?"

Chapter 11

"It's alright," he said. He glanced at the clock. It wasn't even ten o'clock yet.

"Will, you don't sound good. Are you feeling okay?"

Now that it was done, Will knew he had to tell her about his deal. But not now, not after so little sleep. He didn't like deceiving her, but given the circumstances he thought a little white lie was justified. "I think I'm getting sick. I don't feel like myself right now."

"Oh no," she said through the phone. "Do you need anything? I'd be glad to come over and take care of you. I can bring chicken noodle soup. That always makes me feel better when—"

"That's okay," Will interrupted. "I just… Need sleep."

"Oh…" Silence. "Okay then. Right. Well, call me if you change your mind, 'kay?"

"Okay."

Eliza hung up. Will felt terrible; he should have invited her over and broke the news to her. But he was still so *tired,* he wouldn't have the strength to explain. He rolled over and fell asleep, feeling as sick with himself as he claimed to be.

When his alarm went off hours later, Will refused to wake up. He hit the snooze button over and over, until finally he surrendered and dragged himself out of bed. Apparently getting eight hours of sleep didn't guarantee you'd wake up rested, especially when that sleep was during daylight hours.

Barbason was much better that afternoon. When Will groggily left his room he found his great-uncle at the sink doing dishes. Will insisted Barbason get back to bed, and the old man didn't fight it. He was still weak, but definitely getting better. He was even well enough to join Will at the table for dinner.

"I got some pork chops thawin'," Barbason said. "Help yerself to as many as ye want."

Cursed

Will rummaged through the fridge for an alternative. "No thanks. Vegetarian, remember?"

"Oh. Yeah." Barbason scratched the back of his head. "Dun' know how to tell ye this, kid, but ye might want to rethink that whole *vegetabletarian* thing. The Beast don't take to it so well."

Deciding on a boxed mashed potato dinner from the pantry, Will said "Thanks, but I'll be alright." He might be a monster, but the thought of eating an animal was still gross.

Barbason shrugged. "Suit yerself."

But by the end of dinner Will suspected Barbason had a point. The smell of fresh meat sizzling in its own grease was intoxicating. The sight of the pork chops made Will's mouth water. And by comparison, his mashed potatoes were bland and flavorless; he could taste preservatives far more than the "sour cream & onion" the box claimed it to be.

He left the table still hungry.

Will's second night as a werewolf was less eventful, but just as restless. He tried to read. Paced his room. Watched TV. Cleaned the kitchen. He was desperate to find *anything* to pass the time. Even with a day's sleep, he was constantly fighting the urge to nod off when he wasn't active. One thing Will could still do was Sudoku; he was solving puzzles with eerie speed. He wasn't sure why. Most of the time Will was constantly distracted, much like he suspected an ADD sufferer would feel like. But Sudoku was effortless, to the point it barely kept his mind busy.

Maybe the Beast was good at puzzles, too.

As the sun rose and Will got ready for bed, he made a decision. Tomorrow night (or should he say tonight? Will didn't know anymore) he had to find something to keep him occupied. Otherwise, he would slip up and fall asleep. He pulled the sheets up to his chin, and told himself he'd figure

Chapter 11

it out when he woke up.

Eliza didn't interrupt his sleep this time.

When Will finally got out of bed late in the afternoon, he wondered how she was handling this. He thought maybe now he should tell her. But he froze, phone in hand, unable to make the call.

What if she hates me for it?

He wasn't ready to confess. Not yet. But as he held his phone another idea came to mind. He dialed a different number and waited.

"Frank Scott, what do you want?"

"Hi, pops," Will said.

Bellowing laughter rang through the phone. "If that ain't Will! Hey, hey, I got a joke for you, boy. You ready?"

There was no getting around Frank Scott's jokes; it was easiest just to let him tell it and move on. "Sure," said Will.

"Who can shave 25 times a day and still have a beard?"

Will wasn't even going to guess. "I don't know. Who?"

"A BARBER!" The laughter was so strong Will had to hold the phone away from his ear. "Alright, alright, I s'pose you want to talk to my little brat, don't you?"

"Yes please."

A few moments of down time, then, "He didn't force a joke down your throat, did he?"

"Yep," said Will. "The barber one again."

"Geez, that old fart is getting more senile by the day," Travis remarked. "What's up, man?"

He didn't know how to put it. "Can I crash at your place tonight? I've been up late without anything to do."

Cursed

"Hell yeah!" said Travis. "You're welcome anytime, bro."

"Great. See you tonight," Will said. He felt relieved as he hung up. Travis was always a night owl; he would be glad to keep him company. Plus, he wasn't known for attention to detail, so he might not notice if Will acts strange.

Once he let Barbason know where he would be, Will biked down to Travis' house.

Returning to the Scott's little Quonset hut was a comfort. Although B.R. Amon was finally like a home to him, it was under this domed roof Will first felt like he belonged in Elkhorn. Will and Travis spent the afternoon watching TV with his dad and telling terrible jokes. As night fell they migrated to Travis' room, where they didn't do much of anything and didn't mind it one bit. Doing nothing by yourself is boring, but sometimes with the right company there's nothing better.

But around two o'clock in the morning, the questions started.

"Dude, you look like shit," said Travis. "When you going to bed?"

Will intended to blink, but his eyes stayed closed a little longer than he expected. "I'm fine. I'm… I'm wide awake."

Travis put a hand on his shoulder. "You don't have to cover it, bro. I *know* what happened."

Will snapped out of a daze, almost choking on his own spit. "You know? But… How did you find out?"

"Dude," Travis said with his arms out, gesturing towards himself arrogantly. "I'm me."

One of the peculiar side effects of Will's double senses was the ability to smell emotions. The animal side of his mind found it perfectly logical; when a person feels a certain way their body releases slightly different scents, and in

Chapter 11

time you could recognize them. His human side wasn't so convinced; he suspected it was more spiritual than physical. But the source didn't really matter.

The Beast would know if Travis was kidding or bluffing. He was neither.

"And you… Don't hate me for it?" Will asked. It was the question he was most afraid of.

Travis looked offended. "Hate you? Nah. I ain't thrilled about it, but I knew it was coming."

Will sunk into his seat. "I'm glad. I was so worried. But now I don't know what to do. I'm beginning to think I should never have called that demon."

Awkward silence followed. Will looked up to find Travis staring at him, dumbfounded. The air reeked of surprise. "Say that again?" said Travis.

"The other night. You know, when I summoned Moyset," Will explained. He couldn't grasp the confusion.

Travis' jaw hung open. He slapped himself out of shock. "Hell man, I just thought you and Eliza made it to third base!"

Oh no, Will thought. He looked back and saw the misunderstanding, clear as day.

"Alright, now slow that down, assume I'm dumb, and try that one more time. Because right now I'm not liking how this sounds," said Travis.

Too late to backtrack now. "I… took a huge risk the other night," Will said. He explained everything that happened, from the ritual to his pledge.

"Holy hell dude, are you insane?" Travis said. He ran his fingers through his long black hair, processing what he heard. "I mean, people say I have issues. But this isn't like tie-a-preschooler-to-a-pole crazy. This is, like… Coat-yourself-in-pollen-and-run-naked-through-a-beehive crazy!"

Will had nothing to say. He agreed with Travis; what

he did was insane.

"What's it like?" Travis asked out of the blue.

"Huh?" Will lost focus again. He wanted sleep so badly.

Travis rolled his eyes. "C'mon man, what's it feel like to be the freakin' *Beast?*" There was more than a hint of excitement on Travis' breath.

It wasn't easy to articulate. "I only did it once," Will admitted. "And I'm not sure it even counts. I wasn't fully formed, just sort of floating like a ghost. But it's strange. For one thing, you sense *everything*. Nothing escapes the Beast's perception. And you think differently, too."

"Like how?" Travis inquired. He was on the edge of his bed, leaning in as close as he could.

Will didn't know how to put it. "Like, if the Beast were to see you I could look back, later, and know you are Travis Scott. But to the Beast, names don't matter. It doesn't think in those terms. It thinks like an animal, with the intelligence of a human. And when it happens, when you let your mind sink into that primal form… You're free. You can't control it and you aren't even really yourself, but you leave all your worries behind."

Travis chuckled. "Kind of sounds like being drunk."

It wasn't a bad analogy, although Will could only guess; he never had so much as a sip of alcohol. "So, let me ask you again… Do you hate me? I wouldn't blame you if you did." Will bowed his head with guilt.

He considered it for a moment. "Nah, I can't hate you."

"Do you still plan on killing me to stop the Beast?"

"Hell no," Travis answered at once.

Will was surprised. "But, that's what you wanted to do with Uncle Barbason."

"Yeah, but that was different," Travis explained. "He

Chapter 11

was old and creepy anyhow. You're worth saving."

That was one of the few compliments Will ever heard out of Travis. "Thanks… I think," he said. "Now I just have to tell Eliza."

Travis crossed his arms. "Don't."

"What do you mean?" Will said, his head cocked to the side like a puzzled dog.

"She ain't going to understand, especially if you didn't tell her first. Women are possessive creatures, and they get super mad when you do anything they didn't give the stamp of approval to," said Travis. He scratched his head and added "Plus, she might not be so cool with the whole 'deal with the devil' part."

"But, won't I just make it worse by not telling her?" Will asked.

"Only if you get caught," Travis pointed out. "Keep her in the dark long enough and it won't matter."

Will never understood Travis' bizarre logic. Sometimes he made morbid sense, but other times his ideas couldn't even be called half-baked. "And how exactly do we keep it from her while she's helping us fight Moyset?"

"Easy," Travis said with confidence. "Dump her and find a chick who's less hassle."

"That's not a solution," Will pointed out.

"And she ain't worth findin' one," Travis replied.

Rubbing his eyes, Will said "Let's find something else to talk about, okay?"

"Fine, fine," Travis said. "So… If I give you a list, can you scare the pants off a few people? I'll pay you per person!"

Will covered his face with a pillow.

Although he was exhausted, Will rode home at

sunrise.

Travis offered to let him crash the day with him, but he wanted to check on Barbason. They made plans to hang out again that night. As he peddled up Bray Road, Will was caught up in a reverie of beauty he never paid attention to. He had always ignored the shimmering of the morning sun in the leaves, the gentle swaying of branches, the orchestra of animals chirping and squeaking to start their day. The scenery and physical labor were the only things keeping him awake; the last hour at Travis' he had to be shaken from a nap twice.

As he locked up his bike at B.R. Amon, Eliza emerged from her house.

"Where were you?" she asked, hands on her hips and eyebrow raised.

Will got caught, and he knew it. "I spent the night with Travis," he said. Then, to make it sound less severe, he added "No big deal."

"No big deal?" Eliza was not happy. "You told me you were sick. Shouldn't you be resting in your own bed?"

He didn't know what to say.

"You've been acting strange all week. When are you going to tell me what's on your mind?" she asked.

The time had come to fess up and tell the truth. But Will was so exhausted. He would tell her, and real soon, but he needed sleep first. "You're right Eliza. I'll explain… Later, okay?"

Her glare was fuming. "No, Will. Not 'okay.' You've been blowing me off and, honestly, I'm worried about you. We're a team, remember?"

Something stirred in response to her anger. Somehow, Will felt himself *expand*, like he was growing bigger yet the same size. How, Will couldn't explain, but from his perspective he was looking down at Eliza from much higher than he stood. "We will talk later," he reiterated, the sound of

Chapter 11

rage suppressed in his voice.

She backed down. Eliza couldn't possibly know what was happening (even Will wasn't sure), but she must have sensed a powerful shift in Will. "Fine. Later." Without another word she left.

The moment Eliza was out of site, Will was filled with guilt. He shouldn't have lashed out at her. It wasn't like him at all. He knew who to blame for his reaction, and his anger now focused on himself. He went to sleep thinking of a way to apologize.

When Will woke up, he could hear voices.

He first thought he was dreaming. Then, even more alarming, he feared it might be Moyset speaking in his mind, whispering horrible commands. But these voices weren't otherworldly—they were definitely human, but not exactly welcome.

Will recognized one of them.

It couldn't be… Could it? Will got dressed in a hurry, listening closely. There was no mistaking it, not with this uncanny hearing. The same anger that flickered through him earlier rose to the surface. He walked slowly to his door, telling himself to take deep breaths and stay calm. He closed his eyes and turned the doorknob.

"Will! So good to see you, kiddo!"

Sitting on the tattered couch were two people it was *not* good to see; Natalie Elwin and her cameraman. Barbason sat in his easy chair looking agitated and uncomfortable.

"What are you doing here?" said Will. He could feel the demon close to the surface, ready to pounce if given the chance.

Natalie stood up, hand extended. "We were just having a chat with Mr. Amon here. He's been oh so cooperative."

Veins pulsed in Will's temple. His body was going numb, yet there seemed to be a second set of senses coming to the forefront. "Get out," he said in a voice deeper than his own.

"Oh, we won't take up much of your time, promise," she said, winking at him. "We wanted to give our viewers a different point-of-view. You know, most people only think—"

"I said *GET OUT!*" Will said in a guttural roar. A force emanated from him, invisible but strong. Natalie stepped back, her long braid whipped in a breeze that shouldn't be. Eric the cameraman actually covered his face. Even Barbason shuddered.

There was no arguing with that.

"Well, um, right then," Natalie said. She collected her things in a hurry. "I guess we'll just… Leave you two for now. But keep us in mind if you decide—"

Will pointed to the door. "Out," he said again, quieter but no less forceful.

Natalie nodded. "Sure thing, sweetie cakes. Eric! Get your gear and let's go!"

Eric nodded and scrambled to pack up. They were gone in less than a minute.

"Thanks kid," Barbason said once they were alone. "I tried tellin' 'em to bug off, but they wouldn't listen. That woman is some kind o' persistent, alright."

"Don't worry about it," said Will as he took a seat. But he was worried; not about *Monsters of America* but of the monster inside of him. Letting it simmer at the surface felt… Good. That worried him, more than anything.

That evening, Eliza came knocking. The fact that she

didn't call ahead sent a clear message; she wouldn't be brushed aside.

"Can we talk?" she asked when Will answered the door.

He nodded. "Let's take a walk."

The sun would still be up at least another half hour, so they took a stroll down Bray Road. This was the same place Will first told her about Moyset. It seemed like a fitting background.

"Eliza…" Will searched for the words. Instead he came up with more excuses. *No, not this time,* he told himself. *No excuses. Just do it.* "I did something the other night. Something very, very dangerous."

She was nervous. You didn't need enhanced perception to see that. "What did you do?"

"I found the one book with answers," he said. "*Livre de la Bête.* The Book of the Beast. The book that started it all. In it was a way to save Uncle Barbason… But not without a sacrifice."

"You're scaring me, Will," Eliza said. She wrapped her arms around herself like a hug. They were hardly walking anymore. "What was the sacrifice?"

He forced his eyes to look into hers. "I was," Will said. "I summoned Moyset and make a deal. My freedom in exchange for Barbason's. It agreed… And so did I."

They stood in place. Eliza's mouth slowly opened as the devastating truth settled in.

"Moyset has taken me, Eliza. Now, I am the Beast."

Eliza was shaking in place. She couldn't look at Will; her eyes darted everywhere but at him. "No," she muttered. "No, this can't be. You couldn't have…"

Will bowed his head. "I did."

Why…" she couldn't finish.

"I had to. Uncle Barbason would die if I—"

Cursed

"Why didn't you tell me first?" Eliza interrupted.

Will knew this was coming. "I didn't want you or Travis to talk me out of it," he said.

The air was heavy with the scent of disbelief and anger. "Did it ever occur to you that we would be right to stop you? That this was a huge mistake?"

"Eliza, that's *all* I've thought about since I did it. I should have told you first. I was desperate, and running out of time." Will reeked of shame. "But… What's done is done," he said.

She turned away, hands over her eyes. "Is this what I can expect from you? More secrets and lies? Because I've had that before, and I won't put up with it again."

He went to hold her hand but she pulled away.

"Don't touch me!" Eliza shouted. Will caught a glimpse of tears in her eyes. "I thought I knew you! I thought you were different! I… Thought we were in this together."

"We are," Will assured her. "This isn't over, Eliza. I bought us some time, but Moyset isn't gone yet."

She faced him. Never before had she looked so hurt. "Of course it's not gone. It's inside of *you!* How could you put yourself in danger like this? Did you once think of what you're doing to me? You *lied* to me, Will. And you gave yourself up, just when I started to fall in… When I started to care about you."

"I'm sorry," Will said. He wished there were words to show how sorry he was.

"Moyset was killing Mr. Amon," said Eliza, fighting against her tears. "And you expect me to sit by and watch it kill you, too?"

"We will find a way," he insisted.

"No, *we* won't. *We* aren't doing anything." She was beyond tears; now Eliza was crying full-force. "You're on your own Will. I'm done."

Chapter 11

Eliza ran up Bray Road, and away from Will.

The world was cast in hues of red.

Part of it was the sunset. It set the sky ablaze with oranges, yellows and reds, as if the clouds were made of fire.

But there was so much more to it than that.

Will's vision bubbled and rippled like the air over an open flame. He felt his rage physically, circulating from his heart into every nerve of his body. But was it directed at Eliza, or himself? Will didn't know. By this point his anger was beyond reasoning or cause.

He suspected it wasn't *just* anger, either; he was heartbroken.

The old Will, the one who was completely himself, would have locked himself in his room and drown in his own misery.

Not this Will. Not anymore.

Instead heartache and frustration and sorrow all melted together, until all that remained was this highly-refined rage. And on top of that, he was insatiably hungry; for how intense his appetite was, it could have been days since he ate.

He abandoned the road and wandered between the trees. He didn't care if he got lost. Not that he could, with the senses he inherited. He kept walking into the woods, until there was no sign of the civilized world in sight. Will wanted a release from this inferno. He wished he could leave the heat, the rage, and the hunger behind. It felt like he was going to explode from all the fury in his body.

Will spread his arms.

Suddenly, what was hot turned cold, and he was blanketed by a subzero wind. He collapsed, numb at last.

Cursed

My physical coil drops, now an empty shell.

The heat is gone with it. This body pulses with ice, not fire. I let myself rise, stretch my ethereal limbs, and come to understand myself. I am not material, not now. I can become something close when I must, but for now I am formless energy, without the limitations of gravity or dense physical structure.

Freedom.

I examine myself. There is power in every inch of me, such vitality I never knew as a human. My invisible body is malleable, but one shape feels incredibly natural.

The shape of the Hellhound. The Great Wolf.

That is the form I maintain, even while unseen. And ah—what strength! I am not the tired old creature the townspeople are used to. I am greater. I am stronger.

I am a new Beast. A Beast reborn.

But now, to business. No longer is my mind clouded with emotion. I can think clearly enough to calculate. Analyze. Plan. I lift myself above the treetops, swimming through the air like the tides of a nightmarish ocean. I look out into the endless sky, the sun vanishing beneath the horizon.

So many wrongs to make right. So much punishment to deliver.

Where to begin, where to begin?

Chapter 12:
The Duel

The night sky is a world of its own; filled with beauties and horrors scarcely imagined by those of simpler senses.

Tonight, I am one of the horrors.

I ride the wind, following the back trail of the foolish girl. She had a head start, but still I arrive at her home soon after her. At the window, I watch. Tears rain down her face, as if she could purge all the sorrow through her eyes. Such naivety is pitiful. The hurt she feels is by her own hand; it is she who rejected what I am.

A violent gust unlatches her window. She looks up—but does she see what's in front of her? Of course not. But she is afraid. Maybe she guesses at the true cause of the intrusion.

Now what to do with her?

I could strike her down for her disloyalty. But no, that's not right. Ignorant as she may be, the girl is important. She must be protected. The decision is made; her life will be spared, and from the shadows I will ensure no harm befalls her.

Before I leave her to this misdirected misery, I should give her a gift. I call her naïve, for she understands so little. I will give her a

The Duel

glimpse of truth's ugly face.

For a moment, I make myself real. *Not entirely, but real enough for her human eyes to perceive. She screams, the sound alarming family throughout the house.*

Now *she sees what she has rejected.*

As one with the wind, I follow the road through the countryside. Searching. Searching…

There's the scent I'm looking for.

It takes me to a shared home, one where nomads can rest for a night or two before continuing their journey. One nomad in particular catches my interest.

The eavesdropper.

She has stolen the words of those in my territory, perverting them to suit her needs. She has no business here, yet despite my warnings has continued to pursue me. Silently I slide into the room she has claimed.

How to punish her?

If only she were out in the open. It would be much easier to become *if we weren't in such claustrophobic space. I will have to be quick.*

My body explodes, sending waves of ethereal energy in every direction. The artificial lights falter and perish, plunging the room into darkness. Oh, how easy it is to disrupt electricity! The eavesdropper might as well be blind now, for she lacks my level of night vision.

Time for judgment.

I contract my body, tightening the loose and fluid energy I'm made of into something almost solid.

Solid enough to injure. Solid enough to kill.

She hears something in the room. Fear fills her. "Eric? Eric, is that you?" she calls out. Does she really fool herself? Is she still clinging to the hope that she is in no danger?

I growl. The sound petrifies her.

Chapter 12

I go in for the pounce, but mid-air I lose hold of my solidity. Like flexed muscles, it is difficult to keep my body wound so tightly for long.

Plus, I am hungry.

In this condition there's little I can do to the eavesdropper. I will let her be...

For now.

The breeze turns towards the nearest farm. Ah, the outdoors! It's so much easier to hold myself together out here. My body of air becomes semi-solid as I descent upon unsuspecting cattle.

One well-placed bite to the throat, and the creature lives no more.

Blood flows freely, staining the grass. I gorge myself, rending flesh from bone. I devour not just muscle but the animal's other body, the one as intangible as my own. The delectable lifeblood fills me up. My work on the material corpse is sloppy; bits and pieces are littered carelessly. But of its phantasmal self I waste not a drop.

A farmer hears the slaughter and hastens to the field, bearing a long-barreled hand cannon for protection. He sees me, in all my monstrous glory. The farmer knows what I am, or at least has heard the rumors. He aims his weapon and pulls the trigger. The projectile within scatters into a barrage of metal.

I am barely hindered.

With this new, more lively prey in sight, I prowl forward. In a panic he fires again. Although still no threat, at this distance the blast does enough damage to slow my pace. But I do not falter more than a moment.

The man readies his cannon, but he isn't quick enough. I pounce, sinking my claws into the farmer's frail shoulders. He topples to the ground and is pinned, completely at my mercy. He bleeds, and I drink up the invisible energy leaking from the wound.

As I open my maw, the farmer's family join the fray. I pause, calculating their numbers. Two adults, two children, outnumbered five to one if you count the fallen fool. I could lay waste to them all, of this I am confident. But is it worth it? They would injure me along the way. Why cause a fight when I have already replenished?

Must not be greedy.

To give the illusion of worldly existence, I leap off my prey and retreat into the woods. Once I vanished behind the tree line, I became a chilly breeze once more.

The night has taken me further than ever. Such a brilliant array of scents and sights! If I was without cause, I could spend hours relishing every little sensation the world has to offer.

But tonight, I have a purpose.

At last I pick up a familiar trail. I follow it cautiously, unsure if it's the one I'm after. As I get closer, I become confident this is what I wished to find.

The scent of the instigator.

It leads me to a large house, filled to the brim with wasted resources. Earth's most precious commodities cut down, shaped, and hung for display. They serve no use aside from pure aesthetics.

Lowering myself to the ground floor, I peer inside. Four dwell inside; three human, one canine, all sitting around a machine producing false images of life. Such a mix of aromas pour out of them!

The alpha male, sire of the instigator, reeks of hypocrisy. He feels bitterness towards his mate and shame for his child.

The beta, mate to this alpha, smells of repulsive obedience.

Their child—the instigator—has the salty scent of sweat shed to earn the favor of his progenitors. His ambition is pungent enough to numb him to the depths of immorality he has plunged into.

The canine, a mere pet, carries the musk of abuse. It alone senses my presence. It barks at the window through which I spectate.

Stepping back, I analyze the scenario. Life is a puzzle. To move now would be a mistake. Too much could go wrong.

Chapter 12

I must be patient. I must wait until the instigator is alone.
I fall back and let the wind carry me away.
The night is still young. There is much yet to do.

Will didn't wake up until the sun was back in the sky.

When he did, he was still in the woods. Memories came crashing back, faster than he could keep track. He couldn't recall every detail of his night, but he was confident he spent almost the entire evening as the Beast. A sick feeling of guilt came over him, but he tried not to let it; Moyset could break the best of men. It was foolish to think Will would be able to resist for long.

Every muscle ached when Will got up, and he even discovered a few minor bruises that weren't there yesterday. At first, he didn't understand.

Then he remembered staring down the barrel of a shotgun.

Of course. Will had been shot. Twice. The Beast wasn't seriously harmed and neither was Will, but the injury still transferred. He should have expected this, after seeing the effect silver had on Barbason. Considering the damage a shotgun round should have caused, Will didn't feel so bad about a little bruise.

Brushing himself off, Will noticed something else; although he was exhausted, he wasn't the least bit hungry. He tried to keep the blurred memories of attacking a cow from his mind.

Will found his way back to the road, and walked home.

Barbason figured Will spent the night with Travis, which avoided any unwanted questions. Although he was unconscious the whole night, Will was far from rested. When he slept, he slept like the dead.

The Duel

At dinner time, Barbason was cooking steaks. To Will, it was torture; he didn't think *anything* ever smelled so good! His appetite was certainly back. He scavenged through the fridge again, trying to resist, but nothing could compete with that incredible aroma.

Seeing his struggle, Barbason said "Offer still stands, kid. There's more than enough."

After a battle of moral versus need, Will gave in. "Why not?" he said, more to himself than his great-uncle. "After what I've done, I doubt it matters."

He sat down with a big piece of steak. He wanted to be repulsed, but he had to admit it looked delicious. Will took a bite, and his taste buds exploded with flavor. His body tingled as it assimilated the protein and iron and fat. It felt like he digested the bite instantly.

Barbason smiled. "And I gots plenty more, if ye ain't full after that."

Will tore through the steak, a mad-man's glimmer in his eyes. When he finished Barbason cooked up round two, then round three. When they were done, Will felt comfortably full.

Meat was definitely worth it.

With the library out of question and the Scott hut so crowded, Will and Travis spent much of their time at the hideout.

Reluctantly, Will told Travis that it was over with Eliza, and about the night that followed. He wasn't concerned about the break-up, but Travis thought the werewolf rampage was awesome. They avoided too much conversation about the Beast, though; it always led to Will feeling hopeless. They still had no plan, no strategy, and no hope to get rid of Moyset.

Chapter 12

Travis made a habit of bringing his knife and dartboard. He practiced daily, and noticed significantly better aim when he taped Mason's yearbook photo to the bull's-eye.

"We got to use the time we have," Travis said. "Pretty soon we won't be able to hang out here as much."

"Why's that?"

Travis struck his favorite throwing stance; one leg straight and forward, the other bent, his throwing arm pulled back. "The county fair is coming in a few months. Once it gets close they'll have real rent-a-cops watching the place, to make sure no hooligans try their luck at breaking and entering." He laughed. "Not that any hooligans would, of course."

Will watched Travis focus, steady his hand, then throw. The knife *whooshed* through the air. Mason's cocky mug lucked out; he hit the target but missed the picture at the center.

"Can I give that another try? Will asked.

"Sure buddy." Travis pulled the knife from the dartboard and handed it to Will. "I'll be standing over there. Try not to be *that* far off target, 'kay?"

Ten paces away, Will focused on the dartboard. He was seeing through two sets of eyes, calculating the distance with both his human and canine mind. He held his arm back, carefully took aim, and in one fluid motion sent the knife flying. It almost buzzed as it whirled through the air at lightning speed. A loud crackechoed across the room when it met its target.

In the bleachers, Travis applauded. Will did a double-take, and still didn't believe the results of his throw.

The dartboard was cracked down the center, the blade slicing Mason's face in two.

The Duel

In dire need of advice, Will turned to the only place he could think; Julie Baker.

He didn't expect a cure to lycanthropy, or a remedy for a possessing demon. All Will wanted was another opinion, and maybe a little comfort.

But how much could he tell her?

It was true that she didn't live far. All he had to do was go straight down Bowers Road, and he was at her house in less than fifteen minutes. It was strange standing at the doorstep of a teacher. He rang the doorbell and paced the porch anxiously.

Mrs. Baker was surprised to see him. "Well, this is unexpected," she said. "Come on in, Will."

He stepped inside. Mrs. Baker's house was a spacious ranch-style home, roomy but old. It reminded Will so much of his house in Beloit.

"Would you like a drink? Mrs. Baker offered. "I'm afraid I don't have soda, but I make great iced tea."

"No, thank you," Will said. "I won't stay long. I just wanted to talk to you about something... It's stupid, really."

She put a hand on his shoulder. "If it meant enough for you to visit, it can't be stupid. What is it?"

Will avoided her eyes. "Have you seen *Monsters of America?*" he asked. It was the safest starting point he could think of.

Mrs. Baker nodded, but hesitantly. "Every now and then. Of course I had to watch the episode they filmed here. But mostly I just see it while flipping channels. Why do you ask?"

"It's got people talking," he said. "About... You know. The Beast."

She made an attempt to laugh. "Any news is big news in a town like this."

"What do you think?" Will asked her.

Chapter 12

"I think that show is desperate for material," said Mrs. Baker. "A couple weeks ago they did a special on the 'Frog Men of Ohio.' Not the most exciting episode, let me tell you."

"I meant what you thought about the Beast."

The scent of seriousness radiated from her. Mrs. Baker took her time considering her answer. "I have lived in Elkhorn my whole life, Will, and my parents lived here for theirs. Half the people who came forward with sightings have been family friends for decades or longer. They are good, honest people, and that includes your great-uncle. I don't know what they are seeing. But when these friends tell me of an encounter, I believe them. I would sooner believe there is some sort of Beast than believe any one of them is lying."

"What if I told you it *was* true. All of it—the Beast, the rumors about Uncle Barbason, even some of them about me," Will said. His spine tingled from confessing these things. It was exhilarating and terrifying. "What if it was every bit the monster people are afraid it could be? What if I said I know everything about it except how to stop it? What would you think then?"

Mrs. Baker was stunned. She could tell this was no prank, that Will meant every word. Decades of logic threatening to topple over like a house of cards. Will could sense her world shaking at the foundation.

"I… I would believe you, Will," she said at last. Her breath held the cold taste of truth.

Will had nothing to say. He feared he already said too much.

"What is it you know about the Beast?" Mrs. Baker asked.

Now what? thought Will. Nerves were getting the best of him. "I better go," he said. He turned for the door, unable to tell the whole tale.

The Duel

"Wait!" Mrs. Baker called after him. "Will, I understand if you aren't ready to talk. But please, just tell me you aren't in harm's way."

Hand on knob, Will thought of how to answer. "Just… Be careful, Julie. It's not safe right now. Not for any of us."

Before she could reply, Will left.

In time, Will settled into a routine.

His sleep pattern officially shifted. Will counted himself among the nocturnal, sleeping from eight in the morning until three or four in the afternoon.

Sometimes Will slept at B.R. Amon; other times he stayed with Travis. Since Barbason's health kept improving, Will didn't worry so much about checking on him. He became very familiar with the bike route down Bray Road, to the point he knew every hill before he reached it. Now and then Will opted to go on foot instead of bike. It took longer, but the walk was incredibly calming.

Then, of course, there was the issue of the Beast.

In the weeks since Will sold his soul, sightings of the Wisconsin Werewolf reached an all-time high. Even the most skeptical citizens had to admit *something* was going on, although they were running out of sane excuses. Local farmers were the most vocal; their livestock were dying off and they demanded something be done about it. Mostly the Beast targeted cows or sheep, but the ER saw more than one victim of an unusual animal attack.

Will began to wonder if he would carry this curse the rest of his life.

Eliza stayed away from him. Occasionally he saw her in his most vivid Beast-dreams, as if he watched her with an invisible eye. She always had a scent of fear to her, and

Chapter 12

rightfully so. Will was a monster. He hoped that, someday, she might understand the sacrifice he made. But he didn't count on it.

At this rate, he wasn't sure he'd live long enough to earn her forgiveness.

This routine was not ideal, but with it came a certain comfort. It gave him something to expect each day, and in between the anxiety of his guilt Will was able to relax. Even, to a degree, enjoy himself. It wasn't allbad being a werewolf; he was attuned to a world of beauty and wonder, the splendid array of sensations never ending.

But the calm would not last. Not for long.

It was a hot and humid day in late-May. Will spent the morning asleep on Travis' floor, and was headed home. He didn't take his bike; lately he almost always chose to walk. But as he went around the bend at the beginning of Bray, he picked up a scent that did not belong. He kept his pace, but was on guard.

Someone was following him. The only question was—who?

A voice slithered up Will's spine and into his mind.

(The instigator.)

Will knew that voice; in many ways, it was his own. His inner psyche, warped into the primal thinking of the Beast.

Walking at a steady pace, Will let his inner monster do the tracking.

(He will follow until we are alone. Alone, I can enact justice.)

They played this game of cat-and-mouse halfway down the road. When they neared the center of Bray, the pursuer made himself known.

"Lewis!" he called after him. "Just where do you think

you're going?"

It was Mason, after all. Will kept walking, fighting with the voice in his head. If he stopped moving, if he let the Beast have its way… There's no telling what he would do to Mason.

(No one to interrupt us here. The time has come to end this feud.)

"Why are you running, Lewis? What, are you scared?"
(Fight him. End him.)
"Turn and face me, coward!"
(Face him!)
"We've got a score to settle!"
(Settle the score.)

Finally he snapped. Will stopped in his spot, struggling to keep his rage in check. "What do you want, Mason?"

"Don't you dare think this is over, Lewis," said Mason. He kept coming until they were standing face-to-face on a deserted stretch of road. On one side was a patch of woods, on the other a field. There was not another human in sight.

Will craned his neck to meet his eyes. Although Mason was more physically intimidating, Will knew which of them had the upper hand. "Stay out of this, Mason. This isn't your battle. Keep your distance, or you will get hurt."

"'Keep my distance'? Are you joking?" Mason laughed. "You've made a fool out of me. Eliza confused pity for love instead of aiming for the best. She'll come crawling back to me, I guarantee it, but until then everyone thinks *you* one-upped me."

It took all of Will's strength not to respond.

"I know you have that… That *thing* on a leash somehow. Whatever it is—some mutant wolf, an experiment gone wrong, or something weirder—I know you're behind it.

Chapter 12

And I will ruin you with that connection." He gave Will's chest a sharp prod. "Your days are numbered, wolf-boy."

Will's own anger was melding with the Beast's. He couldn't hold it much longer. "Leave now, Mason. I'm warning you…"

"Leave?" Mason shoved him, hard. "Like hell I will! I'm going to teach you a lesson, Lewis. The lesson I should have taught you the day we met; *never disrespect Mason McCree!*"

He threw a punch. Will effortlessly blocked it, his eyes closed. "You are about to make the biggest mistake of your life," Will said, his voice toneless.

Mason's laugh was fitting of an asylum. He made a left hook with his free hand. "I knew the moment I met you, Lewis. I knew then that you were going to be an annoyance." He boxed at Will, who avoided each blow. "It was that look you had. Innocent. Childish. And—above all—stupid. Your mother's fault, no doubt. Always a sign of a pathetic mother when her kid turns out like you."

For a moment, there was no Beast. Only poor, weak Will, feeling the sting of grief. In this unguarded moment Mason's fist met Will's face, and he fell into the dirt beyond the road.

"That's what I thought." Mason cracked his knuckles. "One good blow and you're out. No fight, all talk. What would your sorry excuse of a mother say now?"

Blood turned to lava in Will's veins, jetting through his body at frightening speed. Rage consumed him again, but this time Will didn't contest it. He let the fire burn within, turning him into rage incarnate.

"I don't know," Will said, feeling the line between man and monster fade. "She's dead…" His voice deepened until it was not his at all. The guttural intensity couldn't possibly come from a human throat. *"Perhaps you can ask her yourself, once your body lay scattered and your soul awaits judgment."*

The Duel

That's when fire turned to ice, and Will succumbed to the Beast.

The instigator has incited violence for the last time.

Time for justice.

I burst from my shell like a bullet from the farmer's hand cannon. Although immaterial, the strength of the wave thrusts him off his feet and into the road.

He looks in confusion as my human form falls to one knee, weakened by the separation. His simple mind cannot comprehend what assaulted him.

A vehicle approaches. I must bring this battle to more secluded territory. What's the best way to herd him? Why, all it would take is a look at my true form. I position myself opposite the woods, and pull my essence together.

Now he sees me.

"C—call off your pet, Lewis," he says in a voice oozing with feeble hope and dwindling courage.

I spring to action and he retreats through the trees, right where I want him. I give chase, my speed far greater than his. Once we are veiled from the road I pounce, but my body falters. It takes far too much effort to remain tangible. Ah yes—it is because of the sun.

Daylight hours are my weakest, but it does not matter now. The means to end the instigator are still at my disposal.

I slither out of sight and return to my material shell. At first the instigator indulges in a moment of relief, perhaps feeling the threat has passed. I ride this shell, following the instigator into the woods.

To make my identity clear, I speak through the human lips. "You understand so little."

"This is a trick," he says. "Think you can spook me with a cheap Halloween prank? Well think again. You're dead, Lewis!"

The instigator rushes toward me. Such ignorance! I wrap my immaterial self around the flesh and bone I ride, forming a joined

Chapter 12

existence. Ethereal and material. Body and spirit. The instigator sees no change, but his fist hits both skins, each reinforced by the other, and succeeds only in harming himself. Like hitting a solid wall.

Meeting his eye I say "You have declared this a fight to the death. Then death shall come tonight."

His eyes show fear. His fear proves belief.

This union grants me my full power, even in the glare of the sun. I strike his abdomen with a fist made of flesh and energy. The air is extinguished from his lungs and he keels over. I grab him by the collar and hurl him deeper into the woods. He soars further than should be possible and collides with a tree.

When a man faces mortal danger, does he choose fight or flight? The answer to that question defines a person's very nature.

The instigator gets to his feet and faces me. He chooses to fight. For that, I give him credit.

"I… Don't know… What you are," he says between breaths. "But… I will not… Let you… Walk away…"

He charges, the warrior spirit rekindled. Although his punches are no match for my reflexes, they are not without merit. Were I naught but flesh he would be a great challenge, but he stands no chance against me like this.

This human fighting tactic is much too foreign. Better to fight as the predator I am.

I swing at him, tiny human fingers spread. Oh, the shock as he sees his shirt tear as if clawed! The instigator fumbles back, and I drop to all fours—a canine in the shape of a man. I leap, bite, and snarl at him. Some connect, leaving injuries that couldn't come from any man.

But soon, I find this too is inconvenient. The human shape is ill-suited to battle like a Beast.

Maybe I should compromise.

Back on two legs now. My posture is crouched low, invisible claws out and ready. I growl at the instigator, who grows more fearful as the moments pass. With unmatched speed I strike, but to my surprise he reacts in time to block. Too bad for him—No sooner does the blow

The Duel

connect do I hear bones crack in his arm, followed by a scream of pain. His arm drops, blood dripping from the point of impact.

This agony is so delightfully deserved.

Still the instigator fights on. He makes a sweeping kick to trip my feet. I hop over his leg but was unprepared for this action. My unfamiliar fighting stance leaves me off-balanced, and the instigator tackles me at my moment of weakness. He pins me to the ground, his elbow firmly pressed against my throat.

The instigator swallows his pain well, for he shows little signs of its magnitude. "This isn't about Eliza anymore, either," says he. "Time and time again, you defy me. And I…" He punches the face of my joined body. Hardly any impact penetrates. "Won't… Stand… For… It!" With each word he delivers another blow. His knuckles are splattered with blood, but at last he succeeds in damaging me.

Freeing myself from this grapple would be difficult, if I were restricted to a single body. But I am at an advantage; I have complete control of not one, but two forms. I detach my intangible essence again, becoming a wave of pure energy. Not for the first time he is thrown off of me, landing awkwardly in the dirt. With haste I return to my shell and rejoin my bodies.

How best to prolong his pain? First, disable his mobility.

The instigator's feet are closest to me. I scramble to all fours and pounce in one natural motion. Jaw wide, I bite into his knee. His scream is ear-splitting, and rightfully so; his mangled leg shows puncture marks in the shape of a gigantic canine maw.

Ah, the taste of blood is so fresh! I cannot wait; I must deliver the killing blow, and soon!

Slowly I crawl up his chest until our eyes are level. Finally, the instigator has been brought to tears.

"You have been defeated," says I, a monstrous voice through a mundane mouth. I open my jaw and lower it over his exposed throat, but ever so slowly.

I want him to be fully, completely aware of his death. I want his last living thought to be the cold truth of his mortality.

Chapter 12

As I lean in for the kill, a wind picks up. It carries with it a foreign energy, one I do not recognize. At first it is a mere annoyance, but it quickly becomes disruptive. It separates my ghostlike being, forcing my ethereal energy to grow slack and weak. It is nearly impossible to hold myself together. I'm slipping out of control. Slipping back into submission, back into humanity…

Everything was blurry while Will's reality shifted. Once his vision returned, he was repulsed by what he saw; he was only inches from taking a bite out of Mason's neck.

Will pulled himself up, then tasted blood.

There was so much of it, blood was dripping from Will's mouth. He wiped it with his arm, leaving a dirty red stain on his skin. The memories came back, and Will couldn't repress the urge to vomit. He rolled off of Mason and hacked up his partially-digested lunch. Will managed to stand, but his legs were as steady as jelly.

"Oh, god!" Mason cried out. He reached towards his crushed leg. "Oh god no! No, this isn't happening! What have you done to me, Lewis?"

Will stared at Mason's knee. It was bad; not only did the open wounds continue bleeding, but the leg sat at an unnatural angle. Will could only guess the extent of the damage. He had to look away, otherwise his gag reflex would kick in again.

When he turned, he saw a man watching them.

Panic swelled. Will's eyes raced from Mason, to the stranger, to the blood still covering his own hands.

How could he explain?

"This… Isn't what it looks like," Will said. Which was true in a way; it was really much worse.

The figure took a step closer, and Will got a better look at him. He looked old, but not just in age; he gave the

The Duel

impression of walking straight out of another era, from a time vastly different from our own. It was almost as if he were part of a historical reenactment, but the effect was much too authentic. His old-fashioned clothes rested naturally on his frame like they belonged there. The timeless stranger was in fact elderly, but his age showed only in his wrinkles and thin shape. Otherwise, he moved with the vitality of a much younger man. His head was smooth and hairless, and his eyes were concealed behind a pair of round mirrored sunglasses.

"But of course," said the old man, the hint of a smile on his thin lips. "So seldom are things as they appear."

Mason's wails didn't stop. "You there! H——help me! He's assaulted me! Call the c——cops!"

The stranger knelt beside Mason and gently placed a hand on the boy's chest. "You will receive help, do not worry. But, for the moment, I need you to rest." He was calm yet direct. The inflections of some words carried the trace of an English accent.

"Rest?" Mason said, pointing a finger at Will. "I'll rest when he's rotting in juvenile detention! Oh god, I can't feel my leg… It could be paralyzed!"

The old man waved his hands over Mason's face and began chanting in a strange language. He made a series of hand gestures, reminding Will of when priests cross themselves. Mason's cries softened and his eyelids closed. Within moments, he was unconscious.

The stranger threw a piece of cloth to Will. "Tie that around his arm, my boy," he said, tying another cloth around the injured leg. "Nice and snug, if you please."

Will did as he was told. He wrapped the cloth around Mason's upper arm and made the best knot he could. By the time he finished, the stranger was cleaning the wounds with his handkerchief.

Chapter 12

"Well done," said the old man. "That should slow the bleeding for now."

Will swallowed his guilt. "How bad is it? Do you think it'll be paralyzed or… Or worse?"

He examined the bitten knee. "Doubtful. He might have a limp from now on, but he should be fine with proper medical attention."

"Good," Will said. "Listen, I can explain all of this."

The stranger faced him. Will could see his own bloody reflection in those mirror glasses. "But of course. I've come a long way to hear your explanation. But first, help an old man carry this boy to the car. Sally's waiting to take him to the hospital."

Will was speechless as the words sunk in. "Wait a minute—you… You came here to talk to me?"

He laughed. "You don't think I traveled all the way to Elkhorn to purchase some 'Wisconsin Werewolf' t-shirt, do you?"

Chapter 13:
The Man with Mirror Eyes

After what just happened, Will didn't know what he expected to find waiting at the road. Perhaps a *Monsters of America* truck, eager to snatch up the next juicy part of their story. Or worse still, Sheriff Fillmore leaning against his squad car, handcuffs in hand.

He was shocked to see something as simple as a big, black SUV.

Together, Will and the stranger carried Mason to the vehicle. Will didn't know much about cars, but he could tell it was an older model; it had the distinctive box shape from years past. That was the only thing giving away its age, though. The paint looked brand new, and there wasn't a blemish to be found. As they brought him around the back, Will caught a glimpse of the Jeep name.

The old man opened the rear hatch. The cargo area was lined with boxes of all sizes, none made of cheap cardboard. These boxes had to be antiques, making Will feel like he discovered an alcove of forgotten treasure chests.

Chapter 13

Once a few boxes were moved, they had room to lay Mason down with his leg propped up.

"That should work for the trip," said the stranger. He held up Will's chin to examine his bleeding nose. "I suspect you'll be fine without the aid of a doctor. Here, put this on."

He opened one of the boxes and withdrew a necklace. Attached was a small green-and-black stone, shaped like a heart.

Will accepted the necklace. "What is it?" he asked as he put it on.

"Chrysoprase," he explained. "It will speed your healing."

"Oh." Will wasn't about to argue. They both climbed into the Jeep. Will was surprised when the stranger sat in the back with him, instead of up front.

If the vehicle ever seemed normal, it was purely an external illusion. The moment Will stepped inside he was hit with the smoky scent of incense, which only accentuated the bizarre sights. Rune-like patterns ran across every door, pendants of wood and metal and stone hung from the ceiling, and even more esoteric items lined the dashboard.

In a way, the distinct abnormality of the Jeep and its owner was a relief; here, the idea of werewolves and demons didn't feel like a foreign concept.

"Which way to the hospital, dear boy?" asked the old man.

Will took a moment to get his bearings. "Take a right up there, at Hospital Road."

"Heh. Appropriate." He nodded to the woman sitting patiently in the driver's seat. "Sally!"

"Yessir?" she answered enthusiastically.

"You heard the boy. Bring us to the hospital, if you please."

The SUV's engine roared to life, and they were off.

The Man with Mirror Eyes

The ride was smooth, more like a luxury car than your standard four-wheel drive.

"Forgive my lack of manners, but given the urgency of the circumstance I skipped proper introductions." The stranger offered his hand. "My name is Xavier Orrick."

They shook hands. "I'm Will Lewis."

"Pleased to make your acquaintance, Will Lewis," said Xavier. "I hope our hurried meeting has not set us off to a sour start."

"I was more concerned you would get the wrong idea of me," Will said. "I mean… I wouldn't call that a good first impression."

Xavier laughed. "I've met good people in worse encounters than that."

"That's hard to imagine."

"Even harder to believe the tale."

"I'm sure." Will watched Sally turn down Hospital Road, growing increasingly anxious. "If you don't mind my asking, Mr. Orrick… Who are you, really? And what *are* you doing in Elkhorn?"

A grin slowly crept across Xavier's face. "Phenomenal questions, both of them. Each would take hours to explain properly, perhaps even days. But the answer to one question is old news, irrelevant, while the other is rather imminent. So what do you say we concern ourselves with the latter, shall we?"

Will was glad he liked puzzles; deciphering Xavier's words felt like solving one. "Uh, okay…"

"I have come to Elkhorn, quite frankly, because of you. Or more correctly, because of the thing latched onto you."

Suddenly, fear prickled down Will's spine. Did this man know about the Beast? About Moyset? And if he did… What if he meant to do him harm? The term *werewolf hunter* came to mind, and Will instantly became defensive. "What do you mean, Mr. Orrick?"

"Heh. How coy. Pretending, or perhaps hoping, that I might not know his lycanthrope secret."

Suddenly the Jeep was very claustrophobic.

"How… How do you know about that?" Will asked.

Xavier watched the passing countryside, hands folded calmly in his lap. "We all have secrets. And for good reason; most secrets are best kept from prying eyes. But I believe I can assist you in dealing with yours."

"You didn't answer my question."

"Very observant."

"Are you going to?"

"Perhaps," said Xavier. "But to do so now would be skipping much too far ahead. There is much to tell, and once you hear it you will have a better understanding of more than just how I discovered the abomination clinging to you.

Will was at a loss. He felt trapped next to this stranger, but he could see no way out. Unless, of course, he tried to fight him like he fought Mason, but Will didn't think that was going to work. Not on Xavier Orrick. "Fine. Then when will you start telling me *something?* Or are you just going to string me along like this?"

Xavier pointed a wrinkled finger out the window. "Is that the hospital over there?"

With a sigh, Will nodded. "You're good at avoiding questions."

"A talent that's kept me alive."

The SUV pulled into the Aurora Lakeland Medical Center and parked near the door. Xavier and the driver stepped out.

"Sally, take this young man to the emergency room," he instructed. "You will have to drag him, but someone will assist you once you are inside."

The Man with Mirror Eyes

She nodded. "Yessir!" she said while unlatching the trunk. Will got his first real look at Xavier's driver. Sally was pretty, no one feature was responsible for it. Her prettiness was more a product of her infectious smile and upbeat demeanor.

"They'll wonder what happened," Will pointed out. "You can't just show up with a bleeding, unconscious kid without questions. What are you going to tell them?"

Xavier smiled, as if he thought the matter was trivial. "The truth. If they ask, Sally, tell them you came across him being mauled by a monstrous canine, which retreated upon your arrival."

Sally gave him a thumbs up and a cheesy smile. "Gotcha! Big beast was mauling him, left when I got there, came straight to the hospital!"

"Good girl," Xavier said. "Run along now."

Without hesitation Sally hoisted Mason down, and dragged him across the concrete to the front door.

"She truly *is* a good girl," Xavier said, watching her go. "Grew up with developmental challenges. Doctors say she acts thirteen instead of thirty. Not simple getting through a world that expects conformity when you run at your own pace. But I think that's helped her. She sees the world with the innocence of a child, not the ignorance of an adult."

"What now?" Will asked.

Climbing into the driver seat, Xavier said "Now… You get some answers."

The Jeep was still parked. If Will was going to make a break for it, now was the time. But, he decided, the promise of the old man's wisdom was worth the risk.

"I want my great-uncle with me," Will said. "He's as much a part of this as I am. He deserves to hear what you have to say." Not to mention there was safety in numbers.

The vehicle shuddered softly as it started. "Show me

Chapter 13

the way," Xavier said over his shoulder.

Will directed him to B.R. Amon & Sons, Inc.

Barbason was clearly not expecting company.

He was in the kitchen cleaning knives when they arrived. At the sight of this stranger, he clutched his current knife tightly.

"Who's this fella?" Barbason asked, one eyebrow raised.

Good question, Will thought. All he knew about him was his name. "This is Xavier Orrick. And Mr. Orrick, this is my great-uncle, Barbason."

"A pleasure," Xavier said with a courteous bow.

Barbason was no less confused. "Alright then, what are ye doin' in my house?"

"I have come here, as per Will's request, to share some of the knowledge I hold. Or at least, the portion of it that will aid in your current predicament."

"My... *Predicerment?*" He gave Will a puzzled glance. "Kid, what all does this weirdo know 'bout us?"

"I don't understand how, but he knows about..." Will wasn't sure how to word it. "Our *werewolf* problem."

The stench of fear leaked off Barbason. He unconsciously held the knife at a threatening angle. "Listen buddy, I don't know what ye think ye know, but we ain't—"

"I know that Will here is a werewolf," Xavier said casually. "I am guessing you were too, at one point. I know what *real* werewolves are, as well; not the silly inventions of cinematographers. As such, your bodies remain while your spirits transform. Am I right?"

Barbason didn't respond.

"I also know that a creature, terribly alien and unseen, is the true cause of these events. Now, I have much to say and surely you have a great deal to ask, but this old body is not what it used to be. If you offered me a seat, I would be much obliged."

"Oh… Yeah, o' course, take a seat," Barbason said, choosing a spot on the couch. He was unaware that he took the kitchen knife with him. "That easy chair's got a board loose, but I swear ye could doze off all day in it."

Xavier took the loose-boarded easy chair. "Ahh, case in point Barbason. This chair could act as a spare bed. Very fine quality, still soft yet strong to this day."

Will sat beside his great-uncle. They stared at the stranger, anxious for an explanation.

The old man cleared his throat. "Right then. Where to begin…"

"If you know anything about this demon, start with that," Will said. "Namely, how do we stop it?"

"Hehe, good intuition," Xavier said. "Yes, I know about it. But given the complexity of the issue perhaps I should start with the basics. The backbone, as it were, of everything else I have to say.

"The world as you know it is not the whole picture. Everything we see, touch or smell is but a fraction of what's before us. What you see is the material world, the physical plane of existence."

Barbason scratched his head. "So there are other worlds or somethin'?"

"Not exactly," Xavier explained. "Think of it as different layers of the same world. The common person today knows only one layer, or plane of existence. There are other layers of this world, all of which tied together yet wholly separate from one another. Just as the world is multi-layered, so are people. A part of us exists on all five planes, working in unison to be a conscious, sentient being."

"I'm not sure I follow what you mean by 'planes of

existence.' You mentioned the physical plane, but what are the others?" Will asked.

"Excellent question, Will. Thinking of it as layers, picture the physical plane as the 'lowest.' It is denser and heavier than any other plane, and by far the hardest to manipulate. Oh, transformations do occur, but they are slow. Look at the metamorphosis of infant to adult, seed to tree, etcetera.

"The next layer up, neighbor to the material world, is called the etheric plane. This level is normally unseen, but can interact most directly with the physical plane below it. As I said, part of us exist on each layer. The etheric human body has been glimpsed by cultures worldwide, and given dozens of names. Perhaps the term you would be most familiar with is *aura*. Our etheric body is a mass of spiritual energy connected to us, which some mystics have learned to perceive and control.

"Another example of etheric entities are ghosts. Sometimes we catch glimpses of them, and on rare occasion they even move material objects—I believe the term *poltergeist* was coined to describe such a being. Ghosts are either spiritual stains left on a place or, occasionally, the remains of a person who has died but kept their ethereal form alive."

Will was intrigued. "Is that really possible?"

With a solemn nod, Xavier said "It is. Although this is a rarity; most hauntings are just etheric residue without intelligence. But at times, a person will linger a while after death.

"As we move up this ladder, the planes of existence become increasingly abstract. The further from the physical plane, the less clear it is in relation to the world we are familiar with. That being said, the third layer is known as the astral plane. This is pure perception, with no body as we would understand it. Through the astral plane all of our senses are processed. To *astral project*—a term that has gained familiarity worldwide—is to leave the heavier physical and etheric bodies behind, and let the part of us that perceives wander freely. Because it is so much lighter than the planes below it, the astral body is capable of traveling great distances in exceptionally short amounts of time. Unfortunately, most people do not know how to harness this form independently. But there is no shortage of people born with remarkable astral bodies, allowing them to see and know things they physically could not. In modern times, these people are often labeled psychic. In days long past they were known as much worse.

"One of the highest planes is the mental plane. This is the land of thought—pure and unadulterated. It is a mixed existence, part chaos and part logic. As the two sides clash, ideas are conceived, personalities developed, and thought comes to life. If one were to abandon the lower planes—to *mentally* project, you could say—you would find yourself in a world that bears only the slightest resemblance to the physical plane. This is the land of our subconscious, which we visit almost every night. The mental plane is the land of dreams and nightmares.

"At the very top of the ladder, the highest known plane of existence, is that of the spirit. The part of us which exists on the spiritual plane is, put simply, our souls. If the astral is our eyes and the mental our brains, then the spiritual is the heart that beats life and meaning into everything we do. Even the wisest scholars know very little about this plane; it is one of life's greatest enigmas."

Will and Barbason tried to wrap their minds around the things Xavier was saying. Half of it went over Barbason's head, but Will thought he was keeping up alright.

"Okay, so how do we know this is for real?" Will asked. "Anybody can come up with theories and claim it's

Chapter 13

true. Not to mention all the religions with their own view on things. Why should we believe you? Where's the proof?"

Smiling, Xavier said "There is none. You can't know for sure. Honestly, neither can I. The world is full of mysteries and no one holds all the answers. But I like to think of it scientifically."

Unable to stop himself, Will laughed. *"Scientifically? How is there a scientific way to think of this?"*

"The goal of science is to dissect the world, to prove what is and what isn't, what does and what does not. I do not know with complete certainty all that I told you is true. But I do know that every single thing I have come across in my life functions *as if* it were true. The only way science proves something exists is by process of elimination. You rigorously test it, time and time again, until there's only one answer that none of the results contradict."

"Ye mean to tell me ye've proven this stuff?" Barbason said.

Xavier shook his head. "Of course not. But after decades of trial and error I have been unable to *disprove* it. And that's all any scientist can do. Attempt to prove it wrong from every angle until one arises which you cannot. Fact is merely faith that is uncontested."

Will still had his doubts. "So we're supposed to believe your studies instead of those of thousands of scientists?"

"Of course not. That would be presumptuous."

"And claiming to know the structure of the world isn't?"

"Very observant," said Xavier. "I do not, however, claim that science is inaccurate. Merely exceptionally narrow. It focuses solely on the physical, ignoring evidence of anything beyond. I have simply wandered where most scientists do not dare."

The Man with Mirror Eyes

Will decided to give the stranger the benefit of the doubt. "Fine," he said. "Then how does this relate to us? Where does the Beast and Moyset come into play?"

Xavier raised an eyebrow. "Moyset, is it?"

"That's the name of the demon," Will said.

"Yes. Yes of course," said Xavier, stroking his chin. "I suspected it might be. It did sound like its preferred style. But how did it make it all the way to the United States?"

"My grandfather. It's a long story, you see—wait a minute…" Will considered his reaction. "You've heard of Moyset? I mean, before now?"

"Indeed," he confirmed. "It was one of the most powerful demons France ever housed. I thought the last of its followers were lost back in 1906, but some piece of lore must have resurfaced. No matter, that is all in the past. What's important is the here and now.

"Demon is as good a term as any to describe this entity. Not a fallen angel, per se, but not far from it. I have only theories about their origin, but this much I know for sure; they do not belong in our world. They are from someplace else entirely, a land that plays by a different set of rules.

"These beings still abide by the principles of their world, and hence do not fit within the structure of ours. They seem to be on a denser plane than the physical, 'below' it you could say, making us appear like phantoms to them. They have no physical or etheric bodies, yet can interact with us on the astral and mental levels. That's how they torment our dreams and tickle our senses. To see them as they *truly* are is impossible; they are from a world utterly alien to us, their bodies made of shapes and colors we cannot possibly perceive. When they try to show themselves, our minds mistranslate their appearance as a wholly unnatural combination of beings from our world. That is why demon

Chapter 13

lore is filled with such horrendous descriptions and frightful images.

"Without a body of their own, demons cannot do us direct harm. Instead they must be crafty, and that's where demonic possession comes in. It has to be done willingly; most demons are not strong enough to take control of us by force. We might not understand the agreement, but demons have no power over us unless we open the door for them. But once one has us…" Xavier looked between Will and Barbason. "Well, I think you both know what happens then."

Will shifted nervously in his seat. "Is there a way to, well… End the agreement?"

Xavier shook his head. "It is not so simple. Once a demon is inside, it sinks its claws deep. Not only our material bodies are at risk of possession; Moyset, for instance, has always preferred to tether itself to our etheric forms. Since the etheric plane is more malleable, it can change more easily. Moyset is powerful enough to reshape your etheric body at will, changing it from man to Beast. And without your aura, you are left so weak that remaining conscious is an effort.

"As you already know, you do not transform at the sight of a full moon. But the phase of the moon is worth noting; its cycle affects all planes, the etheric being no exception. Be wary when it's full—you will be more susceptible to Moyset's influence during that time.

"Defeating a demon is possible, don't worry. When you think about it, they are weaker than us. Without a possessed body all that's left is a broken remnant of a forgotten world. Outright destruction of the being is no simple task; our weapons are physical or etheric, and can hardly touch them at their lower plane. But once removed from its host, a demon can be banished or imprisoned with relative ease."

"How?" Will asked.

The Man with Mirror Eyes

Very plainly, Xavier said "With magic."

Will laughed. This was passed the point of ridiculous. "With *magic?* Now I'm supposed to believe in magic?"

"You already believe in werewolves," Xavier reminded him. "And you believe you are being possessed by a demon. Is magic honestly that far from what you have already come to accept?"

"Yeah, but this is stretching it…"

"Is it?" said Xavier. "Why? Is it any more absurd than man walking on the moon? Or the endless applications of electricity? Humans have split atoms, dominated the sky, reshaped the Earth, yet we don't question how it's possible. But none of that is so incredible as our own bodies; is the miracle of life not enough to make you believe? Magic is all around us, Will. You just have to open your eyes and see it."

Crossing his arms, Will considered it. "Okay, assume I do believe. How does this magic work?"

"It works by doing to the etheric what engineers have done with the physical. Magic is the art of manipulating the subtler planes of existence in such a way to achieve the desired results. No, lightning bolts don't shoot from my fingers. But with the proper use of magic I do know how to counter the abilities your demon commands. Which is why that boy is alive in a hospital bed right now, instead of growing cold in a morgue."

That's right. Will remembered the Beast getting weak, until Moyset could not hold on any more. "You did that?"

Xavier nodded.

This was all too unreal. This stranger appeared out of nowhere, at the critical moment they needed him the most. Could it really be possible? "Let me ask you again, Mr. Orrick… Who *are* you? How do you know all of this?"

He sat back in the chair, glasses glowing in the reflection of light. "I am the keeper of the keys, the North

Chapter 13

Star guiding through the night. And I may be the last hope for mankind."

"That's not an answer."

"Indeed it is not," Xavier agreed. "Then allow me to elaborate. I am the Grand Master of Enoc. It is a secret society founded in 1880 by the renowned mystic, Aldric Garlock. Enoc was formed with a single mission; to enlighten the world of the darkness it has chosen to ignore. I am the last living apprentice of Garlock himself, trained personally before his passing. Since then, I have continued to carry the torch he lit over a century ago."

Barbason was skeptical. "Secret societies of wizards tryin' to save the world? Sounds sketchy to me."

"Believe what you will," Xavier said, indifferent. "Regardless, this is where I obtained my knowledge and skill, both of which could save your lives as well as the lives of those around you. It is up to you if you wish to use it."

He made a good point. The more Will thought about it, the more he believed. If you ruled nothing out as *impossible* (and after the last few months, how could he?) then what Xavier said made sense. It was consistent with everything Will came to know about the supernatural.

But if that was true… Then perhaps the man sitting in Barbason's easy chair really *was* the Grand Master of an occult secret society.

The possibility gave Will shivers.

"Alright Mr. Orrick, I believe you," Will said. "Now tell me, how do we put a stop to this lunacy?"

Xavier's smile was almost frightening. "I was waiting for you to ask that."

The next day, Will sped down Bray Road, his bike soaring like a motorcycle.

The Man with Mirror Eyes

Travis had to hear this, and Will needed his help. Barbason was doing better, but was in no shape for the task ahead. And Eliza made it very clear she would have nothing to do with him. That made Travis his only choice, but even then Will believed he was the *best* choice for this job. To ask a cautious, rational person (like Will was, back in the days he thought werewolves were fiction) would be a bad call. This mission required the character flaws Travis had in spades; cunning, fearlessness, and an absolute disregard for the rules.

Before he knew it he was at the Quonset hut.

Frank Scott welcomed him with his usual humor, but Will paid it no attention. He called for his son, and Travis was at the door in moments.

"We gotta talk," was Will's only greeting.

Travis didn't need more explanation than that. His only question was "Where to?"

"B.R. Amon," Will said. And they were off.

During the ride up Bray, Will filled Travis in on the day before. He couldn't contain his excitement over the duel with Mason, especially when the Beast started "kickin' his well-polished ass," as Travis put it. Will also told him about Xavier Orrick and his alleged status as a secret society Grand Master.

"This guy sounds like a piece of work," said Travis as they climbed the hill up B.R. Amon's parking lot. "Did he get around to telling you how we kill the damn thing?"

"That's actually where you come in," Will said. "Follow me."

He led Travis into the house addition. Barbason was fiddling with the TV antennas when they came in. He appeared disgruntled at having another new person in his house.

"Hey, Old Man Amon!" Travis called in a jovial tone. "What's up? Haven't seen you around since the whole, you know… Werewolf-terrorizing phase. You look good though; no hairy palms or pointy teeth. And don't worry, I'm sure that snarl is the next wolfy trait to go."

Without realizing it, Barbason was scowling in a very canine fashion. Embarrassed, he resumed work on his TV.

"That's enough Travis," Will stepped in. "We came here for a reason, remember?"

"Oh yeah," Travis remembered. "So where's our ghost-busting kit at?"

"Very funny," Said Will. He led Travis to the coffee table, where one of the ornate chests from Xavier's Jeep sat. "You aren't too far off this time, either."

He opened the chest and took out two objects wrapped in cloth—one upright, one flat—and set them on the table. He also found several handwritten notes and placed them neatly in a pile.

"Mr. Orrick left this for us," he said, skimming the notes. "He said the first thing to do is 'condition my mind.' I'm supposed to do these mental exercises to build up my ability to hold Moyset back. He said it'll be difficult, but with time I'll feel results."

Travis looked confused. "What exactly qualifies as 'results' here? Is your brain going to grow some Hulk-like muscles, or what?"

"Don't be silly. Results would mean better control over these werewolf outbursts. Once my mind is trained, I should be able to slow the Beast down when it tries to take over. Even stop it entirely, with enough practice."

Will's eyes were deadly serious, and Travis got the picture; the time for fun and games was over. His attitude reflected the severity of the issue.

"If I can slow it down, the Beast won't be able to feed on etheric energies as often. In time, we can starve Moyset. Mr. Orrick says we have to act when the demon is at

The Man with Mirror Eyes

its weakest."

Travis looked at the covered items on the table. "So when Beastie gets hungry, what are we supposed to do with it?"

Will carefully removed the cloth wrapping from the upright object. It was a small jar, maybe six inches in all. The grayish-white metal surface was completely covered in runic designs and patterns.

"Etheric beings can easily pass through *most* physical barriers," said Will. "But some metals, especially ones that are extremely dense, are just as solid to them as they are to us. This jar is made of solid platinum, one of the densest metals known to man. It's also extremely expensive; if it's not alloyed with something, this could easily be worth a small fortune."

Travis stared at it, eyes glazed with excitement. He reached out his hand, but Will slapped it away.

"Don't touch it!" he warned. "Mr. Orrick put a heavy barrier enchantment on it. Handling it with bare skin will weaken the effect."

Travis put up his hands defensively. "Sorry, sorry. So, what do we do with it exactly? I'm guessing it's for more than decorating the bathroom."

Will covered the jar with the cloth. "When Moyset is vulnerable, I have to mentally force it out of me and into the jar. That's where you come in; there's this sealing spell you're supposed to use once the demon is inside. I need a second person to do it, because I might be too weak from the struggle. Without the sealing spell, Mr. Orrick said the demon could still escape, even from platinum."

"Why doesn't high-and-mighty Grand Master guy shut his own damn jar?" asked Travis.

"He couldn't stay," Will explained. He tried to hide his own disappointment; without Xavier's presence, he felt silly even discussing things like sealing spells and mental exercises. Will wasn't convinced he and Travis were up to the job on their own.

Travis scratched his head, then turned his attention to the other covered item. "So what's that thing?"

This was the part Will was most uneasy about. "Do you remember what happened when my silver-plated watch came in contact with the Beast?"

"Yeah," Travis nodded. "Knocked out Old Man Amon's tooth and gave him a bleeding back. Why?"

"Silver is a peculiar metal," Will explained as he slowly unwrapped the object. "It's denser than iron or copper. Nowhere near the density or platinum, of course, but still impressive. Typically it doesn't make good weapons. The material is soft, you see. But it is also the most conductive of any metal, making it extremely dangerous to etheric beings. In fact, even a blunt object of pure silver would be very effective against one. Properly enchanted, it could be devastating."

Travis craned his neck to catch an early glimpse. "What is that thing?"

Will carefully unfolded the last of the wrapping. Lying between them, almost vibrating with energy, was a dagger. The pearly white blade was no less than ten inches long. Hilt included, the length of the dagger was well over a foot.

"This is our emergency self-defense, in case things go terribly wrong," Will said.

Travis blink. "Wait a sec. Isn't silver really bad for *your* health too? I mean, if Old Man Amon is any indication."

Will looked him straight-on. His throat was dry, and his voice hoarse. "If the times comes to use this, it means I won't be making it to the celebration."

Chapter 14:
Bonfires &
Betrayal

That night, there was a bonfire behind B.R. Amon.

Circled around the orange glow of the burning trash can stood Will, Travis, and Barbason.

"Mr. Orrick thought Moyset was gone a century ago," Will said. He thought this would be the perfect ambience for telling a ghost story; instead, they were all living one. "The only way it could have risen again was if something remained. An artifact of a lost cult, who worshipped the demon like a god."

Will held up the book with the tattered leather binding. *Livre de la Bête*. In the firelight, the cover took on the dirty hue of blood "My grandfather found this in France. More than likely, *this* is the only key left that can give the demon life. To stop Moyset for good, we can leave nothing behind that could bring it back."

Barbason and Travis nodded, but didn't dare speak.

"The arrival of this book was the start of the disaster. Its destruction marks the beginning of the end."

Chapter 14

With a flick of the wrist Will tossed *Livre de la Bête* into the fire.

The pages blackened and curled. The leather seemed to scream as the fire consumed it, whistling and crackling in agony. A nauseating and unnatural stench rolled out of the bonfire. They all believed, with complete certainty, that more than a book was burning. They witnessed the death of something evil, alive and malignant in its own right.

"Ye really think we can do it, kid?" Barbason asked, still transfixed by the flames. "We've already lost so much… Me brother and his wife. Yer mom and dad. Almost me too, if ye hadn't stepped in. What makes ye think we stand a chance of stopping it now?"

Will's fists were clenched. He saw the faces of his family dance through the flame. He remembered spending the night with Grandpa Connor and Grandma Eleanor. He remembered all the special little traditions between grandparents and their grandkids. He remembered his parents. His father, stern but kind. His mother, the compassionate caregiver. He remembered everything. Fifteen years of memories, but never more. These memories were all he would ever have with them.

And it was all because of Moyset.

"We will stop it because we have to," Will said. "If we don't, more families will be ripped apart. But if we're going to succeed, we need to make an agreement."

Travis was remarkably at a loss for jokes. "Tell us, man. We'll do it."

"We have to do whatever it takes to defeat Moyset. Let me reiterate; *whatever it takes.* If that means facing the Beast head-on, fine. If we need to take a little pain, we will. If one of us *has* to die to save everyone else… So be it."

All was silent as Will's words sunk in. No one wanted to answer; they all understood the seriousness of this pact.

Bonfires & Betrayal

Travis was the first to speak up. "Alright man. We're in this together, no matter what we have to do. I'm in it until the end."

Barbason closed his eyes. "I ain't never been known for bein' brave. But kid… Ye made the biggest sacrifice ye could, all to save me. I don't think nobody's ever done nothing so nice for me." In the flickering firelight, a single tear glowed on Barbason's cheek. "I'd do anything to repay ye. Anything. Ain't no chance of me desertin' ye at a time like this."

Will turned from Travis to Barbason. They were sincere.

"Then let's do this," he said. "For months we have been under attack. Starting tonight… We fight back."

In the silence of B.R. Amon's garage, Will was training. His body sat motionless, but that was the only part of him which was still.

Metaphor is material, Xavier's instructions said. *In the mental plane, what you imagine is solid as stone.*

That was the premise of Will's training.

First, he had to drown out his senses. The more disconnected he was from his body, the easier it would be.

Second, Will had to create a visual representation of his mind. This, Xavier said, was his battlefield with Moyset. The image that came naturally was the backyard of his old house in Beloit. Here, he spent hours playing or reading under a tree. In this mental plane, the sun was always setting. Will stood on the side of the light. Opposite him, waiting beneath the approaching darkness, was the Beast. Right now, it slept. Around its neck was a collar of bones, securing it to the spot.

Third… The Beast would wake, and they would do

Chapter 14

battle.

The metaphoric struggle was no less precarious than the real one. The Beast got to its feet, revealing that the stake tying its leash to the ground was loose. Will had the hammer, but would have to sneak past the monster to tighten it.

This scenario was suggested in the instructions. At first, Will didn't see how playing it through in his mind would help, seeing as he could just imagine himself succeeding every time. On his first try, Will arrogantly charged the Beast. He pictured himself outwitting the creature with ease, but was in for a shock. The Beast caught him mid-jump, bit hard, and tore him to pieces. Will woke up from that session with his heart pounding, but was otherwise unharmed.

Will learned his lesson. It wasn't just *his* imagination at work here. Moyset had influence over the mental realm too, and the demon was making sure he couldn't simply dream himself to victory.

It's a puzzle, Will came to realize, not unlike the hundreds of Sudoku puzzles he has completed. And like Sudoku, it was never the same twice. The Beast adapted to Will's tricks, forcing him to stay constantly on his toes.

After three weeks, he was getting the hang of it.

Will and the Beast locked eyes, slowly stepping towards each other. Will stayed less than a foot outside of the Beast's strike range, teasing it. The monster snarled as it calculated the distance. Will took half a step forward, putting him just within the danger zone.

The Beast took the bait; it dashed forward, jaw gaping, eyes ablaze. It jumped towards Will, who rolled to the side. He dodged the attack with hardly an inch to spare.

There was no time to waste.

Will sprang to his feet. The Beast's landing tugged at its chain, loosening the stake further. One more good pull, and the Beast might be able to break free. Will sprinted along the chain, but before he reached the end it began to rattle—the other side was on the move. He glanced over his shoulder just in time; the Beast was seconds from pouncing on him. It expected to catch Will off-guard, but he had been fooled by this tactic before. Will flung himself sideways, once again avoiding a deadly collision.

But the Beast's reflexes were quick. It landed lightly on its feet and lunged after Will, all in the blink of an eye.

Instead of getting to his feet like the Beast expected, Will rolled to the side. The unsuspecting Beast wasn't prepared for this, and landed face-first into the grass.

Now was his chance.

While the Beast was down, Will made a break for it. He ran at the stake, pumping his legs with all his might.

"Will! Yo, Will!"

His mind flashed to a cluttered garage, and heard out of physical ears so far away. Will tried to focus, to keep his mind on the stake and the duel, but he lost speed in the distraction. He reached the stake, and felt someone prod his real body. Again Will flashed back to the garage. The backyard was unraveling, the illusion shattered. But the Beast remained, and before Will could help it he felt its giant teeth tear into him.

Game over.

Back in B.R. Amon's garage, Will fell backwards, sweat pouring down his face. Travis squatted next to him, looking mildly curious.

"What's up, man?"

Will shook his head. "Wait until I'm done next time, okay?"

After a moment of thought, Travis smacked himself in the face. "Oops, sorry man. Forgot all about your brain training. I thought you were just *really* bored without schoolwork to keep you busy."

Chapter 14

"It's alright," Will said. He wiped his forehead with his arm, which was no less sweaty. "What brings you by?"

Travis shrugged. "Felt like going over that whole 'catch the canine' routine again. Somehow canning the Beast like some preserved fruit spread doesn't sound so solid to me."

Will rolled his eyes. "It's more than that. You read the notes Mr. Orrick left for you, right?"

"Well of course I did, but I'm still a little iffy about it. You know, watching you fight yourself like a schizophrenic while waiting for an 'unseen entity.' Oh yeah, and I get to carry this weirdo's magical plant pot, which is worth more than my whole house. But wait, it gets better! When 'the entity' is jammed into this portable fortune, I have to say a few magic words and presto—demon eliminated!"

Travis' skepticism was an ironic reversal of roles. Not long ago Will was the skeptic, and Travis the fervent believer.

"Try to take this seriously," Will said. "Everything Mr. Orrick said makes sense. Logically, this should work."

With arms crossed, Travis said "How much do you really trust this guy? Do you trust him with your *life?*"

He wanted to say yes, but couldn't. Will still didn't know what to think about Xavier Orrick.

"No, I don't. I trust *you* with my life," Will said. He didn't realize it until the words left his mouth. "He might be right about everything… Or he might be some crazy old man pulling a sick joke on us. Either way, this is our best chance. But if things don't work out like we expect… Then there's no one I trust more to get us out alive than you."

Travis' expression seemed new to him, as if he wore it for the first time. He never received such high praise, and it left him flabbergasted. Every time he was about to say something, the words escaped him. Finally he was content with his biggest, cheesiest grin. He held out his arm, and the two of them clasped hands.

"Brother," was all Travis could say.

Will smiled. It was the only word that described the connection they had. They weren't related by blood, but in every way that counts they were family.

"Brother."

Against his better judgment, Will took a trip to the hospital.

He knew what he would find. He saw it all happen, viewed from the perspective of a monster. But he went anyway. He had to see it with his own, human eyes.

This would be the summer everyone at the hospital remembered. Victims of "animal attacks" came night after night, forcing them to borrow rooms from other units. Some were lucky, and only needed a few stitches and mild painkillers. But as Will walked the halls, he saw no shortage of patients with severe injuries.

So far there had been no more fatalities. Of that, Will was proud.

Still, faces of victims haunted him. Once or twice he peeked into a patients room and felt a chilling recognition; he remembered causing those wounds.

One thing was for certain; the Beast was stronger now. Much stronger.

No matter how hard Will fought, the Beast always escaped several times a week. And the encounters became so violent, people stopped calling them "sightings"—now, they were attacks. The Wisconsin Werewolf was becoming a full-blown panic, yet still no one could explain the cause.

There was one victim Will wasn't going to visit. At the front desk he asked for Mason McCree's room number, to make sure he *didn't* pass it. His injuries would be the worst, even after nearly six weeks. Will didn't want to know Mason's diagnosis; he had more than enough guilt already.

It was very unlike Will, but he couldn't help feeling a twinge of satisfaction. The Beast won. It defeated an enemy who deserved everything he got. At first Will fought these feelings, believing them to be the influence of Moyset, but eventually had to admit this pride wasn't entirely because of the demon.

Down the hall, there were voices. It sounded like they were coming from Mason's room.

Will paused, his ears perked. The voices were getting closer to the door, preparing to leave by the sounds of it. He looked for a place to hide, but the rooms on either side of him were occupied. There was no choice—he would have to stand his ground. Maybe it was just a doctor or a nurse, but something smelled familiar about Mason's guest. It didn't take long for the scent to become clear.

(The eavesdropper.)

The Beast stirred. Will knew who it was before they came into view. Natalie Elwin and Eric the cameraman. They entered the hall with cheerful faces.

They noticed Will, and got nervous.

"Well, if it isn't Will!" Natalie called out. Her fake smile was less convincing than usual. "What brings you to the hospital, sweetheart? Visiting a friend? Mason McCree, perhaps?"

Will shook his head. "Mason and I are not friends," he stated. He caught Eric trying to click on his camera, and shouted "Don't you touch that!"

Eric jumped back. Natalie raised her hands in defense. "Relax, kiddo," she said. "Old documentary habit, you know. Hard to break. We're totally off the record, just a couple of acquaintances catching up. Isn't that right?"

Eric nodded.

Bonfires & Betrayal

"Now, you said you and poor Mason aren't friends? Then what are you up to wandering around a hospital?" Natalie asked.

Another series of trick questions were ahead. Will thought about leaving in silence, but he was curious what business they had with Mason. "I could ask you the same question, Mrs. Elwin."

"Oh it's just Miss Elwin. No mister in my life," she said with a smile. "But you can go ahead and call me Natalie. Now Eric and I are here reporting. Beast victims are just *lining* up to tell their story. For the sake of journalism, you see. Doing their part to share the truth."

"The *truth?* What you report isn't the truth and you know it." Will's body heat was climbing. The Beast was close to the surface, empowered through anger. Understanding the change made it even more bizarre; he could actually feel his etheric body trying to shift.

He had to stop this.

Will slowed his breathing, playing through his mental exercises. It took all of his willpower, but he managed to calm his other side… For the most part, at least.

"Every story has two sides," Natalie said. "You're entitled to your opinion, just as we are entitled to ours."

A question came, more from the Beast's mind than Will's. "What did Mason tell you?"

Natalie shifted in place. "Well you see, I can't exactly tell you that. Confidentiality and all, you understand."

It was much harder to control the Beast when they wanted the same thing. Will's aura pulsed with invisible energy, causing the lights to flicker.

"What did he tell you?" Will repeated.

The electrical shortage seemed to make Natalie uneasy. Perhaps she felt the same presence now as she did in her motel, when she almost became a victim herself. "His

238

encounter with the Beast was very… Detailed," she said. "His testimony could be the highlight of our follow-up episode on the Wisconsin Werewolf."

Growing impatient, Will turned to Eric. "Let me see the tape."

Natalie jumped between them. "Whoa, hold up now tiger. We can't go giving private showings before the film goes to editing. The network would throw a fit!"

"Even if it's about me?" Will said.

His bluntness caught Natalie off guard. Judging from the nervous glances they exchanged, Will's guess was right.

Once again Will felt like a puppet. He didn't choose his actions—it was the Beast in charge now. He stepped closer, locking eyes with Natalie. *"Air that footage, and there will be hell to pay,"* said the Beast, using Will's voice. *"Do you truly want that blood on your hands, eavesdropper?"*

Natalie shivered. She sensed the predator behind Will's eyes, if only in her subconscious. From her came the scent of a cornered animal. But, in her defense, it didn't last. Within moments she regained her composure.

"I beg your pardon," she said. *"Eavesdropper?* I am no such thing, thank you very much. All of my information comes from people eager to talk. No eavesdropping necessary."

The monster inside wanted to fight back, but Will resisted. If he let anger get the best of him, the Beast would tear her apart. So Will closed his eyes and forced himself to relax.

Meanwhile, Natalie watched him as if he were crazy. "Hello? Still with us champ?"

Will shook his head. "I was just leaving," he said. He wanted to shout one last warning or threat, but he knew it was a waste of breath. Will left the hospital biting his tongue.

Bonfires & Betrayal

As time went by, there was one task Will dreaded more than a showdown with the Beast; confronting Eliza.

It had to be done. Will could not leave things the way they were. He was no fool—he knew there was a very good chance he wouldn't walk out of this alive. The thought of his mortality was the only thing giving him courage to stand in front of the Fillmore house again. He rang the doorbell and waited.

When the door opened, Will and Eliza met each other's eyes for the first time in months. He forgot just how stunning she was. Will's heart fluttered and his knees were weak. It was just like the first time he saw her.

Only this time, Eliza wasn't smiling.

Her eyes were wide with a mix of surprise and fear. She backed up and covered herself with her arms.

"Can we talk?"

She hesitated. Will thought she was about to decline, but instead she gave a weak nod. Will led her outside and started to walk towards the road.

"No," said Eliza. Her feet were planted on the porch. "I won't go far from home."

Will accepted her terms, and respectfully kept his distance. "Eliza, I…" he didn't know what to say. "I've missed you."

No response.

"A lot has happened," Will said. "There's a lot you need to hear."

"You think I don't know anything?" she shot back. "You think, just because I'm not in with you and Travis, I haven't kept up on what's going on? I've heard plenty; animal attacks have gotten out of hand. Even the police department officially suspects one or more large, dangerous creatures are on the loose. They posted a warning to be extremely cautious outdoors.

"You think I don't know what that means? I'm not stupid, Will. I know that's not Mr. Amon out there hurting people. It's you." Eliza's face was turning red.

"I can explain," said Will.

This only fueled Eliza's anger. "Can you? Fine." She put her hands on her hips. "Then explain why the number of 'Beast' attacks have doubled."

Her aggression stirred the slumbering monster. With his mind's eye Will saw the chained Beast perk its ears. A wintry gust blew by. Suddenly Eliza was more frightened than angry.

No, Will told himself. *Not now. I must keep control.* With a deep breath, he calmed the monster within.

"I'm stronger than Uncle Barbason," he told her. "Moyset is taking advantage of my strength. I'm trying to fight, but… It isn't easy."

Eliza averted her eyes. "Can you beat it?" she asked, more concerned than mad.

Will didn't know how answer. "I don't know. We have a plan, and if it works we'll be free of Moyset at last. If it doesn't, well… We have a backup, too."

"So what *is* the plan?" Eliza asked. "Because last I heard, there was none. And judging from how active the Beast has been, I assumed you still had no idea how to stop it."

Her words stung, but Will let it go. He probably deserved it after hiding this from her. "We met someone with extensive knowledge of the supernatural. He taught us how to imprison Moyset."

Eliza was skeptical. "Sounds like quite a coincidence. Where did you find this guy?"

"He found me, actually," Will said. "When we met, he used this trick to weaken the Beast and change me back. That probably saved Mason's life."

As soon as he saw the expression on Eliza's face, Will knew he made a mistake.

"What did he save Mason from?" she asked, a touch of harshness in her tone.

Will braced himself. This could not end well. "Mason attacked me, and well… The Beast defended itself. If Xavier hadn't arrived… It wouldn't have been pretty."

Disappointment swept across Eliza's face. She mouthed words in silence, unable to articulate her feelings. "How bad is it?" she asked.

He couldn't bring himself to answer.

"Well?" Eliza persisted. "You wanted this since day one, didn't you? He picked on you when you were new, and you've been at each other's throats ever since. And now you have the power, more than Mr. Amon ever had, and what happens? Mason gets attacked. So answer the question Will; how badly did you hurt him?"

Will hung his head. He felt sick. "You'd have to ask his doctor, but… His leg didn't look good."

The color drained from her face. Will's enhanced senses picked up her anger and disgust, a smell so pungent it would not be washed away.

"You really are a monster," she said quietly. Tears poured down her face.

Her words cut into him like knives. Inside, Will was heartbroken, but he kept his best poker face. "Believe what you want. But I'm going to put an end to this, Eliza. One way or another, this Beast will be slain."

She shook her head, crying harder by the second. She ran back to her house, never giving Will another look. He went after her, only to have the door slammed in his face.

He came here for closure. Now, at least, he had that.

Chapter 14

The distant sound of crowds, music, and excitement could be heard all the way at B.R. Amon & Sons, Inc.

It was opening night of the Walworth County Fair. According to Travis, all the locals were hyped for the show. The fair brought in people from many miles away, making it one of the biggest events in little old Elkhorn. Will remembered going with his parents when he was young, but he lost interest a few years ago.

This year, the fair sounded like fun. A chance to be a kid again, if only for the night. Any distraction from the constant struggle with the Beast would be nice, but Will decided against going. For one, it would bring up unwanted memories of his parents. But more importantly, Will didn't want to go alone. He couldn't ask Eliza, of course. If he invited Travis, Will suspected he would spend the entire time trying to keep him out of trouble. Barbason might go, but strictly as a chauffeur; crowds were no more his style than following the rules was Travis'.

Still, the sound of laughter in the air made Will a little jealous.

Propped up in bed, Will worked on a challenging Sudoku puzzle. He opted to relax tonight and leave his mental battle for another day. Finally, after months of practice, he was getting better at controlling the Beast. Now it only got out once or twice a week. Soon Moyset would grow desperate, and they would have the chance to strike. But, for now, Will allowed himself a night off. Even if he couldn't go to the fair.

Someone knocked on his bedroom door. Will got up and let his great-uncle in.

"Kid…" Barbason looked pale. "Ye're gonna want to see this."

Will followed him into the living room. He didn't

understand why Barbason was worried, until he saw the ancient television set. On it was Mason's bruised face, with the title *Survived a Werewolf Attack* below his name.

The recording of Mason told the story. "It was horrible," he told the camera. "I was out enjoying a walk, when I heard something behind me. I ran for it, but that *thing* was too fast. It mauled me!"

The voice of a narrator came on. "But the most remarkable part of Mason's tale is the identity of this 'Beast.'"

"I saw it change right in front of me," Mason recounted. "I wouldn't have believed it if I hadn't see it for myself."

The camera panned out, showing Natalie Elwin sitting beside his hospital bed.

"Tell us what you saw," she encouraged.

Mason played the role of innocent victim, but the corners of his mouth betrayed the façade. They couldn't help but curl into a grin. "I saw it transform into that freak, Will Lewis."

The screen shifted to an overview of the countryside. "Will Lewis, 15, has been the focus of controversy ever since he moved to Elkhorn in February. As it turns out, Mason wasn't the first to suggest his involvement with the Wisconsin Werewolf. Will lives with his great-uncle—the town boogieman Barbason Amon—at the heart of Beast territory. When asked for an interview, Will's response left our crew shaken."

"I said *GET OUT!*" yelled the video of Will. His eyes were fiery and insane. It was footage from when they interrogated Barbason.

The scene returned to the hospital. "Is this boy a monster in disguise? Do Will Lewis and Barbason Amon know more about the 'Beast of Bray Road' than they let on?

Chapter 14

And if not… Why are they so secretive?" the narrator said.

"We might never know the truth behind the Wisconsin Werewolf. But rest assured; if there are any developments you will find out first, here on *Monsters of America.*"

Will clicked off the TV.

His blood was so hot, it burned his veins. His heart jackhammered painfully in his chest.

"That be one nasty woman," said Barbason. "Cheer up, kid. Nobody believes them stupid shows, anyhow."

Will knew better than that. If high school taught him anything, it was that people believe anything they see on TV. Will was beyond angry; he was seething. Mason sold him out. And Natalie had the audacity to air the film, even after he directly forbid it. Will's vision was blurred by his fury, so strong he could practically see steam billowing from his nostrils.

And that's when it happened.

Without warning Will's body went into a spasm. The force was overwhelming; normally the change felt like being hit with a wave, but this… This was a tsunami by comparison!

Will saw the mental version of the Beast thrash against its reins. The mental Will had to stop it and fast, but he'd never make it in time. Not that it would matter if he could; the hammer was missing. Fear paralyzed him. He knew what was about to happen.

The stake was unearthed. The Beast was released from its chains. And any control Will had was lost.

The backyard scene shattered. Will went numb as body and spirit split, and the Beast took to the sky.

(I sail through brick and mortar, until I can taste the pale light of the full moon on my skin.

Tonight is the night I have awaited. Mother Moon, bear

witnessed to my lunacy!

The hunt is on. My prey; those responsible for the desecration of my name. I sniff the air, and catch the scent of the instigator. He who so wrongfully survived our last duel. He was defeated in every way, yet chose to strike another blow. Such arrogance will not go unpunished.

Following his trail comes naturally, for I have tasted his blood. Now, there is nowhere he can hide. I soar across the woods and fields, until I see the gathering in which the instigator resides.

Lights and noise and commotion flood the fairgrounds. Oh such sweet, abundant energy!

Tonight will be my salvation. Tonight, my hunger shall be sated.)

A world away, Barbason shook Will frantically.

"Kid! Kid, are ye alright?" he asked.

Will's eyes were distant. He could barely force himself to move. "Help me to the truck," he struggled to say.

Barbason hoisted Will to his feet and led him to the door. "Where we goin'?"

"The Walworth County Fair," said Will. "The Beast is free… And that's going to be its hunting ground."

Chapter 15:
The Fair

In a daze, Will packed the necessary tools. He placed the jar and dagger securely in his backpack, and with Barbason's help made it to the truck.

"Ye sure this is it, kid?" asked Barbason. The sky was still bright enough to drive by. "This be what that old guy warned us about?"

Will thought it over, his mind falling in and out of the Beast.

(So much fresh, tender meat, all together in one compelling buffet. Perhaps the instigator should wait. Yes, first a feast is in order.)

"Not exactly," said Will. "Moyset is supposed to be weaker. But I can... Barely stay... In my own head."

He noticed the full moon, rising against the orange sky. Of course—Xavier told them the Beast would be stronger when the moon was full. Moyset was waiting for tonight, hoping to catch them off-guard.

"We have to hurry!"

Barbason nodded. The speedometer kept rising, until

The Fair

it reached a number Travis would be proud of.

"Wait… Travis!" Will exclaimed. "We have to get him first. Without Travis, we can't complete the seal."

As they drove, Will tried to concentrate on the things around him—the truck, his great-uncle, the passing buildings—but his vision kept slipping behind the eyes of his other half.

(Under the cloak of night I prowl the lanes of this fair. These humans see nothing, like cattle led to the slaughterhouse. No need to rush. Each one I pass shivers, but they do not understand the source of their dread.

I am hungry. The hunt has been slim as of late. Time to select an appetizer, to regain strength for bigger game.

I lift my weightless body to the top of a barn. All the better to watch this stream of delicious morsels.

A little girl drops her toy animal, quickly scurrying after it. Although invisible to the five common senses, she must detect my gaze. The girl stares in my direction, and I zone in on her. All other sensations drown out; I only hear her heart rate climb. Not in spurts, no… It rises in slow, beautiful suspense. The girl's knees tremble. Her hand clenches the toy. The taste of fear, so delectably pure, marinades her tiny form.

I have found my appetizer.

To separate her from her kin, I must be swift. I descend upon her faster than she could utter a shriek, and give myself enough solidity to whisk her away from the crowd. Although weak, my instinct is unmatched; not so much as a leaf is disturbed during her abduction. She is forced through the air like a pebble in a stream, until she washes up behind a barn.

Keeping an invisible hand over her mouth, I bring my body to full tangibility. It takes a great effort, and perhaps I could feed while immaterial, but it was worth it—nothing could match her terror at the sight of my true form!

Oh, I am going to enjoy this.

Chapter 15

My maw opens wide. I take things slow, to make sure she knows what's coming. Unable to scream, the little girl sobs in silence at her impending demise. But just as I go in for the kill, something restrains my jaws. I clench them, tight as I can, but they are held open by some other force. This force pulls my jaws back until they should split from my skull. I have no choice but to let my body disperse into the wind, unfed.)

Will was buffeted as he came back—all of him—to Barbason's pickup. He was glad to see they were almost at the Scott household.

"What happened?" asked Barbason.

He couldn't bear to describe the tragedy he prevented. Instead, Will examined the sky. "I have it under control, but not for long. Once night falls, the Beast will be stronger."

With no regard for conventional roads, Barbason criss-crossed the trailers until they reached the Quonset hut at the end. Will leapt from the truck, his energy temporarily restored.

Several frantic knocks later, Frank Scott opened the door.

"Where's Travis?" Will said, giving no time for jokes.

Frank scratched his head. "Don't know. Went off a while ago. Might've said something about the fair."

With the stakes this high, Will didn't have a second to spare. He ran back to the truck, shouting "Thank you!" over his shoulder.

"Might not have, though," Frank muttered. "Never know with that boy." He shrugged and shut the door.

Back in the truck, Will told Barbason their destination. They could only hope to find Travis before anyone was harmed.

As they drove around the school parking lot to the fairgrounds, the last sunlight left the sky.

The Fair

"This is it," said Will. "The night belongs to the Beast. We're in its territory now." He remembered his mental exercises. *Metaphor is material.* Tonight, that was about to change; what was once merely imagined became all too literal.

Will hoped he was ready.

Werewolf or no werewolf, the Walworth County Fair was an electrifying place to be. The sunless sky had no effect on anybody's vision. Between the vibrant moon and lights at every corner, it was almost bright as day on the main paths. But the real energy came from the sound. The air was full of muffled conversations, mechanical clatter from the rides, and vendors preaching the value of their wares. Screams echoed through the grounds, mostly in the direction of the rides. No one was alarmed by them; in this setting, screams were expected.

This place is perfect, Will realized. *With so much chaos, no one would recognize real danger until it was right in front of them.*

The thought gave him chills.

Tracking down Travis would be no easy task. At school he always made himself scarce until *he* wanted to appear. But Will knew him well enough to know this principle; where there's trouble, there's Travis. But in a place like this, the potential problems a prankster like him could cause were endless.

Barbason parked, and together they examined the map of the fair. Will thought through each option, mentally eliminated less likely places. This was a puzzle, and he was solving it like any Sudoku challenge.

"He'll either be at the ferris wheel or the biggest roller coaster," Will said.

"How do ye know?"

Will studied the map. "Travis will be where the biggest, most exciting things are happening. You can't miss that ferris wheel, and I'd bet anything he's a roller-coaster

Chapter 15

junkie. Looks like the ferris wheel is closer, though. Let's start there."

They ran down the pavement until, without warning, Will was hit with a tidal wave of energy. The attack knocked him off his feet, but he never felt pain. He was gone before he hit the ground.

Shed from that fleshly coil, I can resume my hunt. My patience for appetizers has passed; I am ready for the main course.

Ah, glorious night! It is so much easier to roam the domain of darkness. I waste no time with the vessel or the old man. I need an unsuspecting victim. So I rise above the grounds and calculate my options.

This is a puzzle. The objective? Feed and grow strong, until the human side is left helpless. The obstacle? The vessel is not without the means to retaliate. Just as he stole the meal from right under me, he could prove to be a nuisance again.

I must be quick. I must be deliberate. And—most importantly—I must be without mercy.

On the wings of the wind I prowl. I let my senses scan the hunting grounds while I move, searching for the perfect target. I must find it quickly; or else the human could turn the tables. I am not yet strong enough to attack en masse. So first I must find sheep that have strayed from the herd.

Yes—there's the scent! Raging adolescent hormones pinpoint a pair of humans. Their desire for each other makes them seek privacy; which is the last thing they need.

My first victims.

They frolic behind a barn. The male presses the female against a wall and assaults her with kisses. They live in the moment, intimately aware of one another yet oblivious to the world around them.

Time to strike.

The element of surprise is offered freely, so I don't bother

The Fair

putting on a show; all that matters is sustenance. With a fatal sweep of my invisible hand, I wrench the man's etheric body from him. It is soft and untrained, nothing more than an infant compared to me. The woman sees nothing, other than an abrupt end to their pleasure.

The man collapses in with a spasm. He jerks about on the ground, blood gurgling from his mouth. The truth is far more gruesome than the flesh can imagine; I devour the man's energies, not with a singular mouth but through every touch of my ethereal body. His aura flares, the equivalent of bloodshed. Cuts and lacerations spontaneously appear on his physical form. To his mate, all of this happens with no apparent cause.

She screams.

The woman must be dealt with before she stirs the herd. But oh—how delicious this is! I cannot bring myself to leave this meal prematurely, but it hardly matters. The last of his aura—the true *lifeblood—is nearly finished. And as I take the final bites she merely kneels beside the man and shakes his dead body. That mistake will cost her life; if she ran for help, she might have gotten away. Now… She is mine.*

Having fed so greedily, my power is back to its pre-starvation state. So easily I have undone the vessel's best attempts to weaken me.

Like a clenched fist, I pull myself together. A figure, massive and ominous, appears before the woman. She sees me, and the terror of it forces her against the wall. I rear up on my hind legs, standing like a man in the shape of a monster.

She is about to scream again. I spare her the trouble by ripping open her throat. She barely makes a sound as the lights go out in her eyes. A doctor might declare her dead, but there is still life in her. Life which I will put to good use. I bite into her and taste the warm blood flow over my face. The physical desecration is symbolic; a path to best consume the true nutrients buried beneath the flesh.

Once finished, I step back to examine the carnage. The vessel shares my vision. He must see this, and see it clearly.

The game has begun. Round one goes to me.

Chapter 15

Will's entire body felt like lead. Yet in spite of the difficulty, he forced himself upright.

Barbason was at his side, trying to comfort him. "C'mon kid, ye alright. Ye're stronger than it is."

The images were burned into Will's mind. He didn't just *watch* the Beast commit those unthinkable acts; he *experienced* it. He could even taste the blood, and feel the satisfying fullness of the meal.

Worst of all was what he saw right now. Two innocent people, lying murdered and maimed by his own doing.

(Round one goes to me.)

Will was devastated. He would never forget that scene. He knew he would carry this guilt until his dying day.

Which, he realized, might not be that long after all.

"Travis…" Will panted. "We need… Travis."

With the Beast this strong, they couldn't afford to look for Travis at random. Lives were at stake, and any second the Beast could claim its next victim. Desperate for a solution, Will looked for something—*anything*—that might help. He saw the truck, and the wheels of his mind started to turn.

Could they bring Travis to *them?*

"Help me to the truck," said Will. Barbason walked alongside him for support. Will wished he had his strength back, but Moyset was still riding his aura. With a strange double-vision he could see the Beast as it hunted for its next meal. One eye saw the fair from the ground level, while the other surveyed it from the sky like a hawk.

"What's the plan, kid?" Barbason asked when they reached the truck.

"Drive," Will instructed. "Honk your horn, too.

The Fair

Cause as much commotion as you can. Travis always finds his way to trouble. With any luck, he'll come check out what the ruckus is about."

Barbason didn't seem so sure. "Alright kid, if ye say so..."

The old horn blared across the chatter. Everyone's attention turned to the truck, which was good; it gave them time to move once Barbason screeched the tires and drove into the crowd. People ran and swore as the truck forced its way through. They were causing a stir, alright.

Before he realized it, Will slipped away from consciousness. He found himself watching the truck from a bird's eye view.

A disturbance catches the herd's attention. Since I returned to my ethereal form, I choose to swim through the sky. From this height, I can easily see the cause; the old man's tired steel mount, stampeding aimlessly. Is this the vessel's best strategy?

Pathetic.

Meanwhile, opportunity presents itself for a second course. A "house of horrors" attraction lures the skittish into a show of imitation danger. They seek out fear, but why? Perhaps fear makes them feel alive. Or perhaps they have become so housebroken that they forgot what real *fear is.*

Another easy target.

Inside, only the faintest light guides the herd. The sculptors use darkness as a trick; they make objects hint at danger, then let the imagination fill in the blanks. Little do they know that, in my case, darkness only hides the depths of my monstrousness. If cast into the light, these fools would be in for the fright of their lives. I suppose I could sneak up on my prey. Catch them off guard, and silence them before they know what's coming.

But terror tastes so much better.

Chapter 15

My body tightens until solid, and I prowl the twisted corridors. Already the task of materializing is easier. That is to be expected; the more I feed, the less effort it will take.

There—the scent of humans!

The floor creaks. I make no attempts at stealth—in fact, I want them to notice me. There are three to the group, huddled close despite their claims that this place is "lame." The woman in back notices me first. Hair whiplashes her comrades as she turns.

"Something's there," says she.

One of the men takes a step closer. "If it's another clown, I'm blowing this joint. This place sucks."

They catch a glimpse of me in the strobe light. The woman gasps. The man laughs.

"Ooh, a 'Wisconsin Werewolf' gag," says the bold man. He takes another step closer. "Not very original."

The woman grips his arm. "Don't!" she cries.

"Leave it alone, Josh," says the other man. He remains neutral on the matter.

The bold one, Josh, laughs again. "Chill out. No one's even allowed to touch you in here, remember? I just want a good look."

I growl. Not out of defense, but for sheer entertainment. I shouldn't play with my food, but this amuses me so.

"Well aren't you scary," says this Josh. "If you're so tough, why do you just stand there snarling? C'mon, take a bite! I'm right here!"

Ah, the irony of his taunts! Behind the smell of arrogance, I pick up the aroma of nervousness from his companions. Nerves, but not fear.

Not yet.

The bold idiot, laughing at his own stupidity, sticks his leg out in my direction. Then I do the last thing he expects; I clamp my mighty jaw around his shin, and tear it off.

His friends scream. But the light is still low, and they are expecting cheap thrills. They are not entirely convinced this isn't an act.

The Fair

They stay by his side, caught in the confusion of a show too real to be staged.

I climb atop my prey, and bite into the tender meat of his thigh. Now his wails are too authentic to deny. He pleads for his friends, his language growing unintelligible as shock and terror overwhelm him

Finally the others run, their friend left for dead.

With no further distractions, I finish my meal.

It was impossible to stop the Beast; all Will could do was try with all his might to block out the horrific images. Closing his physical eyes opened them to the Beast, so he stayed alert and focused on the world around him.

They were certainly getting attention. Irate fair-goers shouted obscenities as they cleared way for the truck. Finally, a man working with the Walworth County Fair arrived. He explained that cars were not allowed past this point, and asked us kindly to return to the parking lot. Will commended him for being so level-headed. If Travis was watching, it would surely make him laugh.

Lucky for them, he was.

The pickup truck bounced as Travis hopped into the cargo bed. He tapped the back window, looking bewildered.

Will grabbed his backpack and got out of the truck. "Get people out of here, Uncle Barbason. Do whatever it takes."

Travis jumped down from the truck. "Hey buddy! Ever heard of subtlety? Look, if you're here about Mason and Eliza, you really ain't a knight and this sure as hell ain't no white horse to ride up and save her."

"That's not why I'm…" Will paused. "Wait a second—what *about* Mason and Eliza?"

He raised an eyebrow. "You don't know? Mason guilt-tripped her into coming with him to this thing. I ran into them a couple minutes ago and gave him hell. But if you didn't know that, why *are* you here?"

Will's vision kept shifting. It made him dizzy.

(I prowl behind the barns, fully physical, on my way to the great rotating disc.)

"The Beast is free, and it's here at the fair," said Will. "It's already killed, and I think it's headed for the ferris wheel next."

Travis' double-take was comically expressive. "Holy hell, here? *Tonight?* And I just thought you were hoping to run Mason over with that old clunker!" Another thought crossed Travis' mind. "You said it's headed for the ferris wheel?"

Will nodded. "Yeah. Why?"

"Well… Don't know how to tell you bro, but those two were in line for that when I saw them. They're probably on it by now."

Fear crept over Will.

(The instigator is near.)

The Beast wasn't moving on a whim anymore; it was locked on to its real target.

"We have to go, *now!*" Will yelled. He worked his way through the crowd in slow motion. Every limb felt heavy as stone, but he wouldn't let himself slow down. If he did, he'd have to watch the Beast claim another victim.

Will kept running.

"What's the plan, boss?" Travis asked. He was jogging alongside Will.

Great question, Will thought. Their original strategy was quickly falling apart. "Right now, we have to warn Mason and Eliza. After that… I have no idea."

He became very aware of the silver dagger in his backpack, and of its kamikaze purpose. Will stopped long enough to take out the satchel containing the dagger and tie it to his belt. It was like a makeshift holster. "Take my backpack," he told Travis. "The jar is in there. Hopefully we get the chance to use it."

Travis eyed the satchel. "We better. Because I'll kill you if you wind up dying on me!" In place of humor, his words came across entirely serious.

Will closed his eyes as they ran, letting Travis guide him. He wanted to keep tabs on the Beast's progress.

(The great wheel runs on simple machinery. Ah, electricity. So easy to disrupt with etheric energy.

Now, to locate the instigator. Yes, there he is. Dangling from a basket at the halfway point of the wheel.

Time to strike.)

The moment Will opened his eyes, the ferris wheel lost power.

"The lights are off, but I bet the big bad wolf is home," said Travis.

Thankfully, Will saw all he needed. "Mason and Eliza are halfway up, on the right side." They were almost there, but the Beast beat them to it. "We won't make it in time."

Travis' eyes darted from Will to the ferris wheel. "Maybe *we* won't. But *I* can, if I'm not waiting for you, slowpoke." He patted Will's shoulder. "Hang tight bro. I'll get it off their asses."

With a mad dash, Travis left Will in the dust.

If he had time, Will would have protested. Travis had no defense, nothing to use against such a monster. He could be walking to his grave. But Will couldn't stop him now, so he did the only thing he could; sit down and rest.

When relaxed, Will dissolved back into the mind of his enemy.

Chapter 15

With the lights extinguished and the operator scared off, I am free to resume my hunt.

Fully tangible, I climb the metal railings of the great disk. Some passengers notice a gigantic shadow creaking by. They scream, causing panic to ripple across the entire wheel. It matters not; my prey is trapped. They must either await my arrival or jump to their doom.

There! The instigator. Sitting there, indignant at the disruption of power. And—to my fury—he sits in the company of the foolish girl. She who is mine. Their intimacy is treachery from both ends.

And both shall be punished.

I step close enough to make my shape known, a patch of blackness darker than it should be. But my eyes—those still glow with a haunting yellow light! It would be hard to guess which of them showed more fear, although the scale would likely tip towards the instigator.

As it should.

"Back off, Lewis," he whispers.

My lips part in a canine smile. What a nightmarish vision that must be! Yellow eyes and moonlit teeth suspended in in darkness. The girl whimpers at the sight.

Suddenly, something strikes my rear. An annoying interruption. I turn gracefully on the rail in the direction the object came from. I see the source, and snarl.

The troublemaker.

Clad entirely in black, he blends in almost as well as I do. He balances on the railing rather well, for one of the herd.

"Hey, Cujo! Here boy!" the troublemaker calls. He whistles, and the pitch causes me to shudder. My superb hearing makes the sound unbearable. He grins at my response. "What's wrong, wolfy? Don't like the sound of that, do you?"

This boy is an unnecessary distraction. I have the instigator cornered, and I yield to no man. I turn back to the next course of my feast. The girl weeps, and the instigator stands vigilant. But in the air, there's a scent of uncertainty; he has no plan of action, and knows I may very well finish what I started last time. His demise becomes clearer

The Fair

with each step I take.

That terrible pitch fills my ears again, disabling me. The melody sounds familiar. From a dream long forgotten, I recall the tune being played through an oral musical device—a harmonica, it is called. Another piece of rubble is thrown at me. The lights of the wheel flicker, and in that instant I turn back to the interruption.

The troublemaker. He stands there, stone in hand, whistling his infernal music. He yells beyond me. "What the hell are you guys waiting for, an encore? Get outta here!"

It's time to deal with this fool. The instigator can't go far. There are crutches in his seat, so he must still be slowed from injuries. Besides, I have tasted his blood, and can find him anytime I wish.

But this troublemaker. He must be dealt with. Staring into the face of death, he smiles. This man knows no fear.

"C'mon wolfy," he says. "Let's dance."

Such mockery will not be tolerated. I charge him, but in unison he whistles and throws a stone at me. The pebble strikes me square in the face. Combined with the agony of the noise, I lose my footing and tumble down a series of metal rails. The entire wheel trembles as I hit row after row of metal. Yet the troublemaker climbs away from me, as much at home as a monkey in the treetops.

Rage consumes me when I hit the ground, the depths of which no human could possibly comprehend. Fury transforms me into an embodiment of hatred itself, incomparable in its thirst for destruction. My body becomes a shockwave of etheric power. Sparks fly, and the machinery ignites. Little flames flicker over the controls. My ethereal form conducts the flame like a cloud of gas, turning me into the center of a wild inferno.

I spot the troublemaker at the opposite end, and I shoot towards him like a fireball. The force of my impact catches him off-balance.

The troublemaker falls from the wheel in clothes covered with flames. He should be of no concern anymore.

Still in a blaze of fire, I soar to the top of the wheel. I

Chapter 15

materialize on the highest empty basket, and fill the night with a fearsome howl.

The time for subtlety has passed.

Will opened his eyes.

There it was, for all the world to see. The Beast was howling at the top of the ferris wheel, still slightly ablaze. A trail of dying flames traced its path. From the ground it was a great, foreboding silhouette against the full moon.

Now people started to worry.

Crowds pointed and stared, confirming what they saw wasn't imaginary. They grew nervous, but no one ran. This was still just a spectacle, something they thought could be watched from a safe distance.

How wrong they were.

Will wanted to warn those around him, but he was distracted by his other half; the Beast was on the move again.

(Now, where was I?

Ah, yes. The instigator.

With no further distractions I descend the wheel in his direction. As I suspected, he has not gone far; the girl carefully attempts to climb down the rails, but the instigator remains in his seat. He is crippled. He cannot escape so easily. They see me approach. The girl screams, but the instigator sizes up the situation.

Perhaps he sees how hopeless it is.

"Eliza, GO!" he yells. When she doesn't move, he grabs her wrist and pulls it from the rail. "Jump if you have to, but GET OUT OF HERE!"

Finally, she takes the hint. Caution thrown to the wind, she climbs down clumsily but quickly.

"Leave her," the instigator says. His eyes are locked onto mine. "Don't make her watch. This is between you and me, Lewis."

I cannot speak, but I do slow my pace. That is answer enough.

The Fair

Once the girl reaches the ground, I leap towards him with my teeth bared. But the instigator seems ready; he grabs one of his crutches and wields it like a weapon. How ignorant. Such mundane tools have little effect on the likes of me.

The instigator swings the crutch, and my world explodes with pain.

I topple off course, and crash into the rail supporting his basket. More than simple pain, I am stunned; his weapon shouldn't have affected me so.

The instigator smirks from his seat. "Well look at that," he says. "I guess there's more to the legends than fairytales."

Ah; now I see it! The metal of his crutch shines brightly in the moon's light. That shade, not industrial steel at all.

Silver.

Although immobile in his seat, the length of the crutch protects the instigator's whole basket. I try to strike, carefully, but his aim is true. We are at a stale-mate; neither can harm the other without risking our own lives. I scrutinize the environment, trying to find an angle at which to regain the upper hand.

Angle… Of course.

I jump, not at him but at the bottom of the basket. My claws sink into the side, and with my whole weight the basket flips over. The instigator flies from safety and slams into a metal rail. His weapons fall through the wheel until they hit the ground.

Now, he is vulnerable. Now… He is mine.)

"No…" Will muttered. "This can't be happening."

Despite everything, Will desperately wanted Mason to survive. The other deaths were horrible enough, but they were strangers; the thought of murdering someone he knew was unbearable. Whatever it took, he *had* to stop the Beast before it was too late.

(The instigator lays still. He landed on his back, perhaps too hard for his fragile spine to take. But, ever so slightly, he stirs. He is still alive.

Chapter 15

But not for long.

I climb up to him and announce myself with a growl. He sees me, but his spirit is gone.

"Go on then," says the instigator. "Be done with it."

Within moments I am on top of him. I begin to open my mouth, but—what's this?—some force holds it closed.)

It took every ounce of his strength to control the Beast. Will knew it could be done; he saved that little girl the same way. He pushed and pushed, until he felt nauseous from exertion. His body writhed on the ground, pouring sweat until dirt became mud.

(That human! Trying to stop me from delivering punishment. He thinks he can put me back on a leash, tame me like some kind of pet.

Think again.

I rip open my jaw, a force so powerful it could rend metal. His unseen hands—which bound my muzzle—are thrown off of me.)

Will gasped.

He felt the literal pressure of the Beast. It swatted him away like a fly.

It was too strong now.

(Free again, I look upon my meal. The instigator has given up, but his eyes have not. In them, I see the same burning glare he gave me countless times since my arrival. I can't help but grin to see him like this.)

"No!" Will screamed. Battered and weary, he still fought with all his might to hold back the Beast.

But it wasn't enough.

(My maw opens wide. Slowly, I lower it over the instigator's head.)

"STOP!"

Frantically Will flailed about. He felt insane with terror; his body and mind beyond the breaking point.

(A row of fangs surround his skull. The instigator mutters his

last words.

"See you in Hell, Lewis.")

"NO!"

(One quick, decisive action, and it's over.

Justice, at long last, has been delivered.)

The flailing stopped. So did the screaming. In fact, to Will it seemed like the whole world froze.

Mason was dead.

The truth crushed Will. He lay motionless, too shocked to react. He was a murderer. He murdered a boy not much older than himself. Will's hands—as well as his conscience—would forever be stained with that blood.

He heard someone calling his name.

"Will!" It was Eliza. She saw him by the side of the road and came running. "Will! What's going on? You have to stop this!"

(Ah, such a glorious feast!

The instigator has been dealt with. My next target? That foolish girl.

I leap from the wheel. The ground quakes as I land, and I bring forth a primal howl. The human herd sees me for what I am. They do the only sane thing they can; they run for their lives!

There—the girl's scent. I follow it, walking down the path at a casual pace. No reason to hurry.

I have all the time in the world to hunt her down.)

"Will!"

Eliza shook him. When he came back to himself, Will saw people running everywhere. Panic was spreading in waves. Before long, the fairgrounds would be empty, but until then it was a stampede to safety.

Will got to his feet, even though every muscle in his body was beyond sore. He walked to the center of the road, standing against the current of panic-stricken fairgoers.

"What are you doing?" Eliza asked.

Chapter 15

Will looked at her. "The Beast is coming for you. When it gets here, I'll distract it while you get away. Understand?"

Shaking, she nodded.

"I love you, Eliza," he said. The road was clear of people now, leaving them alone. "I won't let it get you."

They heard a growl.

Down the road, maybe a hundred feet away, was the Beast.

It wasn't moving. It stood there, staring them down. Even from this distance those eyes were piercing. They were too intelligent, and they were too much like Will's. Until now, Will never saw hisBeast in the flesh. It resembled the monster that took his parents, but this Beast was younger. Its fur was a healthy brown, and its body was larger than ever. On all fours, it had to be as big as a horse.

(The human vessel.

Do you wish to stand in my way again? I know you can hear me; we share one mind, remember?

The choice is yours, vessel. We can be allies or enemies. I do not need you intact to survive; so long as your heart beats I remain strong. A little dismemberment might do good for your obedience.

It's your move, human.

Make your choice.)

"What are you going to do?" Eliza asked. She was frozen in place.

With cold certainty, Will came to the hardest realization of his life… He was going to die here. Tonight, on this very road. And a funny thing happens when you accept death; fear becomes a pointless emotion.

"Now… We end this," he said. Will reached into the satchel and pulled out the silver dagger. He held it steady, and met the Beast's gaze.

"I choose to fight."

The Fair

(So be it, vessel.)

In perfect unison, Will and the Beast charged at each other.

Chapter 16:
Showdown

Faced with immediate danger, the human mind goes into "crisis mode." Calm, analytical thinking shuts down completely. Without all that rational thought weighing you down, your brain speeds up and relies on instinct to make hair-trigger decisions. That's why time slows down in a life-or-death situation; you're processing everything twice as fast.

As the Beast approached, Will's brain was on overdrive.

The two halves collided, and the greatest fight of their lives began. Man against monster. Material against spiritual.

The Beast swiped its claw. Will rolled out of the way.

Will swung the dagger. The Beast ducked.

They were eerily in-tune with each other. If anyone else were to fight the Beast, the battle would end quickly. But Will had an advantage others didn't; he could hear the Beast's thoughts. He knew the next move before it happened, and could react in time to dodge.

Showdown

Unfortunately, it went both ways.

So they did the dance of war, each staying half a step ahead of the other. One wrong move for either, and the battle could come to an abrupt end.

Finally, a blow connected.

Will was knocked off his feet. The Beast made a deep cut across his chest, staining his shirt red.

(First blood goes to me.)

The Beast pounced. Will barely made it away in time. It looked like the Beast was right; this shared pain only went one way. The matching place on the monster's chest was unscathed.

Adrenaline held Will's fatigue at bay, but it wouldn't last. He had to hurt it soon, while he had the strength to fight. He needed a plan, but couldn't make one without the Beast listening in.

An idea came to him.

Metaphor is material. That's never been more true than now. What if he could block the Beast out of his thoughts? It was worth a try. By the same principles of his training, Will imagined himself inside a fortress, with the monster locked out. Maybe, just maybe, the metaphor would create a real barrier around his thoughts.

He concentrated on the image, and his mind went quiet.

No more glimpses through the Beast's eyes. Will's thoughts were his own again. It was a trade-off, of course; he lost insight into his enemy. But now, he could do something unexpected. Something the Beast wouldn't predict. That way, he could catch it off guard.

It was time to take risks.

Narrowly dodging another blow, Will tried to think. He was never a daredevil. He wasn't the type to come up with split-second, unpredictable, and in all likelihood completely

Chapter 16

insane ideas.

So he asked himself, *what would Travis do?*

Then it hit him; Travis already *found* a way to fight back!

The Beast's razor claws cut a deep gorge in Will's arm. He groaned in pain, fell back, and saw a row of huge teeth descending quickly.

Will whistled, as loud as he could.

The great wolf flinched, and Will took this moment to swing. Finally, the blade met the Beast's skin. Silver sliced the ethereal flesh with no resistance. Will knew it hit before he heard the Beast's moan; a matching cut opened across his right collarbone.

No time to waste. Will ran, whistling as loud as his strained body could muster.

The Beast stumbled, but the head start wasn't enough.

It took a single leap to clear the distance. Will discovered new depths of agony as its jaw clamped onto his shoulder. He toppled under the weight of the Beast, scraping his face against the gravel.

Exhausted, covered in openly bleeding cuts, bruises, and bites, Will admitted defeat.

His mental wall collapsed. He was too strained to resist any longer. The voice of the Beast slithered up his spine, whispering in the back of his skull.

(You have lost, vessel.

Let tonight serve as a lesson. You bow to *me,* human! *I will not kill you, don't worry. But you must be scolded for disobeying me.*

Now, to choose your punishment…)

Will was released from its hold. He felt the Beast's muzzle sniffing along his back. Then his arms. Then his legs. Will didn't have the strength to struggle. All he could do was wait for whatever gruesome torture the Beast decided on.

Showdown

"Stop it! Don't kill him!"

Perfectly synchronized, Will and the Beast turned toward the sound.

Eliza came back. She held her ground, meeting the Beast's gaze. Her eyes were determined, but her lips quivered when she spoke. "It's me you want."

(The girl.

Yes… The perfect punishment.)

"No!" Will shouted.

The Beast abandoned Will and sprinted to Eliza. She wasn't far. In the blink of an eye the Beast tackled and pinned her to the ground. It raised one claw above its head, winding up for the kill.

(Watch her die, vessel.)

There wasn't enough time. In that second, an idea crossed Will's mind. He couldn't think it over; he either had to do it *right now* or witness Eliza's death. Using the last of his willpower, he stood up.

Will held the dagger, took aim, and threw. It was just like the knife at the hideout. He followed the dagger's trail as it wavered off course, drifting a little too far in front of the Beast. Will panicked—it was going to miss! The dagger flew past just as the Beast's claw arced forward.

A thunderous pain exploded in Will. It stormed through his veins, knocking every single thought from his mind. He was numb to everything but this searing, overpowering agony. Distantly, he heard a *thump*, and looked down to see the source of the noise.

A severed human hand lay before him.

His hand.

Will passed out.

He did not wake up. Not exactly.

Chapter 16

Sight came to Will, but it didn't feel like he opened his eyes. It was more like his eyes simply faded into existence. His mind was blank. No memory. No emotion. Nothing. He did not see himself, nor did he feel a body. Will felt like a self-aware wisp, and had no human reason to think otherwise. So he did what any self-aware wisp would do; he looked around.

Will was surrounded by darkness.

Everywhere he turned was darkness. He was on a patch of grass a few feet around, the only land in a vast, black pit.

"Where am I?"

The sound of his voice, so unfamiliar, brought a flood of feelings to him. Nothing coherent, not like memories. These were more like *shadows* of memory, giving a vague impression without details or meaning. He caught glimpses of a childhood. Of a family.

Of a *home*.

Square, warm lights appeared from the darkness. The outline of a house stood out, illuminated ever-so-slightly by the windows. Even the shapes of trees seemed to flirt with the edge of view. A sense of *déjà vu* sent shivers through his body.

His *body*.

As if all it took was the thought, Will felt the comfortable human form come into being around him. Real memories of early life returned, as well as the indisputable knowledge of where he was.

Will was standing in the back yard of his old house.

One by one details came into view. The sky filled with stars. The house took shape. The neighboring woods became clear. And looming above was a full moon, bathing the yard in a pale glow.

Somehow, this was all wrong. He couldn't be here. But try as he might, Will couldn't think of why not.

Showdown

"Mom? Dad?" he called.

Their names conjured up nostalgic imagery, and it hit him. He remembered the funeral. He remembered the drive home… And he remembered the Beast. The last few months came back to him like a rapid slideshow. Pictures flashed at dizzying speed until he caught up with the events of the fair.

Will realized the dismal truth of his condition.

"I'm dead."

The house now seemed more like a mirage than a solid object, rippling gently like a reflection on the water. Will suspected this whole place was nothing but an illusion. Some kind of limbo as he awaited judgment. He saw the chain and collar, which once held the monster within his mind.

Beyond that, there was movement in the woods.

At first Will thought it was the Beast, back to finish him off. But as it approached, that didn't seem right. It wasn't in the shape of a canine. One feature stood out against the darkness; bright, malicious yellow eyes. At the sight of them, the temperature dropped to a freezing chill.

Something emerged from the trees. Something which should not be.

No description of the Thing could do it justice. There weren't words in any human language to capture its appearance. You could describe fragments of it, maybe even paint a picture of how they fit together. But nothing—*nothing*—could communicate its absolute wrongness. Its very existence was a blasphemy of the greatest offense. Every motion of its body was a sin against all things natural. Your eyes couldn't linger on the Thing; as if your subconscious knew that with every element acknowledged, you slip one step closer to irretrievable madness.

Before he could force his attention away, these features were burned into Will's mind:

It rode on top of a black, emaciated horse. Perhaps

rode was the wrong word; a torso seemed to protrude from where a saddle might sit, like some kind of malformed centaur. The Thing had a head like a raven. A tail like a serpent. One arm was strong and clawed. The other, black and corpse-like. And those eyes, shining with an unholy light.

It was a cancer to our world. Pure evil given form.

There were endless details, each more nauseating than the last. But—thankfully—Will looked away before his sanity was threatened. Most frightening of all, however, was that this Thing was familiar. Will immediately knew what he was looking at.

"Moyset."

Out of the corner of his eye, Will saw the Thing nod. It was sickening to watch it move. To see it *exist*.

"What… *Are* you?" Will asked. Even in the face of death, he wanted answers.

Moyset laughed. It was a grotesque, ear-splitting cackle. The sound reverberated in Will's skull and made his teeth chatter. *"Curiosity. Such a self-destructive human motive. Pitiable creatures, seeking knowledge with nigh a thought of repercussion. But do you truly wish to know? Would you cross the threshold of sanity, and glimpse beyond the peak of madness?"*

Will gulped.

"So be it," said Moyset. *"As of yet we hath played in your mental field. A world comprised of thy recollections."* A vibrant meteor shower streaked across the sky.

"Now… It's my turn, childe."

The night sky ripped away like a painting. There was a flash of light, so bright it left Will blinded and nauseous. He felt the ground tremble and collapse beneath his feet. As he tumbled sightlessly into the abyss, Will was overcome with a sense of vertigo. His center of balance shifted drastically. His body was wrong, all wrong. But all his eyes revealed was a white spot left by the flash.

Showdown

As his vision returned, Will's terror grew.

If ever there was a Hell, this was it. There was nothing but destruction wherever he looked. Celestial flames, hotter than the sun, blazed like a wildfire. Planets of impossible shapes withstood an endless barrage of meteors and asteroids, until they too shattered into a trillion pieces of cosmic shrapnel. Every few seconds, a star would erupt with cataclysmic ferocity.

The universe itself was constant hellfire.

Will's sanity felt loose at the hinges. The sight of the demon alone could send you to the asylum, but this… This was insanity squared, the very birthplace of chaos.

But it was still Will's mind, he was sure of that. Moyset was creating an illusion from *its* memory now. Surely it was just a metaphor; it would be impossible to see this world as it really was, just like we cannot truly comprehend the form of demons.

Which was good; one *real* glimpse of this place would be a fate worse than death.

Through the fire, a black horseman rode.

Will braced himself. The demon slashed its claw at him. As the blow connected, a nearby star exploded. Will was buffeted by the blast, thrown at the whim of this infernal realm. Moyset gave chase, a sinister shadow riding the tides of Hell. Gravity was of no concern; they could move freely through the cosmos.

Already their physical and etheric bodies fought.

Now, it was a battle of the mind.

Will felt no more prepared to defend himself. His mental stability withered away under Moyset's assault. Soon, Will feared, there would be nothing left of him but a hollow shell.

"Arrogant humans," said Moyset. The demon knocked Will into a moon and began to trample him against it.

Chapter 16

"Wasting resources given in abundance. You know naught of our suffering or tribulations."

Will was beginning to understand suffering, alright.

"Ungrateful cretins! We have aided in your growth, your prosperity, yet are we acknowledged for it?" Moyset grabbed Will by its deadened hand and held him up, bringing them face-to-face. *"We gave you power in exchange for worship. And this is how you use it?"* The demon made a bizarre hissing sound.

"Pathetic."

Will opened his eyes. The sight of the abomination, so close, was dissolving any reason he had. Surely he was going crazy; because staring into those alien eyes he made an insane decision.

He was going to fight until his last breath.

Drawing up his saliva, Will spat into Moyset's face. The Thing recoiled, hissing and screeching at an inhuman pitch. The sound was painful, yes—but the demon lost its grip. Will fumbled to his feet, on a moon in the midst of pure, cosmic chaos.

No... This wasn't Moyset's world. Not really.

This was still Will's mind. And he intended to reclaim it.

"Imbecile!" shouted Moyset. *"You shall pay for your insolence!"*

The demon struck Will into the fiery cosmos. While getting his bearings, Will remembered Xavier's lessons. Now that he had the resolve to fight, Will discovered he had complete control of his mental self. He stood, suspended in space.

Moyset charged, wailing an otherworldly battle cry. This time, Will was ready. He shot himself at the demon like a comet, making a trail of imaginary stardust. They collided with the force of a supernova. To both of their surprise, it was Will who remained at the center of the blast. Moyset was thrown into the flames, out of sight but not out of mind.

With every breath, another piece of sanity returned. It was bizarre—his insane determination was actually mending his mind. Will felt like himself again.

Out from the fire came Moyset. The abomination was on the attack, seething with diabolic rage. But Will wasn't afraid; in fact he felt strangely calm. No matter what Moyset tried, it could not lay a hand (or claw) on the boy. He couldn't explain it, but Will didn't feel weak at all. Actually, now that he thought about it… He felt *great!*

Maybe there was still a chance.

Another star died in a blinding explosion. When the flash cleared, that hellish universe was gone. They were back to the yard where Will grew up. The demon looked around, confused and aggravated.

"What audacity is this?" it shrieked. *"Submit to me, impertinent human!"*

The moon was setting. Behind Will, the first signs of dawn started to show. "No," he said plainly.

Moyset's steed stomped. *"Excusez-moi?"*

Everything was making sense. "You aren't the Beast, Moyset. I am. You're nothing but the master commanding by whip and chain. You turned me into a monster." Will stepped forward, smirking. "I bet you fooled everyone into thinking they were powerless. Starve the physical body—the only one they know—while feeding the etheric. Your victims usually don't understand that side of them. You always had free reign, didn't you?"

Demonic eyes glared into him. *"You underestimate my cunning."*

Will took another step, and to his amazement the black horseman backed away. "I think you have underestimated *me,* Moyset." A beautiful sunrise crept over the horizon, forming a halo of light around Will.

Chapter 16

"Imbecile!" it shouted. *"Should thee manage to dispel me, I need just clench the soul of another hapless human to reap my vengeance!"*

"Really? And how do you plan to do that?" said Will. The sun was a metaphor. As it rose, so did Will's strength. Realizing now that he and the Beast were truly one, he could tap into the power of his other half. It was revitalizing. "I know a few things about your kind. You can't take control without consent. With your book destroyed, the only others who know about you are Uncle Barbason, Travis, and Eliza. My *friends and family,* in other words. Remember the terms of our agreement, Moyset? I let you in, but you were forbidden from taking them. Maybe you were lying, but I don't think so. Seems like there are twisted rules you have to follow."

The horse and its rider reared up. *"I have devastated humanity for centuries! Wrought death and destruction on countless mortals! Stained the soil of two continents with the blood of all who defy me! Such hubris, that a mere boy would challenge me."*

Light became part of Will. He felt the sun's rays melt into his body. His skin took on a soft, orange glow.

He was an avatar of sunlight.

Moyset kicked and clawed and fought, but Will was beyond limitations. He was master of his own mind again, and the demon couldn't touch him. In fact, the mental version of Will wasn't even in human shape; it was a formless mass of light, pure and vibrant and good. It was the polar opposite of Moyset.

When Will spoke, the words didn't come from his mouth—they boomed from every direction, as if spoken with the voice of God.

"Be gone from here."

The luminous being lifted Moyset off the ground and carried it into the sky. Fury didn't begin to describe the demon's stare; it was full of hatred so intense, no human could understand. Those eyes were made of hellfire, pulsing with the chaotic destruction of the world that made them. And it was all focused on Will. That look of otherworldly malice burned a scar into his very soul.

"This… Is not… OVER!" Moyset shouted.

The body of light exploded. Glorious colors cascading everywhere, like the grandest firework ever seen. Moyset shot into the sky like a bullet. It writhed and screamed, until it was lost beyond the stars.

Once the light faded, darkness returned. It swallowed everything up until there was nothing left. No yard. No house. No horseman…

And no Will.

Chapter 17:

In Memoriam

Darkness.

A soft hum.

Slow, gentle beating.

It was like drifting through the ocean on a starless night. Waves rock the piece of wreckage you ride. Maybe there was a ship once. It's gone now. All that remains is darkness and the ebb and flow of the tide.

This must be death.

Dying was no fun, but death itself seemed peaceful. If all Will had to look forward to was the feeling of being adrift, he could deal with that. He took comfort in the thought that the hard part was over. Will accepted this fate, and indulged in the numb tranquility of the afterlife.

Sometimes, faint images or sounds came from across the waters. They were muffled, but often very familiar. Maybe they weren't sounds at all, just memories from distant shores floating on the wind.

Time was immeasurable here; hours, days or years

could have passed and Will wouldn't have known. It *felt* like he was here a very long time, but there was no means to gauge just how long it's been.

Finally, something new happened. Light flooded onto Will and stung his eyes. He blinked until he adjusted to the brightness. The sky was white, which made no sense at all. But then again, this was death. Who was he to say what was sensible?

Then he realized; that wasn't the sky.

It was a ceiling.

Eyes still watering, he looked around. It was definitely a ceiling. He could even see a window, and out of the corner of his eye some strange machinery.

He was in a hospital.

"Kid! Ye're awake!"

Barbason's weary face filled his view. At first he rejoiced at the sight of Will, but once he got a good look the old man gasped.

"Nurse! Nurse, come quick! Somethin' ain't right!"

Will was drifting again. But before he fell into the black ocean, he thought… *Maybe I'm not dead, after all.*

Although time was still lost, Will was definitely floating back to consciousness more often. Slowly, he was becoming himself again.

Eventually, Will woke up completely. He glanced around the hospital room (despite the soreness in every muscle) and saw his great-uncle dozing in a chair. Barbason sprang to life at the first sign of movement.

"How ye feeling, kid?" he asked.

Will fought to find his voice. When he did, two words said it all. "I'm… Alive."

Barbason began to cry. "That's right, kid. Ye're alive.

Chapter 17

And thank God for that! I thought I was goin' to lose ye."

"What happened?" Will asked. "The last thing I remember I was at the fair, and the Beast was about to get Eliza…" The memory of that horrific moment returned. Dreading what he might find, he lifted the arm that threw the dagger.

All he saw was a bandaged stump where a hand should be.

He turned away, barely suppressing the urge to vomit. This couldn't be real, it just couldn't be. As long as it was out of sight, he could convince himself there was still a hand there. In fact, he swore he could still feel fingers resting at his side.

The old man's relentless tears told otherwise. "I'm so sorry, kid! I wish this ain't never happened to you!"

Holding his breath, Will risked another glance. He could feel his right hand, just like always, but there was no denying what he saw. The bandage wrapped around his forearm, then came to an abrupt end.

"How?"

"I didn't see it," Barbason said. "It was just Travis and Eliza when I got there, and they ain't said much. Eliza's been worryin' herself to pieces. They'll want to see ye, kid. They visit every day."

Something still wasn't right… Every time Barbason looked at Will, he got spooked and turned away.

"What's the matter?" Will asked.

Barbason was uneasy. "There's somethin' else. I ain't so good at explainin' this sort o' stuff though… Probably best ye see for yerself." He handed over a small mirror.

Will examined his reflection. He looked awful, which was expected. Then, he saw what Barbason was talking about. The mirror fell to the floor. His heart rate monitor sped up in panic.

In Memoriam

His eyes, which were always a calm shade of blue, had no irises.

They were pitch-black.

Later, Will's doctor explained his condition.

His right hand was lost. When they found him, it had been cut roughly two inches from the wrist up his forearm. They tried to reattach it, but the nerves wouldn't take. Out of either respect or confusion, no one asked the circumstances of its removal. The good news was that the cut was clean and healing nicely.

It's amazing what qualifies as "good news" at a hospital.

All the same, Will was glad. He tried not to think about what life with this injury would be like. The time for worry would come, but he would think better once the shock wore off.

His eyes were an anomaly. The ophthalmologist said it was a condition called aniridia, which literally meant "without iris." Normally, you have this disorder from birth, but in very rare cases it can be caused by injury. The ophthalmologist was amazed to find Will's vision was as good as ever—aniridia was usually accompanied by other eye disorders.

Will slumped in his bed. *Great,* he thought. *I've got one hand and perfectly black eyes. And people thought I was a freak before.*

Will slept without dreams. When he caught the scent of roses, it was a solitary sensation.

He woke up one feeling at a time. First was smell. Next came the touch of soft hands. Then the gentle sound of his name. Sight was last. With it came the blurry image of

Chapter 17

Eliza's face.

"Will? Will, are you awake? I think he's waking up!"

Each blink cleared his vision. Soon, he was as clear-headed as you can be while taking pain meds through an IV.

"About time, sleeping beauty."

Will didn't even notice Travis. He stood on the opposite side of the bed. "Hey," Will said. It was all he could manage.

Eliza flung her arms around him, which hurt more than he would admit. "Will! I'm so glad you're okay!"

Travis patted him on the shoulder. "Have a nice nap?"

Will nodded. "Are you two alright? Did the Beast hurt you, Eliza? And Travis… How did you survive that fall?"

Travis laughed. "That was nothing, man. Trust me, I got good at landing *long* before I got good at climbing. Lots more practice falling off of stuff. It's all in how you take the impact."

Laughing hurt, but Will could afford to chuckle. Typical Travis. He turned back to Eliza. "I need to know… What happened to you and the Beast?"

She let go of him. "It was going to kill me. I knew it… I couldn't stand to watch, so I closed my eyes—and then it screamed! It stumbled backward in pain, slowly fading away until there was nothing left. That's when I saw you…" Eliza was pale. "There was so much blood…"

"That's about when I limped over," Travis chimed in. "You know—after I stopped, dropped, and rolled like a good burning boy. I didn't think you were going to make it, bro. I tied my belt around your arm, because people always did that on TV, but I wasn't too hopeful."

Travis and Eliza exchanged a nervous glance.

Whatever was bothering them, they didn't know how to say it. "Then what?"

In Memoriam

"Then things got weird," said Travis. "Right when we thought you were a goner, you started to spaz out. You were shaking, foaming at the mouth, and muttering like a lunatic. We were freaked."

Eliza nodded. "Then, just as suddenly… You were calm. After a few moments you gasped deeply, and—I don't know how to describe it—something came out of you."

"Something came *out* of me?" said Will. He was shocked.

"That's one way to put it," said Travis. "It was strange. We didn't *see* anything. But—man, how can I put it?—we *felt* something. It was invisible, but when we looked at you we could almost see it. The air above you was somehow… Thicker. It made me think of that funky mystical mumbo-jumbo. You know, the 'unseen entity' and all. So I did the ritual thingy I was supposed to."

Travis pulled the platinum jar out of his backpack.

"I don't know if it did anything, but this thing has felt icky ever since," he said. "I try not to touch it. Just feels so… Wrong."

Will saw the pieces fit together. It was too good to be true.

"Guys… I think it's over," he said. "Moyset had been locked up for good."

Eliza beamed. "You really think so?"

Will told them his experiences after passing out. He didn't offer any description of the demon or its realm. He stayed strictly on the topic of what happened. When he finished, Eliza said "So, we must have seen Moyset. Which means…"

"It means I got that bitch sealed up like a pickle in here," Travis said, smirking. "Serves him right."

As much as he wanted to celebrate, the platinum jar made Will uneasy. It stood out against the background in

Chapter 17

stark clarity, looking so crisp and sharp as to not seem real. It exuded an aura of wickedness that was impossible to ignore.

"What should we do with it?" asked Eliza. She was also staring at it.

Will hadn't planned this far ahead, but knew who to ask. He was willing to bet that, like it or not, the one with the answers would visit him soon. "For now, take it to Uncle Barbason," he said. "Tell him to guard it with his life."

"Good call," said Travis. Using a gloved hand he packed the jar up. "I'll get right on that. The sooner this is someone else's problem, the better. I think I got my first gray hair carrying this thing."

He left, and Will and Eliza were alone.

There was a long, awkward silence. Finally she said, "You saved my life."

Will didn't know how to respond.

"I really thought you were dead." Eliza's eyes were getting watery. "I haven't been able to sleep. Every time I try, I remember yelling and calling you a monster. I couldn't stop thinking that, if you died before I could apologize… I wouldn't be able to live with myself."

"You were right to be angry," he admitted. "I shouldn't have kept this from you. You had the right to know that I planned on bargaining with Moyset."

Eliza shook her head. "But I should have tried to understand *why* you did it. Back then, all I could think about was myself and how hurt I was. I never even considered how much bravery it took for you. After seeing you at the fair, I realized just how hard you were willing to fight. You were doing everything in your power to protect us. I saw what you *really* are—a hero."

Hero? Will never thought of himself as a hero. "I watched people die, Eliza. No, worse—I killed them! And I hurt many, many more. I'm no hero. If I died out there, well… I was the only one who deserved it."

Without warning, Eliza kissed him. The tenderness caught him entirely off guard.

"You are a hero to me," she said. Her eyes glistened with sincerity.

Eliza gently ran her fingers through Will's hair. This time, silence was blissful. No medication could have relaxed Will as much as her light touch and loving gaze. She didn't avoid his coal-black eyes, but looked straight into them with acceptance.

"So… Do you forgive me?" Will asked.

She smiled, but a tear finally crept down her face. "Only if you can forgive me for shutting you out when you needed me the most."

Will leaned up (despite his aches) and gave her a kiss. "Deal."

With that one word, all tension evaporated. Eliza stayed with him for hours, sometimes talking but mostly just holding his one remaining hand in her lap. He might not have died, but Will knew this feeling was a piece of heaven.

After three days, the visitor Will was most anxious about arrived.

Xavier Orrick.

He entered after a brief knock, and strolled gracefully to sit next to Will. He brought a duffel bag, and left it beside his seat. Xavier's face was unreadable behind his round sunglasses.

"Hello Will."

For days, he could think of nothing but questions for this mysterious man. Now that he had the chance, Will didn't know where to begin.

"May I ask what happened?" said Xavier.

Chapter 17

"It didn't work," Will told him. "Starving the Beast wasn't enough. Moyset waited until I was angry on a full moon. It must have had strength in reserve, because it overpowered me long enough to feed."

As he explain the trail of events, a horrible suspicious crept into Will's mind. "But... You knew that would happen, didn't you? You knew Moyset would try this."

Slowly, a terrible grin crossed Xavier's face.

Of course he knew. He was the Grand Master of a supernatural society. Xavier seemed to know *everything*.

"Why?" Will's voice was pleading. "Why didn't you tell me? If I had known, I could have been ready. I could have saved those people. I could have saved Mason..."

Xavier's reflective gaze turned to him. "Telling you would have done far more harm than good."

Will was angry. "How can you say that? People *died*, Mr. Orrick! They died because of you. I'm a murderer because of *you!*"

The old man raised a hand. "Easy, easy. I believe you misunderstood me, Will. Did I suspect Moyset could try a move like that? Yes, it was likely. But did I know a mere fifteen year-old boy could defeat a demon that powerful on his own, and walk away relatively unharmed? No. I never imagined such a thing."

"Unharmed?" Will held up his stump of a hand. "You call this unharmed?"

Xavier's stare was icy. Invisible energy pulsed, making the lights flicker. For the first time, Will was afraid to be near him. "People have lost *far* more than that fighting for this cause," he said in a fierce tone.

Will shrunk back.

"My apologies," Xavier said. He recomposed himself as quickly as he lost his temper. "Allow me to start anew. When I met you, I sensed great potential. You reminded me

In Memoriam

of someone I knew a long time ago. He would have made an exceptional mystic if given the chance. But, if I sat you down and taught you all that I could, you might never realize that potential. Or worse, we might discover too late that your abilities were not as I thought. The only way to learn was a trial by fire.

"So yes, I gave you incomplete information knowing it could turn into a blood bath. I was nearby, worry not. If things went too far I was prepared to step in. Yes, I did stand by as those poor people lost their lives. But if I held your hand, do you truly think you would have found the strength to defeat Moyset? What you did was exceptional, Will. You were pushed beyond your limits, pushed to the very brink of death, and discovered that you had the power all along. All you needed to do was recognize it.

"Their lives are a tragedy, that goes without saying. But think of how many lives you can save with this newfound power."

Will felt sick. "And if I couldn't defeat Moyset… Would you have helped before it killed me? Or would I have been another sacrifice to your cause?"

Xavier sat back, his fingers crossed. "If you were unable to save yourself… Then there was never anything I could do to spare you. You would have been doomed the moment that demon entered your body."

"Then what do you want with me?" Will asked. "You keep saying I have potential. Apparently, it was worth taking innocent lives to find out if I lived up to your hopes. Why do you care about any 'inner strength' I might have?"

His smile was like no other, equal parts inviting and unsettling. "I have a proposition for you. One which, at first, you might not like."

"You have my attention," said Will.

Xavier stood up and walked to the window. "I would

like you to join Enoc, Will. I want to take you in as my apprentice."

Will couldn't believe what he was hearing. "You watched as I murdered people in your name. You were prepared to let me die… And now you want to mentor me? You're out of your mind!"

He chuckled. "Yes, I supposed I am." Xavier looked over his shoulder. "So, what do you say?"

This was unreal. "Why should I?" Will asked. "My life can finally go back to normal. I can try to forget this ever happened."

"Back to normal, you say?" Xavier strolled across the room. "Do you really think things could ever be normal again? After what you've seen, what you've experienced, do you believe an ordinary life would hold any appeal to you? You can't forget what happened, no more than you can pretend you are not crippled."

"I won't forget," Will pointed out. "But that doesn't mean I should throw myself back into danger. I can use what I know to stay away from anything demonic."

"True. But here's the part that'll really keep you up at night… With the knowledge of your remarkable ability… Could you do nothing? Could you go about your life peacefully, knowing that other lives are being destroyed? You have the power to vanquish evil, Will, especially with proper training. So the question is… Could you live with yourself if you walked away now?"

Will didn't think it was possible to have such mixed feelings about one person. He hated Xavier. Feared him. Respected him. He was even in awe of his knowledge. But regardless of his opinion, Xavier was right—Will's life would never be the same again.

"I'll think about it," Will said. "Is that good enough?"

"That will do," said Xavier.

In Memoriam

"May I ask another question?"

"Always."

"What will happen to the Beast?" The question was burning in his mind since he woke up. "I was the Beast all along. Moyset controlled and manipulated me, but it was still my etheric body. Now that Moyset is gone… Will the Beast come back?"

Xavier studied him. "That depends. The demon did the same thing to your great-uncle, but his aura was never as strong as yours. It is gradually returning to its original state. If you do nothing, the same should happen to you.

"However, this does pose an interesting possibility. You have already learned the transformation. With practice… I think you could do it again, this time without the influence of Moyset."

The idea made Will nervous. "Why would I want that?"

Xavier laughed. "Why? My dear boy, you saw how powerful the Beast was! Now, under the control of a demon it was a monster. But as your own master… That power could be used for good."

That reminded Will of another important matter to discuss. "What should we do about Moyset? We think the seal worked, but we aren't sure what to do now."

"Ah, yes," said Xavier. "With your permission, I believe it would be best if I take it from here. As I said, demons are difficult to destroy. But in the meantime, I have a very secure place to keep it, where escape is all but impossible."

Will could think of no better option. "Alright."

"Excellent," Xavier said. "Now, might I ask another question of you, Will?"

"Go ahead."

"What did you see?" he nodded towards Will. "Your

eyes have changed. I suspect that is more than a medical coincidence. I find it likely you saw something while fighting Moyset. Something that human eyes were not meant to see."

Will looked away. He was reluctant to relive that horrifying part of his journey. The details were so painful, he didn't even share them with his closest friends. "Moyset gave me a glimpse of its memories. It showed me a universe on fire. There was death and destruction around every corner. Everything about it was wrong somehow. I... I can't describe it."

Xavier's mirrored gaze drifted away from Will. "I see..."

"Do you know where that was?" Will asked.

"Perhaps," he said. "I have my theories, but they are based on more assumption than fact. When the truth becomes clear, I would be glad to give you the explanation you deserve."

Will wasn't sure he *wanted* to know the truth about that place. The brief glance he got was more than he could handle.

"Now then," Xavier sat down and reached into his duffel bag. "Before I depart, I have a gift for you. Something I thought could prove very useful."

"A gift?" Will couldn't imagine what the Grand Master of Enoc might have for him.

Grinning, Xavier pulled a metallic hand from the bag.

Will's eyes widened. "Is that... A prosthetic?"

"The finest *myoelectric* prosthetic available, giving you the best possible motor skills. Made of solid silver, blessed myself, to guarantee you always have a weapon handy against etheric threats." Xavier smiled proudly as he offered the prosthetic to Will. "Do you like it?"

Will examined the hand. The silver was so perfectly shiny, it appeared to glow. "I can't take this."

In Memoriam

"Don't be silly, dear boy," Xavier shook his head. "If you accept my offer of apprenticeship, this will be essential. And if you decline… Then think of it as an apology for what my mission has cost you."

He thought it over. This prosthetic had to be expensive, but he couldn't deny it would be helpful. Besides, Xavier didn't appear to have any shortage of funds. "Thank you."

"I will return Christmas Day," Xavier said as he stood up. "Take the next few months to put your life in order, and consider my offer. You can make your decision then."

As Xavier turned to leave, Will said "Wait!"

He looked back. "Yes?"

It sounded childish, but Will couldn't help it. "Are there really more monsters out there? Monsters like Moyset and the Beast?"

The Grand Master threw his head back and laughed. "My dear boy, they were only the beginning!"

By the first snow, things were very different in Elkhorn.

Will distantly remembered the boy he was when he moved here. Now, not even a year later, he felt like a new person.

With no imminent crisis, Will and Barbason lived together very well. He was even cleaning the garage and talking about reopening B.R. Amon. He still carved wood, but they were never wolves.

Rumors flooded after the public attack—and sudden disappearance—of the Wisconsin Werewolf. Will's name always came up. Some people theorized Will lost his hand in a heroic fight with the Beast. Others believed he was in fact a werewolf, and got his wound in wolf-form. Will and Travis found the accuracy amusing.

Speaking of Travis, he became the town advocate of "Werewolf Awareness." He spread the word that the Beast was not an ordinary wolf, as the police department claimed. Many thought he was crazy. Those who attended the fair believed him.

Monsters of America contacted Will for a follow-up interview. He never returned their calls.

Eliza visited the hospital every day. After Will was released, she was always by his side. With Eliza's help he practiced all of his daily tasks left-handed, and slowly got used to his prosthetic. Will told her she didn't have to. Eliza said she would have it no other way.

As December approached, Xavier's return became all too real. He needed to think. He needed to remember.

He needed to make the most important decision of his life.

In the silence of night, Will crunched through the undisturbed snow of the fairgrounds. It was a ghost town—the streets were unplowed and the barns were long abandoned. The snow was deep, but he wasn't going far. Within moments he saw what he came for.

The Wiswell Center. Or—as he came to know it—the hideout.

Hanging on the outside wall was a large memorial plaque. It was barely visible under starlight, but it didn't matter; the words were etched into Will's soul as deeply as they were etched into metal.

In Memoriam

In honor of those who lost their lives to the "Wisconsin Werewolf." Your sacrifice will never be forgotten.

~

Mason McCree

Josh Stiles

Adam Mills

Wendy Baldwin

Every time he read it, Will's heart felt like a lump of coal. Compared to tragedies that claim lives by the thousands, a death toll of four might not sound too bad.

But to Will, these names were not a statistic. The people who loved them took no comfort in the number of casualties—all that mattered was that your friend, or child, or parent was gone forever. These were four human beings, most of them not much older than Will. They had a whole life ahead of them, a life that was buried with their remains. Each death was a tragedy beyond measure, a ripple of pain and suffering to everyone who ever cared about them.

The first name haunted Will the most; Mason McCree. From the moment they met, he couldn't stand Mason. But in a way that made Will's guilt more crushing. At school, Mason always had the upper hand—he was strong, and deviously clever. He used these talents to antagonize, and force his way to whatever he wanted. Will despised him for it.

But in the end, Will became something much worse. And he loathed himself for it.

When he left the hospital, Will's first priority was to order this plaque. He got approval from the families, but insisted he would pay for it. The words were carefully chosen,

Chapter 17

a secret apology to his victims.

Will *was* the Wisconsin Werewolf.

And he would *never* forget what he did.

Tears froze on his cheeks. He tried to hold himself together, but after a year of trials and sorrow, he broke. Will collapsed into the snow. Memories consumed him, forcing him to replay everything that happened since Connor's funeral.

His parents death.

Countless hours at the library.

Learning the truth behind the Beast.

Becoming the Beast.

Then, finally, facing his inner demon. And winning.

Will stood up. He wiped his tears. And he left the fairgrounds with his head high.

He made his decision.

Christmas Day was here.

As their neighbors gathered around to open presents, Will and Eliza stood in the parking lot of B.R. Amon. The snow was surreal—the flakes were too big, falling too slow. It was like being in a giant snow globe.

The boxed shape of an old SUV appeared through the snow. It drove up Bray Road and pulled into the parking lot beside them.

Xavier stepped out.

"Will," he said. "You look well."

Will nodded. Eliza held his arm tightly. This was her first meeting with the Grand Master. She was understandably nervous.

"How is that prosthetic treating you?" asked Xavier.

Will held up a gloved hand and flexed it. "I'm getting used to it."

In Memoriam

"Good, good." Xavier stepped closer. "We both know why I am here. Have you come to a decision?"

"I have."

"And what have you chosen, my dear boy?"

Will took a deep breath. "I want to go with you. I want to join Enoc."

"I see. That means leaving Elkhorn for long periods of time. Are you prepared to do that?"

He gave a tentative glace to Eliza. "Will I be able to come back?"

"Yes. But you will be gone more than not. Months at a time, perhaps even years." Xavier put a bony hand on Will's shoulder. "I can offer no promises, dear boy, except that this road is paved with peril. We are fighting a war, you see. A war against ignorance. I'm afraid I have never been good at recruiting; if you are unsure, you can still walk away. But once you start down this path, there is no turning back."

Will stared at his reflection in Xavier's glasses. There was not a trace of doubt in his face.

"I'm ready."

The old man grinned. "Very well."

Will pulled Eliza into a tight hug. Tears stained his shoulder as he whispered into her ear. "I'll be back."

Mid-embrace, Eliza kissed him like never before.

"I'll be waiting."

Reluctantly, Will let her go. Giving Eliza one final glance, he climbed into the Jeep. They drove away from B.R. Amon. Away from Eliza. And away from everything Will ever knew.

Will wondered what was ahead for him. But most of all, he wondered if he would ever see this place again.

They weren't even out of Elkhorn when something attacked the Jeep.

Immediately, Will's guard was up. He knew life would

be dangerous, but he didn't expect danger to find them so soon. Something pounced on the hood of the car, a dark shape in a flurry of snow. The figure pressed its face against the window, and Will gasped—it was the last thing he expected!

Travis was looking through the windshield, giving him a thumbs up.

The Jeep pulled over, and Will got out. "What on earth are you *doing?*"

Travis made himself comfortable. "Where we headed?" he asked.

Will sighed. "We talked about this. You knew I was leaving today."

"Yeah, I know," he confessed. "But then I got thinkin'. Why should you have all the fun? You weren't the only one fighting the Beast, bro. If it weren't for me, we'd never have caught that demon dude. I told you months ago. 'In it until the end,' remember?"

Will couldn't believe his ears. "You're an idiot, Travis."

He puffed out his chest. "Exactly! I'm just the kind of idiot you need!"

"Look, this is very brave of you, but it's not my call," Will said. He was amazed Travis would offer, but he couldn't ask this of him.

Xavier came around the car. "You are right. The decision is mine."

"You're the hocus-pocus guy, aren't you?" Travis asked. Xavier humored him with a nod. "So what do you say? Can I tag along?"

His reflective eyes examined Travis. "Are you fully aware of the danger that waits down this road?"

"Oh, don't worry about that," Travis said proudly. "Danger and I are old friends. We visit each other daily."

In Memoriam

Xavier laughed. "Then you may accompany us."

Travis' expression lit up with childish delight. "Really? Aw man, you won't regret it! I'm an expert at the whole daredevil thing. Will told you about the ferris wheel, right?"

Will could only laugh. Before long, they all joined in a chorus of laughter.

"Let us go, gentlemen," said Xavier. "Your futures await."

Travis hopped off the hood. Will climbed into the back, next to his best friend.

Will didn't know where they were going, or what challenges they would face, but he wasn't worried. Not anymore.

A new tale was about to begin.

Epilogue:
The Beginning

News of the Beast was about to come full circle.

A messenger traveled across France. The journey took her to the outskirts of Mende, a commune hardly bigger than the town of Elkhorn.

It all began here.

The messenger followed a path taken only by the most desperate. Each cobblestone down this road marked a dream broken or hope shattered. No person of a sound mind would ever approach the clinic at the edge of town.

Only one doctor was there. He was a specialist in hopelessness, and had his masters in despair.

Here worked Dr. Jacques DuPuis.

Knock, knock, knock.

The doctor answered immediately. He expected this visit.

"Come in."

He led the messenger through twisted, illogical corridors into his office. The second the door was locked, the

The Beginning

messenger spoke her warning.

"Moyset has fallen," she said.

Dr. DuPuis took a seat behind his desk. He showed no reaction.

The messenger continued. "That American doctor's grandson captured it. How could a human child vanquish the Great Wolf? It's absurd! I don't think Moyset has been that powerful since the *Gévaudan* massacre of 1764. The Great One must hear of this. Maybe it's not too late to—"

"That's enough, Merle."

The messenger, Merle, was stunned. "Excuse me?"

"The Great One already knows," Dr. DuPuis said. "You really thought we trusted Moyset? Hardly! It is much too rash. The Great One was nearby the entire time, in case something went wrong."

Merle considered this. "So… You expected this?"

The doctor smiled. "Of course. When Dr. Amon arrived at my door, I knew he was perfect. Humans are so easily manipulated—*especially* humans in love! Handing Moyset to him was but the first move in a carefully-executed plan."

"And what of the boy?" Merle asked.

"The boy?" said Dr. DuPuis. "Oh don't worry, his time will come. But he is of no concern to us now."

Laughter cut through the air. His laugh echoed in the nightmares of innocent minds all over the world, sending waves of irrational fear from coast to coast.

"This is only the beginning."

Thanks for reading
Tale of the Wisconsin Werewolf!

If you enjoyed it, would you mind taking a few minutes of your time to leave a review on Amazon? It doesn't take long, and it makes all the difference. I know I look at reviews before picking up a book, and I'm sure future readers will appreciate hearing what you have to say.

And don't worry—as Dr. DuPuis said, this is only the beginning. There's a lot to come in the *Enoc Tales*, and I can't wait to share it with you.

If you want to keep up on all the news and cool stuff related to the series, why not subscribe to my newsletter? The sign-up form is on the official website, **www.EnocTales.com**.

Again, thanks for joining me in this adventure. Looking forward to our next one together!

Edison T. Crux

edison@wisconsinwerewolf.com

Find Edison on **Facebook**, **Google+**, **Twitter**, & **YouTube**.

Read an excerpt from

Tale of the

Gévaudan Beast

Prequel to Wisconsin Werewolf

This is an excerpt from **Tale of the Gévaudan Beast**, the prequel to *Wisconsin Werewolf*. It follows the story of Dr. Connor Amon, Will's grandfather.

This excerpt is from Connor's visit to France, and his trip to the mysterious clinic of Dr. DuPuis.

To read the entire story of Connor, pick up the Tale of the Gévaudan Beast. Available online & in select bookstores.

www.EnocTales.com/Gevaudan-Beast

Excerpt from

Tale of the Gévaudan Beast

There is no beauty like the French countryside. I went through many lovely cities and towns, enjoying the culture. The further south I went, the fewer towns I saw. The road wound through vast mountains and fields. It was like traveling back in time, to a land less touched by civilization.

Finally, nestled amongst the mountains, was Mende.

With only 12,000 residents, it was hardly larger than Elkhorn. But it was a metropolis compared to the miles of open country I had journeyed through to get here.

I spent the night at the *Hotel Du Pont Roupt,* a lovely little hotel on the river.

The next morning, my search began.

I had an address for this clinic, but couldn't find it on a map. My hope was that the locals could confirm its location. I first went to the receptionist, who was very cordial, even to this ignorant American. I asked (in the best French I could manage) if she knew of a Dr. Jacques DuPuis.

Suddenly, her expression changed.

Tale of the Gévaudan Beast

"Je ne sais rien," she said. ("I know nothing.")

Her response was strange, but I didn't press the matter. I expected no trouble; surely someone would point me in the right direction.

As the day went on, I discovered how wrong I was.

I went to the visitor's center. The *Centre Hospitalier de Mende.* Even the local market. No matter where I went or who I asked, nobody would admit such a clinic existed. I would have believed them, too, if it wasn't for the look of fear in their eyes.

It was like they were hiding something.

I had dinner at the *Restaurant Grill de La Tour,* hoping some food and drink would ease my growing worries. After I ate, I joined the locals at the bar. Perhaps with a few drinks, the locals would loosen up.

"Est-ce que…" I said, pausing to think over my translation. *"Quelqu'un sait de docteur Jacques DuPuis?"*

The room went silent. All eyes fell on me.

"Le Diable médecin!" one man cried from down the bar.

"The… Devil's Physician?" I said in plain English. The man nodded vigorously, as if he understood.

Chatter erupted. I couldn't translate everything; they were talking too fast and their speech was too slurred. What little I could understand was troubling.

Evil!

The witch-doctor!

He is cursed, I say!

Practices Black Magick.

Devil's Physician.

Cursed!

"So…" I said, interrupting the commotion. *"Il existe?"* ("He exists?")

No one spoke. The brute of a man sitting next to me put a hand on my shoulder. *"Monsieur,"* he said slowly, making sure I understood. *"Pour votre propre sécurité, laisser ici. Le médecin que vous cherchez est un mythe."*

("For your own safety, leave here. The doctor you seek is a myth.")

Fearing a panic, I said no more. But I had confirmed one thing; Dr. Jacques DuPuis was real.

The next day I hired a taxi. I gave him the address and explained I wasn't sure of the exact location. The driver was wary. I sensed that he too might pretend he is ignorant, so I offered to pay double his rates, up front. Reluctantly, he took my money and we drove out of town. The road wrapped up the side of a mountain, with a great view of Mende.

To be honest, I wasn't entirely surprised by the locals' reaction. This land felt lost in time. Here, you could easily cling to the superstition of the past. Curing the fatally ill might be seen as witchcraft, and the doctor a devil worshiper. If he was a recluse by nature, that would only further this local belief.

But I had dealt with my share of unpleasant doctors. I wasn't afraid.

The road went on, rolling through woods and hills. It was a beautiful scene, but I must confess I was a little unsettled once the town was lost from view.

My driver was also getting nervous. He eventually pulled over and said, *"Gardez votre argent, américain. Je n'irai pas plus loin."*

("Keep your money, American. I will go no further.")

How unprofessional! I insisted this was silly, but the man couldn't be persuaded. He said if I followed this road, I'd find it. Thoroughly annoyed, I slammed the door shut and

III

continued by foot.

Several miles I walked. It was rough going; the path went uphill, and my shoes were unfit for hiking. When I saw a building nestled among the mountain, I was overjoyed; that had to be it!

As I approached, I saw a sign on the door. If, after all this trouble, I ran into a "Sorry, we're closed" sign, I would have been devastated. But I regained my spirits as I translated.

Welcome!
Please excuse our lack of staff. If you would kindly register at the front desk and take a seat, the doctor will be with you shortly.
Thank you for your cooperation.

Interesting. I went inside, and found the place to be surprisingly modern. I expected some run-down facility, but this clinic was as clean as any in the States. The lobby was decorated with potted plants, white tile floor, and large paintings of France's finer cities. At the front desk a computer stood facing the lobby, with a message similar to the door.

All I had to do was enter my name, and I was in queue to see the doctor.

How wonderfully efficient! If Dr. DuPuis didn't have many patients (and I couldn't imagine he did), this automated system would keep his costs down by removing the need for staff. I took a seat, feeling better already.

To pass the time, I checked the reading material left out. There weren't any magazines, but the table was littered

Prequel to *Wisconsin Werewolf*

with newspapers and a bible. I picked up a paper and had a read.

It seemed there was a terrible accident at the 24 Hours of Le Mans motor race. One of the cars crashed, sending pieces of debris into the crowd. 8 spectators and the driver were killed, while 120 were severely injured.

But something was strange… This paper was dated June 13th, 1955. Why would he have such a dreadful back issue lying around?

I looked for something better to read, but noticed a trend. Another newspaper was dated September 22nd, 2001, with a front page article about a deadly chemical factory explosion. The one American publication was for December 16th, 1967, the day after the Silver Bridge collapsed in Point Pleasant, West Virginia. That accident led to forty six deaths.

I put the papers away. I lost my interest in reading.

There was something unsettling about those articles. If I didn't know better, I would have thought they were deliberately chosen to show great disasters. I took a better look around, hoping to ease my nerves.

The plant next to me wasn't doing so good. Many of the leaves were brown and eaten. When I touched the leaves, I made a strange discovery; the plant was plastic. And tucked away within the leaves was a hungry, plastic locust.

Why put a fake dead plant in a clinic?

My heart began to pound. I turned to one of the paintings. Paris was painted in remarkable detail, with the bustling streets and lavish buildings. But something was wrong... The people in the street weren't walking—they were *running,* and behind them stood an executioner with an axe. Decapitated bodies lay at his feet.

Panic crept through me. Nothing was as it seemed here. I began to feel like this whole clinic—from the friendly message to the benign décor—was all an act. A cheap mask to hide some horrific truth.

I reached for the bible, hoping to find comfort in its verses. But when I flipped it open, I gasped.

Every page in the bible was blank.

Beep.

The sudden sound nearly sent me into shock. There was a new message on the computer. Cautiously I approached the screen and read.

The doctor is ready.
Please follow the door to your right

A door creaked open, all on its own. I was filled with irrational fear, and had to fight the urge to run. The words of the locals ran through my mind, as dread quickly overcame me.

If it wasn't for Eleanor, I never would have walked through that door.

The hallway wasn't straight; it veered off at a strange angle. It made you off-balance, like one of those tricks at a fun house. Only this wasn't fun, not at all. I stumbled to the door with Dr. Jacques DuPuis' name on it.

Before I could knock, the door swung open.

"Hello, Dr. Amon," a voice said from inside. It spoke perfect English, without a trace of an accent.

I looked up and froze. A nightmare sat in the chair before me, its lips curled into a sinister grin.

"I've been expecting you."

Order Now!

Pick up your copy at
EnocTales.com/Gevaudan-Beast

Acknowledgements

I'd like to give thanks to all the people who made this book a reality. I couldn't have done it without you.

To Katie Crux, my amazing wife, for believing in me since the beginning.

To Devin Peltier-Robson, my brother and friend, who has supported my dream in more ways than I can count.

To Morgan Ashire, who inspired one of the most memorable and entertaining characters in this book.

To my parents, Mark & Camille Peltier-Robson, who always let my imagination roam free.

To Christopher Spencer, who made sure my French made sense.

To Wyldraven, whose beautiful stock images made the cover come to life.

But most for all, I give my thanks to you—the fans. Without you, none of this would mean a thing.

Further Reading

The Beast of Bray Road by Linda Godfrey. This is the book that started it all. Linda tells the true story of the Wisconsin Werewolf; from the first sightings to a national media sensation.

Monsters: An Investigator's Guide to Magical Beings by John Michael Greer. This fascinating book inspired the "physics of the supernatural" in this setting. John has a way of explaining fantastic things (werewolves, vampires, and more) in a way that really makes sense. Definitely worth a read for any enthusiast.

The Book of Were-Wolves by Sabine Baring-Gould. This is the classic academic study of werewolf history and folklore. Several of the real-world werewolf trials were used in *Tale of the Wisconsin Werewolf*, including the true discovery of Moyset.

About the Author

Edison T. Crux is a storyteller, devoted husband, loving daddy, and coffee enthusiast. He grew up in Beloit, WI, living in a haunted house across the street from a cemetery. Although his writing can be dark or serious, in person Edison is a very upbeat and silly guy. He currently lives with his wife and children in Beloit, WI.

Contact the Author

edison@wisconsinwerewolf.com

Find Edison on

Facebook, Google+, Twitter, & YouTube.